THE WARNING

A NOVEL FOR THE NUCLEAR AGE

THE WARNING: A NOVEL FOR THE NUCLEAR AGE
Copyright © 2021 Thomas F. Lee

Typesetting by FormattingExperts.com

THE WARNING

A NOVEL FOR THE NUCLEAR AGE

THOMAS F. LEE

The evil that is in the world always comes of ignorance, and good intentions do as much harm as malevolence, if they lack understanding. On the whole, men are more good than bad ... but they are more or less ignorant ... the most incorrigible vice being that of an ignorance that fancies it knows everything and therefore claims for itself the right to kill.

Albert Camus, *The Plague*

The following is a work of fiction.

However, it includes sections of nonfiction printed in a different font intended to emphasize certain facts within the harsh context of the story.

PREFACE

The Virus arrived suddenly. It worked its way through the world's population, despite all efforts to stop its advance. Most cooperated in the struggle against the Virus, although a sizeable minority did not. They were in the thrall of the destructive president of the United States. He railed against efforts to protect the American people from infecting each other with the deadly disease. Death and grief followed in the wake of his senseless objections to the simple expedient of wearing a mask in public and keeping away from crowds.

The Virus was a deadly pathogen that had no regard for borders, for international agreements, for walls, or for anyone's family, loved ones or communities. It had been allowed to burst into full force in the United States because of the president's negligence, incompetence and disregard for advice.

In addition, as soon as he had begun his term, he began to decimate regulations protecting Earth's fragile environment from the real threat of oncoming climate change. He managed, with the cowardly acquiescence of fellow Republicans, to remove protections from our water, air, soils and forests. As the next election approached, it became clear that the results of the vote would determine the very future of our democracy.

However, an even greater threat lay hidden deep in the background of the daily news, a far greater plague than even the dreaded Virus. Across America, patiently waiting deep in underground silos and in aircraft hangars, and far beyond its shores, and carried silently under the world's oceans, thousands of deadly nuclear weapons listened for a command from one solitary individual. At his word, they were prepared to answer the summons, leap out from their confinement, and hurtle towards whomever the president and his cohorts had decided was the enemy. At their release, in a few moments of horror and unimaginable suffering, billions of human lives would be extinguished, and the environment poisoned with radioactive debris, rendering Earth almost uninhabitable for any survivors.

The pace of the Virus slowed soon after the president was afflicted with it. He managed to recover after serious complications. The country's gradual emergence from the crisis was due in part to renewed efforts by a frightened president, and also to a new societal attention to prevention measures as well as the development of a vaccine. People began to slowly but cautiously emerge from their isolation. A new sense of optimism spread across the country. The president paid little attention to the difficulties that other nations were experiencing with the Virus. Without international efforts and co-operation, a practice anathema to the president and his supporters, the world's sufferings would continue.

Hopeful of reelection, the president never mentioned nuclear weapons during his campaign, except to threaten several treaties that attempted to control their spread.

Life in America was returning to a more normal

rhythm. Schools were back in session. In Texas, the Dallas School Board unanimously rejected a request to add Daniel Ellsberg's 2017 book, *The Doomsday Machine: Confessions of a Nuclear War Planner,* to the local high school social studies curriculum. An earlier effort by a local peace activist group suggesting using Howard Zinn's classic, *A People's History of the United States,* in Dallas history classes, had been even more forcefully denied.

In late 2020, in a command center on the freezing plains of North Dakota, a young airman sat at his silo control panel, while at the same time watching a streaming video of warm, sunny climates. In a nuclear missile-laden submarine, a sailor lay in his bunk, idly dreaming of shore leave after his long tour of duty deep in the Pacific Ocean. In an airplane hangar in Louisiana, a crew member suffering from a nasty hangover typed a text message to his girlfriend as he walked to a waiting plane about to take off on a practice nuclear bombing run above the Arctic Circle. In Virginia, a Catholic military chaplain felt honored to be invited to help christen a submarine carrying Trident missiles. He knelt in his chapel, composing a brief prayer that would ask God to bless this instrument of His peace.

Meanwhile, the nuclear weapons, unspeakably powerful and unutterably dangerous, rested quietly. Only a few citizens gave them a thought. Of those that did, most regarded them as a deterrent to enemy attack. They had become a security blanket. But within minutes, with little warning, they could transform our vibrant, living Earth into an inferno.

During the last, annihilative orgy of destruction of World War II, "precision bombing" of military sites had long since given way to the targeting of civilian populations. Under the direction of Maj. Gen. Curtis LeMay and Secretary of War Henry Stimson, Japanese cities were bombed into oblivion under the guise of their being "industrial urban areas" and "worker housing."

Those cities had limited defenses against the swarms of B-29 Superfortress bombers sent by LeMay, leader of the 21st Bomber Command in the Pacific. The slaughter began in the evening of March 9, 1945, when 334 B-29s swept in over Tokyo. Each plane was loaded with almost 2,000 incendiaries—firebombs filled with oil and gel drenched in gasoline. Tokyo erupted in flames. Firestorms swept with hurricane force across the mostly residential city, as air temperatures rose to eighteen hundred degrees Fahrenheit, creating a superheated wind that killed those who were not already incinerated or trampled by stampeding crowds of panicked women, men and children.

A U.S. Strategic Bombing Survey reported that "probably more persons lost their lives by fire at Tokyo in a six-hour period than at any time in the history of man." This massive raid was not a unique event. Between December 6, 1944 and August 13, 1945 there were 65 aerial assaults on Tokyo. According to that city's police statistics, 137,582 people were killed, 787,145 homes and buildings were destroyed, and 2,625,279 were displaced.

Tokyo was a horrendous example, but by no means the only target, for indiscriminate death and injury. Firebombing was extended nationwide across Japan. Overall, 66 Japanese cities were attacked and burned, killing more than 300,000 and wounding over 400,000. Throughout this carnage there was little public revulsion on the part of the American public for this wholesale killing of Japanese civilians on a scale unparalleled in the history of bombing. While the ethics of mass extinction of non-combatants by "area bombing" had been debated throughout much of World War II, by the firebombing of Japan it had become a fixed method of war for the American military. In fact, this merciless approach had its origin in the revered Winston Churchill, who, as British War Secretary after World War I, encouraged "aerial policing" by relentless bombing of Iraqi villages. By the 1940s he would be encouraging the "carpet bombing" of German cities, killing more than 600,000 people. This practice continued unabated in subsequent "conventional" wars, such as in Korea and Vietnam. It would become part of the legacy of the "Good War."

The worst was yet to come. In 1939, intelligence reports had disclosed that Germany was rushing to develop a terrifying new type of bomb—a "nuclear" weapon. This project would, if successful, produce an explosive device that could unleash the energy that holds atoms together. They would be "split" to release destructive forces that dwarfed anything that humans had ever imagined possible.

President Franklin Roosevelt initiated the early stages of a research effort that would evolve over the next four years into the Manhattan Project. The efforts of some 130,000 Americans, almost all of them ignorant of the exact goals of the top-secret endeavor, resulted in the first "atomic" bomb. It went by the nickname, the "Gadget."

The final concept was simple, yet technically complex. A 13-pound ball of plutonium, a highly radioactive element made from uranium, was surrounded by over two tons of high explosives. When these exploded, the resulting crushing forces

5

compressed the plutonium into its "critical mass," a density at which the core of the atoms burst, releasing particles that triggered adjoining atoms to split, a process that continued in a "chain reaction."

At 5:29 a.m. local time on July 16, 1945, attached atop a 100-foot tower in a remote desert near Alamogordo, New Mexico, the Gadget exploded with a force equal to 21,000 tons of TNT. Over 200 tons of toxic radioactive sand and ash rose seven miles into the sky and fell gently over 1,000 square miles. The U.S. Centers for Disease Control and Prevention would conclude that thousands of families were exposed to radiation levels that "approached 10,000 times what is currently allowed." None of the residents had been warned of the upcoming blast which stunned those within a 50-mile radius. "Official" explanations included the story that an ammunition dump had exploded.

Physicist J. Robert Oppenheimer, the head of the scientific team component of the Manhattan Project, said that after he had witnessed the blinding explosion in the desert, a thought from a Hindu scripture occurred to him: "Now I am become Death, the destroyer of worlds." Harvard's Kenneth T. Bainbridge, the director of the test, was more direct. He said, "Now we are all sons of bitches." Quite the opposite thought occurred to Niels Bohr, the Nobel Prize-winning Danish physicist who was in-strumental in discovering the structure of the atom. The day after the successful test in the desert, he exclaimed excitedly, "Now there can be no more war!" (One hundred years earlier, during the Civil War, Richard Gatling created the Gatling gun, a deadly automatic weapon. He thought that it would make battles so inhumane that wars would cease. Soon, even more powerful rapid-fire weapons replaced his invention.)

Scientist Leo Szilard, another important contributor to the Manhattan Project, responded by sending a petition, signed by

70 co-workers, to President Truman, urging that the president not use the bomb on civilian populations in Japan. Moreover, they recommended that, after the war, this weapon should be placed under international control to prevent an arms race. The petition was a moral plea, warning that the United States could "bear the responsibility to opening the door to an era of devastation on an unimaginable scale." A month earlier, a committee headed by the German scientist James Franck issued a report pushing for the United States to first demonstrate the awesome power of the bomb to members of the United Nations.

Neither plea reached the desk of President Truman. The lofty aims of the Szilard petition not only were disregarded, but by 1946, nuclear bomb testing began in the Marshall Islands. It would continue there and elsewhere until 1992, contaminating lands, oceans and populations. Testing was halted, but the production of the weapons continued. Since 1945, 10 countries have built over 134,000 nuclear devices. By 2020 there were "only" 13,400 of these, but vastly more sophisticated and powerful than the Gadget, and waiting for the word that would unleash them into the world once again. Nuclear-armed countries appeared little interested in ameliorating the threats that the mere existence of these weapons posed to the lives of humans and the health of the environment.

After the successful detonation of the Gadget in the New Mexico desert, The U.S. had two designs for atomic bombs, and they had enough material to produce two of them. One used plutonium and the other uranium. The latter bomb type had not been tested, but it would soon become the first nuclear weapon to be used in war against humans. By July, 1945, Germany had surrendered, and the attention of the world turned to the battle against Japan in the Pacific. Allied leaders asked for Japan's unconditional surrender or face "utter and complete destruction." Much of that devastation had already been accomplished in the widespread firebombing. As Japan debated their response, and Allied preparations continued for a land invasion, the 509th Composite Group, a special group of B-29 pilots and crews, was busy practicing for a special, secret mission on Tinian, a small Pacific island about 1500 miles south of Japan. Their code name for the island was Papacy.

Late in the evening of August 5, 1945, crews loaded a uranium bomb dubbed "Little Boy" onto to one of the B-29s, the Enola Gay. That plane was named after the mother of pilot Paul Tibbets, Jr. Workers had written their names on the bomb casing, and at least one message, "Here's to you." Protestant Chaplain William Downey invited the crew to bow their heads. His prayer included the following: "Almighty Father ... Guard and protect them, we pray Thee, as they fly their appointed rounds ... armed with Thy might may they bring this war to a rapid end ... In the name of Jesus Christ, Amen."

The aircraft took off, accompanied by two others, one to measure the blast and the other to photograph it. Six hours after takeoff, as the planes flew over the city of Hiroshima, Japan, the bomb bay doors opened about eight miles above Hiroshima, and Little Boy was released.

Hiroshima, lying on six islands formed by seven rivers, was then a city of about 250,000 people. Located 423 miles from Tokyo, most of its population lived in the four-square miles at its center. In the early morning of August 6, a number of Hiroshima residents were busy clearing fire lanes in anticipation of being firebombed. They paid little attention to the sound of the trio of planes passing overhead. They were accustomed to being observed from the air and knew that firebombing involved great numbers of planes.

When the 10-foot long, 9,700-pound Little Boy reached an altitude of 1,968 feet above the city, it exploded. This was the height that was calculated to do maximum damage to people and property. A chain reaction began that immediately attained a temperature of several million degrees Fahrenheit, hotter than the sun's surface.

A massive fireball over 1,000 feet in diameter formed instantaneously, setting off a shock wave swifter than the speed of sound. Estimates of the grim aftermath differ, but at least 90,000 people were killed instantly, and over the following days, weeks and months, perhaps 180,000 more had succumbed to their wounds or radiation sickness. Two-thirds of the city's 90,000 buildings were demolished. Everything combustible ignited.

Little help was available to the victims of the bomb, many thousands of whom were severely burned. Ninety percent of the doctors and nurses were killed or injured, and only three of the 45 hospitals were functional. Much of the city was reduced to ashes, while the agonized survivors had no one to help them. Many would succumb over the following years to cancers triggered by their exposure to radiation.

Sixteen hours after the devastation in Hiroshima, President Truman issued a statement warning the leaders of Japan to accept unconditional surrender or "they may expect a rain of ruin from the air, the like of which has never been seen on this earth." Even as this challenge was offered, preparations were underway for a second atomic bombing.

Early in the morning of August 9, 1945, just days after Little Boy detonated over Hiroshima, three B-29s lifted off from

Tinian Island. The bomber "Bockscar" carried "Fat Man," an eight ton, 10-foot-long bomb packed with a plutonium device whose explosive force was equivalent to that of 21,000 tons of TNT. The planes headed for the city of Kokura. That site was obscured by cloud cover, so they continued to Nagasaki. Fat Man exploded at an altitude of 1,650 feet. Almost 40,000 people were killed instantly, and much of the residential city was reduced to smoldering ruins. By the end of 1945, the death toll had risen to 74,000. Back on Tinian, scientists began to assemble another plutonium bomb in anticipation of being assigned another target population. Instead, on August 14, the president ordered a massive raid of over 1,000 bombers on multiple Japanese cities.

By the end of those attacks, the Japanese Emperor Hirohito admitted defeat. He said, in an unprecedented radio announcement, that to continue the war would lead to "the total annihilation of human civilization." The Japanese people, who had offered countless lives in his service, had never before heard his voice.

A twelve-foot-tall black obelisk stands on the site of the world's first nuclear explosion. Located on the hot, barren plains of the bombing range at the U.S. Air Force Base at Alamogordo, New Mexico, 120 miles south of Albuquerque, the site is a national historical monument. As the test preparations were underway in 1945, the Manhattan Project head, J. Robert Oppenheimer, reputedly had given the site the code name "Trinity." As the story goes, he had been reading a poem by John Donne at the time—the sixteenth century English writer and cleric—and was struck by the line, "Batter my heart, three person'd God." Oppenheimer would later claim not to remember the incident. This site remains the center of a worldwide arms race, a proliferation of nuclear weapons whose cumulative explosive power is sufficient to destroy all human life on Earth. Since Trinity, there have been more than 2,000 nuclear bomb tests.

In 1985, Father George Zabelka, a Catholic priest who had been one of the chaplains in 1945 on Tinian and had ministered to the pilots and crew who bombed Hiroshima and Nagasaki, delivered a homily in which he begged for forgiveness for his complicity. He admitted, "To fail to speak to the utter moral corruption of the mass destruction of civilians was to fail as a Christian and a priest ... Hiroshima and Nagasaki happened in and to a world and a Christian Church that had asked for it—that had prepared the moral consciousness of humanity to do and to justify the unthinkable."

CHAPTER 1

Monsignor Timothy O'Malley was visibly upset. Pacing back and forth in his spacious rectory office, he could feel his blood pressure rising. His reddened face almost matched the delicate piping on his black cassock and the brilliant pom on his beloved biretta. "Father Tim," an appellation he despised, although that form of address was an inescapable part of the changes that had taken place in his beloved Church, was apoplectic.

His young curate, freshly ordained Father James Sullivan, who rather enjoyed being addressed as Father Jim, looked at the elderly prelate with alarm. He had assisted the monsignor at the four p.m. Mass the previous evening and celebrated the eight that morning. Now they were both waiting for the new assistant to join them for breakfast after the 10 o'clock Mass. Years earlier, back when there typically had been three curates serving under a pastor, a middle-aged "housekeeper" would be busy preparing a hearty brunch for her charges. Now, it was up to Father Jim to do his best to prepare the rectory meals, a chore that was punctuated by frequent calls to his mother for advice.

"What's wrong, Monsignor?" he asked anxiously. "Was it those messages?"

The pastor, because of his advanced age, had only reluctantly entered the digital era. A few minutes earlier, he had been sitting at his large rosewood desk, reading the latest communications on his iPhone. Suddenly, he rose, grabbed his silver-headed cane, and began to limp across the plush Persian carpet.

"I don't know if they were messages, but they were texts. And they were sent before Mass was even over! From parishioners that were there! Including Mrs. Murphy and Billy O'Connor from the Knights! Jesus, Mary and Joseph!"

Father Jim, seeing his pastor so agitated, was tempted to take his arm and help him back to his seat. However, he was too newly hatched from the seminary to allow himself the freedom to touch anyone.

"Please, Monsignor, calm down. Come on now, sit down and tell me what's wrong and what I can do to help." He began mentally to run down the list of principles he had learned in his seminary counseling class.

The monsignor assented and eased himself back into his chair.

"I reminded that young whippersnapper only yesterday that this is Trinity Sunday, a day when we celebrate the deepest mystery of our faith. You know that I told him to give a sermon—I mean a homily—that explained the meaning and the significance of the triune God and emphasized to our parishioners how Jesus is consubstantial with the Father. God knows there aren't that many left."

The curate was confused. "You mean Gods?" he asked.

"No, you dope," the priest thundered. "I mean parishioners. We are losing them left and right. First, it was that damn Virus. Half the people who were afraid to show up for all those months didn't bother to come back to the pews when the bishop loosened things up. And by the way, their money stayed away as well from our beautiful Saint James. It's bad enough that we had to board up the parish hall because we can't afford to heat the darn place. We haven't even run a school for the last ten years. And now we have all these liberals taking over, and half of them think they can worship God without following His rules, like keeping the Sabbath and coming to Mass in their duly appointed parish. Some of these people are wandering around looking for churches where they feel 'comfortable.'"

"So, that's the problem? Missing people? I mean, it's true that pretty much everyone at Mass has grey hair."

"Father Sullivan, just keep quiet and listen to this. Here's a text from Mrs. Murphy. She writes, 'I just had to leave Mass early—too upset at that new priest. He started talking about the Trinity, but then he switched to something else entirely, and he sounded like he was criticizing our men and women serving their country in the military. I just couldn't understand it at all.' And here's another one from Billy O'Connor—he's the Deputy Grand Knight of our Knights of Columbus. 'Monsignor, I think we have a Communist on our hands. Where did you get this guy?' And there's a funny picture at the end that looks like a face with a frown."

The Reverend John Fain, OSB was a Benedictine monk, a member of the monastic community who owned and operated Saint Oliver College, situated on the banks of the Merrimack River in Manchester, New Hampshire. The school was named in honor of Oliver Plunkett, Archbishop of Armagh, Ireland. Falsely accused of treason, he had been hanged, drawn and quartered in 1681, an uncomfortable exit that qualified him as the last Roman Catholic martyr to die in England.

The monks who founded the college in 1867 emigrated from Ireland in order to minister to their fellow Irish, persecuted as they were in America. The monks' early attempts at education had grown into a relatively small but highly respected college, numbering some 2,000 students. Saint Plunkett was remembered in the form of a fragment of his backbone that rested in a gold reliquary behind the main altar of the chapel. Each college commencement featured a procession led by the Dean of the Faculty carrying the precious remains three times around the quadrangle, accompanied by the student officers of the Hibernian Society.

Amid the tumultuous times of the early twenty-first century, the school had earned a widely favorable reputation for the breadth of its curriculum and high academic standards. Among the faculty there was the varied mix of opinions and philosophies typical among college and university professors. However, being a Catholic college, it leaned more heavily toward hiring graduates of Notre Dame than, for example, Berkeley. The 20 priests and 11 brothers in the monastery were drawn from ethnic groups that favored Catholicism. However, among the students there were four African Americans, all male, and two Indians, all converts. The abbot was perplexed at how difficult it was to find a black Catholic who could shoot a three pointer. The administration, in response to

the tenor of the times, had formed a Diversity committee, which was developing a five-year plan to "increase
the numbers of students who are disparate members of
the global community."

Father John—he cringed when anyone addressed him
as Father Jack but remained polite—had earned a Ph.D.
after being ordained, with a specialty in American poets. His modest ambition, befitting a dedicated monk
who had taken vows of stability and obedience, was to
live out his days in the serenity of the monastery, and
to introduce his students to the pleasures of reading
Whitman, Dickinson, Frost, Stevens, Plath, and other
favorites—but more recently, Berrigan, Berry, Stafford,
and even Ferlinghetti and Ginsberg.

Word of his growing interest in the latter "protest"
poets had reached Abbot Richard Flynn, to whom the
monk owed his education and his strict obedience. The
abbot, often referred to as "kindly" or "benevolent" by
the trustees and alumni, was not necessarily thought of in
those terms by, for example, a monk who might want to
go on to further studies in art history and was told in no
uncertain terms that he was destined to become a theologian, or the brother who simply wanted to go home to
visit his mother and was told to wait until Easter.

In the matter of Father John, Abbot Richard decided,
after prayerful consideration, that it would be a good
idea to immerse the monk in the mundane affairs of
parish life during his summer break from classes—not
only to distract him from these troublesome tendencies,
but also to give him a feeling for the common man, so
to speak—the everyday patriots loyal to the red, white
and blue of Old Glory. The abbot would not want to

interfere in Father John's academic freedom, of course, but some of the notions that might be planted in the students' minds from reading those poems? Well, who knows where they might lead? And that Berrigan fellow—a renegade Jesuit—and his brother Phil, a priest who ran off with a nun!

The whole business was made a lot simpler when the abbot's old friend Monsignor O'Malley called him one Sunday afternoon in late May during the ninth inning of a Sox-Yankees game. The abbot took the call reluctantly, not wanting to miss the action on the radio on the slim chance that the Sox might tie the game, but his new iPhone had miraculously revealed the identity of the caller. It turned out that the monsignor was in desperate need of another curate—a kind of "relief pitcher" as he put it. It seems that the young fellow he had been presented with—fresh out of the seminary—seemed to have no idea how to handle the job. His homilies were taken directly from his theology class lecture notes, and even worse—he had a tendency to faint whenever he visited the sick. Did the abbot have a priest he might lend out for a while to shape up this kid? Somebody, he pleaded, who could talk to people at their level.

This urgent request meshed perfectly with the abbot's plans for Father John. The academic year was over, and the priest had no teaching duties during that summer. He was told to report to Saint James parish on July fifth. He was to come directly from his annual visit to his mother up in Berlin, New Hampshire. The priest's father had died suddenly two years earlier, but his mother was alive and well, still living in the home where she had raised John, their only child.

The home visit went well, as usual, and Father John arrived at the Saint James rectory door on a warm, sunny afternoon, carrying a small, battered suitcase. Father Lucas, the Prior, had offered him the bag from the store of commonly owned articles stored in the monastery basement. He was dressed in a somewhat uncomfortable departure from his accustomed monk's black, hooded tunic, with its broad cincture tied at the waist. The latter lately had begun to accent Father John's expanding middle, despite his attempts to moderate his appetite for the peanut butter and crackers always waiting in the refectory. Now, his short frame was draped in clericals several sizes too large, as was the Roman collar which hung around his neck like some sort of necklace. He had managed to retain his familiar black, scuffed shoes.

Lacking a housekeeper, and with his young curate off on an errand, the elderly monsignor answered the chime of the doorbell and opened the heavy oak door. The vision of Father John, wearing a broad grin and sporting a mere fringe of red hair on his otherwise bald head, was not what he had expected. Monsignor O'Malley looked down at this apparition from his spindly height of six feet, four inches, topped by the blessing of many an older Irishman—a shock of white hair in no danger of ever disappearing. His young curate may have been a disappointment so far in his priestly duties, he thought, but at least he presented himself in a proper way, with polished shoes, neat clothing and that nice touch—those French cuffs on a clean, white shirt.

Nevertheless, he greeted Father John amiably, and the monk was soon settled in an upstairs room about four times the size of his simple monastic accommodations.

The towering brick and granite church of Saint James had been built in the late 1870s after years of fund raising among the mainly Irish Catholic immigrants, most of whom were then working in the busy textile mills that stretched along the east bank of the river. In its early years, a grand edifice like this could expect to be filled with worshippers every Sunday, and its primary school would be packed with children studying under the stern eyes of a dozen nuns.

The church, overlooking those mills from its perch on the high bluff lining the western shore of the Merrimack, required a matching rectory as well as a convent. The former needed to be spacious enough to house a pastor and at least three curates, as well as afford space for a secretary and a housekeeper whose duties included cooking. The convent would have to house at least 12 nuns, and the school would need—well, given the Irish proclivity for large families—space for several hundred children.

Now, sitting on the edge of the unfamiliar bed, Father John tried to imagine the hustle and bustle of those long-ago days. It appeared that the heyday of the American Church had quite a long run. But about twenty years before I was born, he thought, at the Second Vatican Council in Rome, the assembled bishops and cardinals (all men) tried to follow the urging of Pope John to move the Church to dialogue and engagement with the modern world.

They did such a good job, he mused, after the good pope declared that he wanted to "throw open the windows of the Church so that we can see out and the people can see in," that many inside saw the new exits and climbed out. The convent of Saint James was now condos, while the school had been converted to low-income apartments, to the consternation of the neighborhood.

Standing, he sighed and began to unpack his sparse possessions—some underwear and socks, a spare shirt, his breviary, and a small wooden crucifix given to him by his late father. He smiled to himself as he thought how his old man would be happy to see him in the role of parish priest instead of "locking himself up" in a monastery. He remembered the trouble he had convincing his father, who "came over" from Galway in 1960 to look for work, that getting a Ph.D. in English was not such a waste of good brain power.

Well, he thought, here I am, ready to prepare a homily for what is left of a parish. After all, despite its mission, the Church has always been a mix of the sublime and the sheer messiness brought about by the fallibility of human beings. I'm just one of those humans, but I hope I can come up with a few words that will help out. I'm used to giving lectures to college kids, so I'd better tone down the rhetoric and keep it brief. Maybe I'll use the classic speaker's trick and glance at my watch halfway through, so they'll think I'm almost done. Well, time to stop worrying. My mother's favorite expression is "Worry is a useless emotion." I'll just keep soldiering on. He stopped short, almost dropping the crucifix he was propping up on the mahogany bureau. Why the heck did I use that expression? I'm trying to avoid using military terms, but they keep materializing.

He sat down again, this time on the leather recliner facing an incongruously large flat panel TV. He had already promised himself that he would hide the remote.

He thought back to his graduate student days at Notre Dame, when his comfortable existence had turned upside down. He entered the monastery at Saint Oliver upon graduating from the college in 1998. The next few years spent first as a novice, and later in studies leading to his ordination to the priesthood, offered little opportunity to engage in the "world," as his spiritual advisor Father McGhee labelled pretty much everything outside the monastery walls.

Even the traumatic bombing of the World Trade Center and the calamitous onset of the Iraq War in 2003 did not disturb the steady cadence of his scholastic and spiritual development, although certainly, in their daily prayers, the monastic community ritually remembered the victims of that terrorist attack, as well as America's fighting men and women. The newly minted priest, ordained in 2004, had been raised as a loyal Republican, as his father had been. One of his first assignments after ordination was to serve as the moderator of the Young Republicans Club, a group of 12 students who seemed quite pleased at the war's "progress." He had felt unprepared for his charges' questions and comments, and so began to frequent the library periodicals room. His father had often warned him against wasting his time with The Boston Globe, or above all, The New York Times. There had been no newspapers in the Fain household, except, of course, the New Hampshire Union Leader.

Father John was busy scanning the latest editions of those banned publications in preparation for a discussion with his Young Republicans, when the word came from the abbot that he had approved John's request to study at Notre Dame. Two days later, he was off to

South Bend, one week late for the beginning of the semester. To his surprise and consternation, he found his fellow graduate students to be a group with which he was totally unfamiliar—friendly, outgoing, inquisitive Catholic liberals. They soon made a habit of relentlessly challenging his conservative views, chiding him for his Republican roots. Every Friday, they would gather for beer and pizza, where they would dissect the latest news while pillorying the President, George W. Bush.

John's discomfort at this dissing of the Republican Commander-in-Chief was soon overwhelmed by the sheer weight of the evidence of Bush's tragic deceptions. While the earlier wars of the twentieth century were only history to him, the daily reports of death and destruction in the Middle East shook his conscience. How could he reconcile the peaceful message of Jesus with the atrocities of the battlefield? And after all, wasn't the war opposed publicly by the U.S. Catholic bishops? He couldn't recall hearing about that from any pulpit.

While he did not turn away from his well-ordered prayer life and spiritual reading, during the next four years he would find himself transitioning from John of the Cross to John Dos Passos, and from Beowulf to Berrigan. The poetry of pacifists like Robert Lowell and William Stafford spoke to his conscience as well as his intellect. He became especially fascinated with Daniel Berrigan. After all, Berrigan was a priest like himself. In 1968, in an act of moral outrage over the Vietnam War, he and eight others including his brother Philip—also a priest—stole files from the draft board in Catonsville, Maryland. They dropped them in a parking lot, poured homemade napalm over them, and set them on fire.

John could easily imagine what the reaction would have been in the New Hampshire monastery if anyone had proposed inviting Dan Berrigan to be a commencement speaker back then—that is, after he had been released from prison. Father Berrigan's many volumes of poems were added to the young monk's rapidly expanding bookshelf.

By his second year at Notre Dame, he had, as he told his friends one Friday evening, "grown a conscience as well as a beard." It was easy enough to find other students and professors who disagreed with his newfound Christian pacifism. In their friendly but intense discussions, his rhetorical challengers inevitably brought out the old standby, the just war theory. Traced back to Augustine and Aquinas, its arguments for the standards by which one could practice a Christian acceptance of violence had become a familiar rationale for placing Jesus Christ at the side of the soldier, putting his blessing on the slaughter.

John came to realize that, particularly in the nuclear age—begun at that moment in 1945 when the U.S. atomic bomb flashed beyond the brightness of a sun as it incinerated thousands of ordinary citizens in Hiroshima, Japan—the moral decisions surrounding war were even more critical. Had that vicious attack been a "last resort" and "proportional to the means used?" as that theory required? Faced with the fact that Jesus taught us to love our neighbors, he reasoned, how would it be reasonable to express that love by wounding, mutilating, and killing them?

His evolution to these pacifist views was buttressed by his growing conviction that to follow Jesus required a commitment to nonviolence. He even found himself sometimes linked arm in arm with dozens of other students as they marched in protest against the escalating wars in Iraq and Afghanistan, as well as in Darfur.

He felt a new sense of community with this small, vocal gaggle of young men and women, dedicated to peace activism.

As soon as he arrived back at Saint Oliver, Ph.D. in hand, and took up the familiar rhythms of daily monastic life, his life as an activist began to seem like a remote dream. Back in the classroom, he began the fall semester teaching a class in creative writing and one section in First-Year English. There was little chance to share his views on much more than adverbs, alliteration, and especially, the proper use of commas. There were a couple of lay faculty members who were outspoken with their anti-war opinions, but the reaction of his fellow monks and especially the abbot to those professors was enough to discourage him from joining their ranks. It did not take him long to settle into the comfortable role of a liberal-leaning, moderate academic.

However, as the years moved along, and the wars he had marched against were supplemented by new, bitter, bloody conflicts—Syria and Yemen among them—he felt that, as a matter of conscience, he could no longer remain still. This was especially the case when the nation elected a man who proved to be unstable, intensely narcissistic, and vengeful. No one, neither a domestic political foe nor another country's ruler, escaped the president's wrath if they dared to criticize him. Although the president cared little for details of history or global diplomacy, he was entrusted, as were presidents before him, with the permission to launch a nuclear attack—at his own discretion, despite whatever his mental state might be.

This simple act, which could condemn to death millions of innocent humans and destroy the world's civilization, could be brought about merely by means of activating the nuclear launch codes. The codes were carried by a military aide accompanying the president at all times.

He had planned on spending some time over the summer preparing to teach a seminar on Shakespeare's sonnets—every darn one of the 154, many of whom he found terribly dull. Well, at least they were short. In addition, he would introduce—with the support of the Curriculum committee—a course for senior majors he was labelling "The Poetry of Protest." That would at least be a more organized way to introduce the notion of pacifism to his students by way of having them read his favorite peace poets, followed by discussions where the subjects of war and militarism would come up naturally. Yes, he might even use this chance to discuss the poetry of a few "radical" priests like Dan and Phil Berrigan, or maybe Thomas Merton.

Wait a minute, he thought, breaking out of his reverie. He experimented with the recliner until he suddenly found himself flat on his back, staring at the ceiling. Struggling back to a more comfortable orientation, he reminded himself that he was due to deliver a homily on Sunday. But what would be an appropriate topic?

He reasoned that it would probably be best to seek the advice of the pastor. The old fellow seemed affable enough. Funny, the Church doesn't make monsignors anymore, he thought. No more chances to wear those cool clothes. There really isn't much need for ecclesiastical ambition these days, is there? There are so few priests left that a youngster could become a pastor in no time flat. Of course, he would find himself asked to be a chief executive, bookkeeper, preacher, confessor, fund raiser, and if there was time, visitor to the sick and all-round holy and wise man. He felt a pang of guilt, thinking of his quiet existence at the college.

Enough, he thought, time to get downstairs and get to meet the curate. He should be back soon. I wonder where the kitchen is. Well, "Once more into the fray." Darn, not again! I wonder, do these guys drink coffee? He walked down the carpeted stairs, and found the young curate waiting to greet him.

Father John walked into the monsignor's office, where he found him perched behind his large desk. The slim, young Father Sullivan, looking a bit pale for the season, sat down on one of the black wooden armchairs facing the pastor and John took the other. Mounted on the wall behind the desk there was a large oil painting of the Blessed Mother, clad in a blue gown, her arms outstretched. Father John had often wondered why Mary always appeared to be a perfectly beautiful Caucasian. He knew enough about geography to know that she could not possibly have looked like that. He stifled a brief impulse to start the conversation with a comment on that incongruity.

The atmosphere warmed up considerably as soon as the monsignor introduced the two, adding a brief, somewhat formal bio of both. It turned out that the Sullivans and the Fains both were families with Irish roots living in New Hampshire communities with far greater numbers of French-Canadian Americans. By the time little Jimmy and John were born, the old frictions among ethnic groups were a thing of the past. However, their grandparents kept the memories of the clashes between the Cotes and the Connors, and the Murphys and the Moreaus alive in the minds of the kids. Saint James church was a monument to those old days, as was Saint Theresa's across the river, whose nineteenth century donors made sure that its steeple was just a bit taller than that of Saint James.

The two priests laughed as they had to admit that more than 100 years later the latter was still considered to be the proper place for those with Celtic genes, and the former was more for the French. True, they knew that, in contrast to when they were kids, Manchester's demographics had changed considerably, and those parishes were beginning to look "more colorful," according to the pastor. Wanting to get in on the conversation, Father Jim pointed out that these newcomers, mostly Spanish speakers, were far more apt to attend Mass further towards the south end of Manchester. There, Our Lady of the Angels parish had the good fortune of having a young priest from Mexico to celebrate Mass in Spanish. O.L.A., as the locals called the small wooden church, was built in the '60s during a brief boom in church attendance. It boasted a busy soup kitchen as well as "Mary's Closet," where volunteers distributed donated clothing. The monsignor did not mention that he had been asked several times to set up similar sites at Saint James, but had declined, saying, "It's just not my style."

The topic turned to the coming weekend's liturgy.

"Now, you are both aware," the monsignor said in a serious tone, "we will be celebrating Trinity Sunday. This is one of my favorite topics, and do you know why?" Neither priest knew what to say.

"Because it is the biggest mystery of all, that's why. And if there is one thing we need to get across to the faithful, it's that we must get used to accepting things we cannot prove or even understand, and yet we know, through revelation, that they are true. I like to think about the Trinity as a kind of division of labor—God the Father as a kind of C.E.O. The Holy Spirit does the day-to-day work, and Jesus is the Savior. What do you two think?"

There was an awkward pause. Father John, who was becoming painfully hungry by that point, could only respond with, "Well, yes, I suppose ..." Father Jim, at first nonplussed at hearing this unique approach to the Trinity, sounded suddenly enthusiastic.

"I believe Saint Gregory of Nazianzus would have perhaps, in his own style, possibly have thought along those lines ..." He stopped, not sure how to proceed.

"Of course," said the monsignor, who had not paid a bit of attention to either of their replies. "Let's divide this particular labor as follows. James, you will try to explain the Trinity as best you can and conclude by telling the parishioners that you really can't understand it at all. And nobody can! That really gets across the whole idea of mystery!"

"Now, John, I want you to get a bit more theological. Remember how we used to say that Jesus is 'one in being' with the Father, and now we say Jesus is 'consubstantial' with the Father? You're a professor, so the people will pay attention if you get into the whole word thing—you know, like the Greek and Latin origins of the word, right?"

The monk nodded in agreement, hoping that ending this meeting meant that he might be able to get something to eat.

"Then it's a deal," the monsignor announced. "Fellas, let's celebrate our new trinity of priests right here with a good meal. John, you are probably not a vegetarian, but I have been for years, and I have been able to convert Jim here to the good life. Jim, I think there's some of that kale salad left over, and I know there's plenty of tofu. Let's eat."

The words of a familiar poem by William Stafford suddenly came back to Father John. It was in the last poem that Stafford had written on the day of his death. "You don't have to prove anything" my mother said. "Just be ready for what God sends." The trio headed for the dining room and the long oak table with seating for eight.

CHAPTER 2

That night, spent in and out of an uneasy sleep in unfamiliar surroundings, did little to put Father John's mind at ease. He woke for the final time at six and spent the next half hour staring at the ceiling, reviewing his meeting with the monsignor. It seems, he thought, that I have been given my marching orders. No, not again! The next thing you know I'll be "rifling" through my drawers and gathering "ammunition" for my sermon. Or maybe homily, which is now preferred, it seems. Anyway, what do I have to add to anyone's notion of the Trinity?

Suddenly, he heard a fragment of poetry in his head. It made him sit up, wide awake. He listened as the poem said: "Their voices were stilled across the land. / I sought them. I listened. / The only voices were war voices."

Yes, I know those lines, he realized. That's Stafford, from World War Two. What comes next? Wait, it goes ... He scrambled out of the bed and began to pace the floor. Yes, that's it. Stafford's poem then goes on to ask: "Where are the others?"

Well, where are they? Where am I? Where have I been since I returned from grad school? I suppose I have been nonviolent; I have taught my students what the books say they need to know, but where is my voice, the voice

I had in the streets and the seminar rooms and the pubs at Notre Dame? As soon as I was back here, I became a chameleon, taking on the color of my environment. True, after years of putting it off, I have been planning to teach a course this next semester where I use poets to introduce the idea of Christian pacifism to my students. Even that mild rebuke of militarism—a bunch of complaining poets—was enough to make the abbot banish me for a while. I guess he thought that a few months in the "real world" would straighten me out. So here I am, ready to give a homily on the Trinity to a bunch of Catholics who are probably quite comfortable quietly accepting arguments for justifying violence, even the unspeakable violence of modern war. Well, after all, that's why we're called "Roman" Catholics, isn't it?

Wait, he said out loud, "Trinity. The bomb. Oppenheimer, that poem—what was it again? Yes, that's the connection."

He dressed quickly, walked quietly down to the kitchen and made himself a mug of instant coffee. Returning to his room, he perched on the comfortable recliner, put the mug on one of its broad arms, and picked up the note pad and pencil he had discovered in the desk next to the television. An hour later, his coffee was cold, and the note pad was almost full.

Standing, he caught a glimpse of himself in the tall mirror on the opposite wall. He saw a man in his mid-40s, less than medium height, and a bit too heavy. The early morning light glanced off his bald crown. That's great, he thought, grinning. Just the man to inspire the flock. He remembered his father, who had retained even less red hair than John had, reassuring him about his appearance, saying, "Don't worry, you look as Irish as Paddy's pig."

Well, that might help with lots of parishioners, he mused. But I might need more of a boost than that. It's time I had the courage of my convictions and handed out some bran instead of Pablum. Wait, that's unfair. There's plenty of nutrition in Pablum. But I think I need to graduate from theology to morality.

Sunday arrived under grey, rainy skies, with a hint of chill in the air unusual for a New Hampshire July day. Father John hurried over to the church from the nearby rectory at 9:30. He decided to go in through the main entrance, to get a good look at his new temporary home. He walked through the spacious narthex, featuring a broad baptismal font topped by a golden dome, and opened the large wooden doors. The interior of the church was quite spectacular. The sacrifices of those early parishioners were expressed in columns of variegated marble supporting a lofty, arched ceiling illustrated with paintings, quite faded now, of angels ministering to Saint James. Backing the chancel, with its scarlet carpet, the elaborate white altar, replete with gold candlesticks, now acted merely as a mute backdrop for a simple marble table where Mass was offered. The traditional altar rail was gone, but the original tall pulpit remained. It was the bane of each of the aging pastors who inherited the massive structure. One had even broken a hip descending the four steps leading from the speaker's platform. However, the donors—the Shanahan family—had left quite a tidy sum for its maintenance, so it remained, looming over the nave whose dark pews could hold at least 600 worshipers.

He found that at least a dozen of the faithful were there already in the front pews, spaced about six feet apart out of habit. Four were wearing masks. He could hear the sounds of the Rosary rising from the group. Every parish had its "God squad" he thought, and here they were, getting ready to hear from the new temp. He walked quickly up the side aisle and ducked into the sacristy. The monsignor hadn't thought to give him a tour, but he was able to find the proper vestments easily. He was vested and ready when a dark-haired young girl walked in.

"Hello father, I'm serving today. My name is Fiona."

"So, you're the altar boy?" he replied with a grin.

He knew immediately that he had made his first mistake of the day.

"No, I think we are called servers now," she answered, with a withering look.

He patched that up as best he could, and soon they were proceeding together out towards the altar, watched closely by a congregation of nearly150 souls. The faithful were scattered throughout the roomy interior, with the majority towards the rear. As the familiar cadence of the liturgy began, the worshippers had no trouble hearing the ceremony, thanks to the small microphone that Father John had remembered to clip onto his green chasuble at the last moment.

It was time to read the Gospel. On this Trinity Sunday, it would begin with the stirring words, "God so loved the world that He gave His only Son ..." The congregation stirred when the priest bypassed the pulpit, descended the three stairs leading to the altar, and positioned himself in the wide center aisle. He said, "Good morning everyone" in a loud, jovial tone. As soon as he began speaking, he felt both at home and already a bit concerned. His years of lecturing in front of a class had given him the teacher's ability to gauge the reactions of his audience and respond to them.

He instinctively looked out over the assembled faces, many of whom were still wearing a mask. Almost all of them appeared to be beyond or near retirement age. To his immediate right there were two nuns in full habits, each somewhere around 90 years old but sitting ramrod straight, exactly six feet apart.

He began, "How many of you have heard of John Donne?"

His listeners, unsure if this was a rhetorical question, remained silent.

"Well, you probably would have liked him. He was raised a Catholic, and he and his wife had twelve children. Of course, that sort of thing was more common back in the fifteen and sixteen hundreds, but still ..."

Walking a bit further down the aisle, moving out of the visual field of the nuns, he went on.

"Anyway, John Donne was a poet. And that's where the Trinity comes in. Now I know that you have heard lots about the Trinity—the Father, Son and Holy Spirit. Most of you probably remember when we used to say the Holy Ghost, eh? Well, I want to talk to you about another trinity, and that's where John Donne comes in. It seems that Robert Oppenheimer was a John Donne fan. Maybe you remember Oppenheimer's name from your history books. Oppenheimer was a leading force behind the Manhattan Project back during the war. No, not 'the war to end all wars.' That was the first one—I guess that didn't work out, did it? No, it was during World

War Two, the so-called 'good war.' The Manhattan Project was the years-long, highly secret effort to build the first atomic bomb. And they succeeded, thanks to Oppenheimer and lots of other scientists, and the urging of Albert Einstein."

He detected the first stirrings of response. People began to shift slightly, and he could see looks of surprise and confusion here and there, even on the masked faces. He went on,

"By July nineteen forty-five, this new bomb was ready to be tested. The scientists placed a thirteen-pound ball of plutonium on top of a tower out in the New Mexico desert, and detonated it. The explosion, which challenged the brilliance of the sun, had the force of over twenty-one thousand tons of TNT. Oppenheimer had assigned a code name to this test. He called it Trinity. Historians trace the inspiration for this name back to Oppenheimer's recollection of a poem by John Donne that begins, 'Batter my heart, three-person'd God ...' The poem beseeches God to renew the writer in his faith. Ironically, the poem goes on to ask God to 'break' and 'burn' him to bend his will towards his creator. The fiery strength of this first nuclear weapon would soon be used to break and burn not only houses and buildings but humans—well over two hundred fifty thousand of them, although we will never know the exact number—when the U.S. dropped an atomic bomb on Hiroshima and another on Nagasaki, Japan. All pretense of destroying military targets was abandoned. These horrendous attacks and the earlier weeks of firebombing of over sixty Japanese cities were aimed at killing civilians. Now, what are we as Catholics to make of all this? This was not just a tragic episode in history. Our nation now has thousands of these nuclear weapons, far more powerful than the bombs that incinerated Hiroshima and Nagasaki. And so do other countries, including Russia. In the U.S. these weapons are waiting silently in underground silos scatted across the southwest, in airplane hangars waiting for the call to load them onto planes, and on submarines cruising across the world under the oceans. Young men and women in the military are assigned to wait for the call to unleash these weapons upon being given an order. How can it be morally justified to use such weapons against our fellow humans created by the triune God? If it is wrong, then how can we even possess them and base our defense policy on the threat to use them? And what is the burden on the consciences of those asked to follow such orders?"

Father John stopped for a moment when he saw five or six people stand and begin to move towards the door. There was a low murmur beginning to spread throughout the pews. He advanced a few steps and continued.

"My friends, I am going to tell you something that I am sure will surprise you. It will come as a surprise because you probably never hear this from a Catholic pulpit, or aisle." He added this with a smile—with not a bit of feedback.

"Well, I can tell you that Pope Francis, three years ago, told a Vatican conference on nuclear disarmament, speaking of nuclear weapons, 'If we also take into account detonation as a result of error of any kind, the threat of their use, as well as their very possession, is to be firmly condemned.' And did you know, by the way, that Nagasaki is the center for Roman Catholicism in Japan? That city's current bishop is part of an international effort to rid the world of these instruments of death. The pope's statement, I should tell you, went far beyond his predecessors, who maintained that, although we should strive toward nuclear disarmament, we have the right to keep these weapons as a deterrent—a way to prevent others from attacking us. I can say more about that at another time."

He paused for a moment and looked to his right, and then to his left.

"Remember," he said, firmly and slowly, "morality is not confined to following the teachings of Jesus. In the end, it is based on our human understanding and instinct that we owe each of our fellow humans dignity and respect. In other words, we all have a right to life. I am sure that sounds familiar to all of you. Nuclear war—even just assenting to the threat of it—is far removed from any kind of morality. And so, as we offer this Mass today, Trinity Sunday, let us ask God the Father to send us wisdom through the Holy Spirit to inspire us and enable us to follow the nonviolent path of His only begotten Son, Jesus Christ."

When the Mass ended, Father John offered a friendly goodbye to Fiona. She nodded and left without a word. The priest stood in the quiet sacristy, removing his vestments slowly. Perhaps, he thought, I can avoid the flock that I am sure has gathered outside, wanting my spiritual advice. Besides, he added, I am really getting hungry.

He left through the side door and headed towards the rectory. He had already given up the dream of bacon and eggs, but maybe ... The cluster of parishioners who were waiting outside the main entrance spotted him. "Father, wait," one of the women shouted as a female trio approached him. The rain had let up enough so there was only a light drizzle. Each of the three elderly women held a parish bulletin over her head to protect her perm.

The tallest of the three spoke first.

"Father," she said, a bit breathless from hurrying across the grass. "Maybe I misunderstood you. We need those bombs to protect us from the Russians. They have lots more than we do, and you can bet they would use them in a minute if they knew we didn't have any. And this crazy story that the Russians helped to elect our president! Why in the world would they do that? He's very strong against them."

"Well, Mrs. ..."

"Oh, sorry, Father. I'm Mary McCarthy, and this is Irene Murphy and Kathleen McIlroy."

"Glad to meet you all. You know, when it comes to war, we always have to keep in mind that wars really are between governments. The people—like you, me, and the Russian citizens, for example—are always stuck in the middle. The innocent citizens are told to do the fighting and dying. Please remember that a nuclear war could, in just a few minutes, incinerate and obliterate millions of innocent people caught up in a political struggle between governments—in fact, realistically, between a few individuals who happen to be in power."

Mary sniffed. "Well, Father, it's not that I would want the soldiers to actually drop the bombs and things, but they should at least be able to threaten to do it. It's like challenging a bully. If he thinks you mean it, he will probably back off."

Irene looked up at the priest from her height of five feet, two inches, just three inches lower than Father John's bald head, now well moistened.

"My husband Frank was in the service for twenty years, in the Army. He must have been willing to use lots of weapons to kill the enemy, like guns and grenades and things. What's the difference?"

"First of all," he answered, "It's nice to meet you, Irene. You have the same name as my mother, and her mother! I am sure your husband served his country with dedication. Actually, I would say that he served his government, not his country. Most of us have little to say who our government decides is the enemy. But once that decision is made, the leaders don't go into battle, the people do."

Kathleen, whose face had grown redder as the conversation continued, glared at Father John.

"With all due respect, Father, do you mean to say that you are against war? How else are we supposed to defend our way of life against the rest of the world? There are forces out there—and even inside our own country—that want to take away our precious freedoms, and I don't mean just our Second Amendment. I may be an older woman, but this Lady Derringer in my pocketbook is mine, and no one is going to come and take it away from me!"

He edged away from Kathleen just a bit.

"Now, Kathleen," he replied, gently, "I am never sure what people mean by 'our way of life' but let me ask you this. The Virus that's still around here and there. Most of us have been trying to protect each other from getting it. I mean, now that the vaccine's here, we still try to wear a mask if we are indoors in a crowd. Our instinct is to keep ourselves safe, but also everyone else as well. Can't we feel the same way about the whole world, all our human brothers and sisters everywhere? Don't …"

Kathleen cut him off.

"That whole Virus thing was a hoax. I never believed it for a moment. Anyway," she said, smiling sweetly, "we've taken up too much of your time, Father, with all of us standing here getting wet. Maybe we should have you come to the Lady's Sodality meeting so we can talk some more. We'll be in touch through Monsignor O'Malley."

The monsignor, accompanied by Father Jim, was waiting for him in his office. The elderly pastor stood up and pointed at Father John.

"Jumping Jehoshaphat, boyo, where in the world did you get those ideas? What in the world were you telling those people—mind you, the ones still going to church on a regular basis, but maybe not any longer after that performance?"

"Were you there?" John answered, puzzled.

"I didn't have to be. I kept that camcorder going that we installed to put the Mass online when people were still cowering in their houses, so afraid of that Virus. Well, it didn't hurt me, and I'm eighty-two! So, I heard every word. Mister, if I wanted Gandhi, I would have hired a Hindu. I wanted you to be a mentor to Jim here, but it looks like you could learn a few things from him."

He sat down and turned to Father Jim.

"Give the peace monk a sample of what you preached at the eight."

40

Father Jim, looking a bit pale, cleared his throat. "Well, I …"

"Speak up, we can't hear you."

"Alright, well, because the homily is meant to be a commentary on the Gospel, and it was—or still is—I mean, the Feast of the Holy Trinity, I tried to emphasize that the Trinity is a great mystery, and so we need to approach it with reverence and … well …"

"You see now, Reverend Fain, what a homily is supposed to be. You sounded like you were talking to the bloody ROTC! And if it's peace you want, you should be telling the people to pray for the peace that Christ gives, and to trust in Him for everything."

He paused, a bit out of breath. The monk answered in a calm voice.

"I certainly agree with our need to seek such peace. But remember that old saying: 'Pray as though everything depended on God; act as though everything depended on you.' You know, Monsignor, I was reminded of that quote when I saw a group praying the Rosary before Mass. I'm sure some of their intentions included peace in this warring world. I guess I am used to being a professor, so I tend to think preaching about peace has to include teaching and then action based on that teaching."

"But for heaven's sake, how did you veer off talking about atomic bombs? I know the prophet Isaiah advised that we beat swords into plowshares, but that's Old Testament advice. Besides, they say that he ended up being sawed in half!"

"Well, I did think you would have approved my quoting the pope about nuclear weapons. If I knew you were

41

listening, I would have added the U.S. bishops' recent statement in which they stated they were 'firmly committed to nuclear disarmament.' They called that a 'moral goal.'"

Father Jim, even paler than before, spoke up.

"But look, John. Those are fine ideals, but how are we supposed to defend ourselves against the forces of evil? What if we get rid of all those bombs—although I don't think there are as many around as you say—are our regular weapons like guns and tanks and things a match for other countries, like Russia and … and maybe China? And by the way, I really haven't heard all that about the pope and bishops making such strong statements. We had a class in the sem about papal pronouncements, but they didn't mention what you are talking about."

The monsignor added, "The Church is not supposed to get involved in politics. Period."

"Well, I can tell you this much," John answered, "back in two thousand seventeen, the United Nations approved a treaty that called for the abolishment of nuclear weapons. The Vatican became the first state in the world to ratify that new treaty. Oh, and you might be interested to know that Ireland has signed it also."

Monsignor O'Malley sat back and sighed.

"All right, now listen to me. After you have been a parish priest for half a century like I have, you'll understand that the people don't want to hear about what's going on outside the walls of their nice, peaceful church—out there in the world, which has always been a mess because of Satan and sin. They want to hear something encouraging and useful for their lives. Jim here gave a great little homily a couple of weeks ago about the widow's mite. That's always a great story, and it moves the listeners to action. The collection was about seven hundred bucks! And with the way things have been going, we are on the edge of not being able to send the bishop our monthly obligation to the diocese. He'll be on the warpath. Oh, sorry, Father. So, let's call a truce. Now, here is what's coming up this week for you two. Jim, you and John will concelebrate the daily seven-thirty. I know that we get only about fifteen folks, but I want them to get to know our new assistant. Besides, most of them are the 'pillars of the church' as they say. Which reminds me—John, I want you to show up at the Knights of Columbus monthly meeting on this Wednesday. When they heard a monk would be spending some time here, they hoped you would give them some spiritual advice. Will you be telling them to 'Praise the Lord and pass the ammunition?' by any chance?"

Father John managed a weak grin. This turned into a smile, but it lasted only a moment. The monsignor announced, "Well, boys, time for our Sunday brunch. Jim, make us some of that avocado toast. I'll break out the herbal tea. John, we've got some great chamomile."

The Knights of Columbus meeting was held downstairs in the church, in a small meeting room previously used for the parish office. Now that the roomy church hall was closed, and its spacious kitchen was no longer available, the Knights each brought food from home—far more than the 15 older gentlemen could possibly eat.

The meeting proved to be a veritable oasis for Father John. While his monastic refectory was not exactly a haven for a gourmet, he was not sure how long he could hold out on the rations served in the rectory. The meeting started, to his relief, with a delicious meal. It wasn't until the feast was approaching dessert time that any earnest conversation could get underway. Billy O'Connor, the same Billy that left the priest's Sunday Mass early, was the president of the Knight's chapter. He began by offering a warm welcome to the assembled, and quickly got down to business.

"Well, gentlemen," he said in a hearty tone that retained a bit of an edge, "Father Fain, as many of you know, comes to us from the college. If any of you attended last Sunday's ten o'clock, you probably heard him give a talk that was, well, a bit different from what we are used to." He looked toward a tall, thin man still wearing his tweed scally cap. "Jimmy Murphy, I'm thinking your wife would agree, eh? So, I thought I would invite Father here so we could get to know him better and give him a chance to give us a few words of spiritual development, so to speak. Father do you know much about the Knights?"

"Well now, Billy, I know a good deal about the Knights. My uncle Sean was very active up in the North country when I was growing up. I used to envy that great outfit he wore with the cape and the feathered hat and all. I can understand why many of you miss that getup since you have modernized the look a bit. I must say, though, I am sorry that you've kept the sword—it is just such a symbol of violence that it doesn't seem to fit in with what you guys do—some really great charitable work. And that was why an Irish priest started your organization many years ago. Why he would choose to honor Columbus instead of a saint is puzzling to me. How do you all feel about that? And the whole Knight thing. Don't get me started on the Crusades. You don't want to be here all night. Now, I know we are supposed to beat those swords into plowshares, but I guess it would be pretty tough to hang one of those on your belt, right?"

He saw a few scattered smiles, but not nearly enough.

"Father," said a gravelly voice from the far end of the table, "We named our son Christopher after Columbus. As in Saint Christopher, the one who protects travelers. And you know, Columbus discovered America—the country my son serves right now in the United States Marines." Most of the assembled Knights clapped.

Father John smiled. He felt grateful that he was fortified by food, sugar, and caffeine. "Well now," he said, in what he hoped was a firm but friendly tone, "I certainly don't mean to say anything negative about your great work. From what the monsignor tells me you have helped many struggling families in the parish, and that's wonderful. But I have to admit that as a priest first, and then as a professor, I can't help but be honest and straightforward with you when it comes to talking about the teachings of Jesus, and I also have this nagging sense of needing to be accurate."

A few listeners raised their hands, but he continued.

"Good old Saint Christopher didn't make the cut. He has not been an 'official' saint for years. The Christopher on the medals is a mix of a few facts and lots of legends. My mother doesn't agree, by the way, but that's another story. And you know, Christopher Columbus didn't discover America, he bumped into it. But he did discover that people were already living there—people that he decided would make great slaves. He was there in a search for gold and other riches, and for the forceful conversion of the inhabitants. Columbus is actually a great example of how far Christianity had come since the first few centuries after the death of Jesus. When Constantine, the Emperor of Rome in the fourth century, was converted to Christianity, there was a drastic change in Christians' participation in the violence of war. Jesus had taught nonviolence, so his followers naturally chose to preserve life rather than put an end to it. When they were suddenly no longer a persecuted minority, and became the official religion of the land, they were swept up into the violence of political and religious conflicts. So, Christians who were in a position of political or religious influence began to construct elaborate arguments for defending violence in all sorts of situations. Now, it has become so natural for Catholics to think that 'God is on our side' that it has become tough to defend the original dedication to nonviolence—to pacifism."

"What about defending our country?"

"Great question. I can tell you this, right now in the twenty-first century, the risks of a war that will kill possibly billions of humans and destroy so much of our environment are so great because of the existence of nuclear weapons. Those weapons are waiting, armed and ready to go, as we speak. We need to make the right choice between diplomacy or war, and reconciliation or revenge. If we choose war, then we are doomed. If we choose another path, we have at least a chance, and the lessons of Jesus point the way. Remember Albert Einstein? He encouraged the invention of the atomic bomb, but after the horrors of Hiroshima and Nagasaki he and many other scientists who had worked on the project deeply regretted their participation. Einstein is said to have remarked that World War Four would be 'fought with sticks and stones' because there would be so little left after a Third World War."

He looked at the questioner. "To answer you about defending our country, I can only say that violence against another human, whether it is by using a rifle, or hand grenade, artillery, tanks, napalm, a nuclear weapon, or a spear, club or sword is an act that is contrary to the teachings of Jesus. I know you don't want an hour lecture here but let me make one more point. And remember, I am not talking about a principle just for followers of Christianity. Nonviolence is the only way for humans to ever achieve lasting peace. As soon as we start to talk about 'just wars' you can bet that we will end up in one. Discussions or arguments about these topics usually include someone who maintains that, even though these 'nukes' are dangerous, we need them for our protection. That's the principle of 'deterrence.' And if they attack, we attack back in revenge. That's referred to as MAD, or 'Mutual Assured Destruction.'"

Billy O'Connor interrupted. "That's right, Father, they know that if they shoot at us, we will shoot right back, and with everything we've got, and that's a lot."

"You're making my point, Billy. That is exactly what would happen. And then the world would turn dark, at least what was left of it. There would be a 'nuclear winter,' as scientists call it, where the skies would be choked with ash, the temperature would drop, and crops would not grow. Of course, we are not sure how many humans would be left to suffer starvation. Remember, every moment that we maintain the posture of MAD, we are assenting—giving our permission—to use those nukes against other humans. That is immoral. OK, speaking about starvation, we need to get to some delicious dessert and coffee, so let me leave you with this scenario. When we talk about MAD, we tend to picture a situation where a country like Russia or North Korea decides for whatever reason to try to pull off a surprise attack, and we are left helpless. But what if we had a leader—I won't name names here, I don't want to get into politics—who was in, let's say to be polite, 'cognitive decline,' and decided to go to war and strike first? Or maybe he just got drunk or forgot his meds and pushed the button? Or maybe the whole thing starts with an accident. My point is that by their very existence, and by our very willingness to use them, nuclear weapons pose an unacceptable threat to humanity and to our consciences."

"Wait a minute, Father," said the gravelly voice. "My name is Frank Fallon, and my son is Christopher, the Marine I mentioned a minute ago. Are you saying he shouldn't be in the military? Then why does his unit have a Catholic chaplain?"

"Frank, that is a complicated question. You probably have heard that old saying, 'There are no atheists in foxholes.' Well, there are plenty of pacifists in foxholes, or at least people who don't agree with war, or maybe just that particular war. And yet they fight on, especially because their training has instilled in them a fierce dedication to each other. I don't mean to suggest that men and women in the military are some kind of conditioned robots. That would be terribly unfair. It's just that, in order to go to war, governments need to convince their people that the cause is just, noble and in the nation's vital interests, despite any evidence to the contrary. Over the centuries, governments have developed a system of military recruitment and training that drowns young men and women in a sea of rhetoric and sends them off to do what their instincts rebel against—kill and maim whomever their government and superiors identify as the enemy. And you wonder where PTSD comes from?"

Billy stood up. "Well, Father, we'd better end here. Thank you for coming tonight and sharing your thoughts with us. As we do with all our speakers, we've recorded your remarks and I'll be posting a link to them in the parish bulletin. There's an Irish proverb that goes like this, 'To a man prepared for war, peace is assured.' Oh, and there's another one. 'Many a time a man's mouth broke his nose.' Let's get to those pastries."

The following Sunday morning was warm and dry. Father John headed over to the church, giving himself just enough time to start Mass. The waiting altar server was Taylor, a tall, skinny boy who had little to say beyond his name, and appeared nervous. John could not help wondering if the kid had talked to Fiona.

He had spent the last couple of days visiting parishioners who were in nursing homes. The atmosphere was still one of great caution. While the spread of the Virus had slowed, the decline in case numbers was due in part to increased vigilance in those vulnerable sites. He wore a gown, gloves, a mask, and a face shield. One of the nurses pinned a large plastic cross to his gown to signify that he was a clergyman and not a doctor or nurse, or maybe someone who disinfected the floors. Twelve parishioners had succumbed to the Virus in the two local homes. Their families all awaited a time when they could have a funeral for their deceased loved ones.

On Saturday evening, the monsignor, instead of offering the expected stern warning about John's upcoming homily and forbidding him avoid any mention of war, appeared to have forgotten about his earlier diatribe. Instead, he pointed out how the Gospel for that Sunday's service fit in so well with John's nursing home visits.

"Now, you know, Father, that you will be commenting on how Matthew tells us about how Jesus went about healing people from all kinds of diseases, physical and mental. I'm sure that you can come up with some useful remarks about how all that fits in with this terrible Virus business. They had their plagues then and we are battling ours now. You need to remind people to ask God to shield us from illness. And by the way, Jim tells me that he noticed quite a few more worshippers at the four o'clock Mass this afternoon. That just may be a sign that his preaching style speaks to their lives—if you get my drift."

When John walked out to the altar with the reluctant Taylor, he could see immediately that there were half as many in the pews as there had been on the previous Sunday, and the elderly nuns were nowhere to be seen. However, a few minutes later, as he approached the center aisle to begin his homily, and looked out at the congregation, which now seemed to be huddled towards the rear of the church, he spotted two women off to his left. He immediately recognized them as nuns, but not the nonagenarians of the previous week. Sisters, he thought to himself, they can't fool me!

The two women had that indefinable air about them that he recognized as a fellow post-Vatican II, liberal religious. Both had short, gray hair. One wore a white blouse, the other blue, with their black skirts reaching well below the knees. The real giveaway was the small, gold cross each wore around the neck. "Mercys!" he thought, looks like I have some backup!

His years of social activism at Notre Dame had given him a keen appreciation for the Sisters of Mercy. Whenever he had been in the street in some sort of protest, usually antiwar or against some human rights violation, there would always be some Sisters of Mercy marching and carrying signs. Along with like-minded Methodists, Unitarians, Presbyterians, Quakers, Buddhists, and pro-testors from other religious persuasions, the "Mercys" could be counted on to show up and support peace and justice actions. Any lingering reluctance he may have about his message that morning disappeared when he spotted the Sisters.

"Good morning, everyone" he began, followed by a low, muffled response.

"Well, those of you who were fortunate enough to be here in this beautiful church last Sunday will remember that I talked to you about the Trinity—the Father, Son and Holy Spirit. I hope you also remember that I brought up another trinity in order to talk about a mortal danger that you and I, and in fact, every human being, face every day—a danger that is both physical and spiritual. I talked about the first nuclear bomb test, labeled with the code name Trinity, and how from that beginning in nineteen forty-five these weapons of mass destruction, which have only been used twice against our fellow human

51

beings—and only by this United States of America—have spread like a cancer across the world. Nine countries now have nuclear weapons—a total of over thirteen thousand of them. And why, in a homily delivered in a Catholic church, did I bring up this subject? Well, as I told you last week, our pope thought it was important enough to move him to visit both Hiroshima and Nagasaki just recently. Let me read to you a bit of what he said then. 'In a world where millions of children and families live in inhumane conditions, the money that is squandered and the fortunes made through the manufacture, upgrading, maintenance and sale of ever more destructive weapons are an affront crying out to heaven.'"

He paused for a moment and caught a glimpse of the two Sisters nodding to each other.

"With those words," he went on, "the Holy Father underlined the threat that these weapons pose, should they ever be used as tools of war, to the lives of billions. He also emphasized in no uncertain terms the real injustices that they cause each and every day, as governments squander money maintaining and improving those weapons, money that could be used to alleviate poverty and all its attendant suffering. Note that the pope pointed to the 'manufacture' and 'sale' of those nuclear weapons. There are fortunes to be made in the business of not only nukes, but in all the instruments of war. We have come a long way from clubs and spears. War is now based on sophisticated technology, a situation that has spawned whole industries dedicated to producing and selling products designed for the same old-fashioned purpose as the spear or sword—to kill and maim humans. I am not talking about some far-off scenario. Why, here in New

Hampshire, we have two major companies—and some smaller ones—who are principal contributors to what President Eisenhower warned Americans against—the 'military-industrial complex.' Both Raytheon and BAE Systems, not far from here, play major roles in developing and selling the technology of modern war."

Four people stood and walked out, a bit more noisily than was necessary. Father John continued. "That reminds me of two other trinities. By the way, I just violated a rule for preachers. Never say how many points you intend to make. Instead of thinking that you might be finished, they will know how much you have left."

Only the two Sisters smiled. He went on.

"The first trinity is one emphasized by that great American hero, Dr. Martin Luther King, Jr. He literally gave his life speaking out against another trinity—the three evils of militarism, racism, and economic oppression. The other comes from the author Jonathan Schell back in the nineteen-eighties. In his book, *The Unconquerable World,* he pointed out how nonviolence can give power to people trying to resolve conflicts, from local to international. He wrote, 'Peace, social justice, and defense of the environment are a cooperative triad against the coercive, imperial triad of war, economic exploitation, and environmental degradation.' Now, I know all this is a lot to digest at one sitting. I have introduced a lot of topics, but they all have in common the fact that they are moral issues—issues that speak to our consciences and demand decisions on our part. I hope to elaborate on what I have been talking about this morning in future homilies. Or maybe we can even start up a discussion group if there is enough interest. What do you think?"

He paused and scanned the congregation. To his right, a teenaged boy slowly raised his hand. His father nudged him, and his son quickly lowered it. John continued.

"Today's Gospel talks about the healing ministry of the Church. We need to pray every day for healing, not just for our illnesses—our physical suffering—but for the wisdom and courage to speak out in opposition to, and to act nonviolently against, the very existence of nuclear weapons. Next Sunday, I want to tell you about some of your fellow Catholics who have put their freedom on the line in doing just that. Some of them are in jail today for taking a moral stand, so please remember them in your prayers."

The two nuns entered the sacristy as Father John was putting away the "visitor's" unadorned chalice. He had preferred to leave his own chalice back at the monastery for safekeeping. Although he had pleaded with his parents to "keep it simple" when they presented him with a chalice at his ordination, they had sold their car to purchase a gem-studded gold cup that looked to him like it belonged at the Vatican. He didn't agree with the choice, but he loved them for it.

The taller of the duo said, cheerily, "Hi, Father. It's great to meet you. I'm Eileen Healy and this is Mary Lyons. We are Sisters of Mercy from way down south in Nashua."

"Well, what do you know. And I thought you were Bedford housewives. You have Mercys written all over you. How the heck did you end up here listening to my eloquent preaching?"

Mary Lyons answered with a broad smile. "The word on the street, Father, is that there is a radical priest in town, and we needed to come up here and see if it was true. Looks like our no nukes friends were right. Next thing you know, you'll be leading some lefty rabble down the street towards Raytheon."

"Wait a second, I just got here last week," he said, laughing. "And what are you two doing down in the Gate City?"

"Right now, we are really busy with a few things," Mary explained in a more serious tone. "We operate a food pantry in conjunction with the local Catholic Worker, we also have what we call a 'Clothing Closet' where we give away donated items, and lately we have been busy helping immigrants with English language instruction and generally helping them get settled. New Hampshire's immigrant population is changing the face of the Granite State—and we love it. We both spent ten years working in Central America."

"Man, that is impressive, and I really mean that. I'd better warn the monsignor that you're in the neighborhood."

"You mean that old curmudgeon, Timothy O'Malley?" Eileen asked. "I wouldn't want to bad mouth your boss, but Timmy tried his best to stop the Catholic Worker from setting up shop in Nashua. He still thinks they are Communists. But beyond all that, when we listened to your homily this morning, we knew that the scuttlebutt was true. It looks like you are a prime candidate for joining our crowd of misfits when we do a CD against Raytheon next month. We could use a priest in his collar out in the street with us. What do you say, Father?"

The priest hesitated a moment, then replied, "Sisters, this is not something I expected this morning. To be honest with you, I have been keeping a low profile since I get back to the college. In fact, when they asked—I mean, when the abbot told me to help out here this summer, I had been trying to figure out how to sneak social justice issues into my English classes. When I realized I would be giving homilies here every Sunday and talking with parishioners about their lives, I realized I didn't have to wait for the fall semester to start being a rabble rouser again."

"Father, I didn't realize you were new to the game here," Sister Eileen said, surprised. "So, you were in grad school?"

"Yup, Notre Dame for four years. I went out there right after ordination. I arrived full of theory, and I fell in with a bunch of bright, scruffy ne'er-do-wells in the English department. They managed to turn my theological principles into action in the real world. I have to admit to you that I'm no stranger to CDs—all nonviolent, of course. However, I was always in mufti. I didn't need the abbot getting hot under the hood, you know what I mean?"

They both nodded.

"We do," Sister Mary said, "Don't forget, we have a Superior. But she's not an obstacle. She just got out after doing six months for a sit-down at the School of the Americas in Georgia. Sorry, they changed the name to the Western Hemisphere Institute. I guess that sounds more innocent. Anyway, Father, you are a sight for sore eyes, as my Irish grandmother used to say. I can say with confidence that you will take the prize for being the youngest troublemaker in our group. I mean, Eileen and I were running around with signs at the Clamshell Alliance demos over at Seabrook back in the day, so we are on the other end of the spectrum."

"OK, I tell you what, Sisters. I am really happy that you got in touch with me on this. It's about eleven-thirty, I 've got low blood sugar, and I've got to face the old fella over in the rectory. Just tell me how I can contact you and I promise to get in touch very soon. And I want to hear more about that Catholic Worker. I'm going to have my students read Peter Maurin's *Easy Essays* this semester."

Sister Eileen handed the priest a card with the community's email address, cell phone number, and the link to their blog website.

"This will get you to Sister Bridget. And if you talk with her, please ask if she can find a donor who will upgrade that phone. I mean the iPhone 5 was really cool at the time, but really. Great meeting you. See you soon, we hope!"

Father John walked back to the rectory slowly, anticipating another emotional session with the monsignor. No problem, he thought, he calmed down pretty quickly last time. I'm sure he can put up with me until September. But for sure, I won't bring up my new radical nun friends. He doesn't need another bee in his biretta.

He opened the rectory door and headed for the office, where he expected Monsignor O'Malley and Father Jim to be lying in wait. Instead, before he reached the office door, he almost tripped over an object on the floor at the foot of the stairs. It was his suitcase, which appeared to be packed and ready to go.

Father Jim walked slowly out of the office and approached John. He appeared to be trembling. John felt a sudden surge of sympathy for him.

"Jim, relax, I already got the message. Looks like my tour of duty is over—darn, there I go again. I have to admit that I didn't think your boss would take this so seriously."

The young priest, red-faced, spoke quickly. "I have been told by Monsignor O'Malley that he has been in touch with Abbot Richard, who is expecting you back at the monastery today, ASAP. The monsignor, by the way, is lying down on the davenport. He needed one of his nitros after he heard your homily this morning. Oh, and Billy O'Connor was in with him for an hour this morning. I'll give you a ride back to the college. We just got Monsignor's Escalade back from the mechanic's. I just want you to know …"

Father John cut him off, with a smile. "Don't worry, I do know. Anyway, that bed upstairs was killing my back. Let's go."

The world is awash in nuclear weapons. The first of these, invented to kill Japanese citizens and discourage Japan from prolonging World War II, had a destructive capacity far less than the weapons that are now dispersed across the Earth, waiting silently for a command or accident to trigger explosive forces that could destroy civilization.

During the Cold War—the long, bitter political rivalry between the United States and the Soviet Union and their respective allies which began shortly after World War II—both sides amassed enormous numbers of nuclear weapons. By 1986, the joint stockpiles of those rivals totaled more than 64,000 warheads. (A warhead is the "tip" of a nuclear weapon. It contains the explosive material.) That number has been reduced in keeping with several treaties. The United States and Russia possess the majority of the many weapons that remain. However, a new "arms race" was well underway in the early 21st century.

Back during the Cold War, the Army, Navy, Air Force and Marines all had nuclear weapons, and each branch vied for superiority in numbers. For example, in 1950, the Army told Congress they needed 151,000. The Air Force claimed to need 10,000 intercontinental ballistic missiles (ICBMs), while the Navy thought that perhaps 100 nuclear-armed submarines would fit their needs.

As of 2020, those numbers seem absurd. However, the large number of nuclear weapons and their destructive power still distributed among nine nations represents an immediate danger to civilization. The reduction in their numbers was required by several international treaties, which are now in peril. Increased tensions between the United States and Russia have led to the design, research, and deployment of numerous "improved" nuclear weapons and delivery systems.

The estimated global nuclear warhead inventory in 2020 was approximately 13,410. Ninety-one percent of them were owned by the United States and Russia. Their exact number is a closely held national secret, but we have a good approximation, as follows, for the totals of nukes earmarked for use: Russia (4,312), United States (3,800), France (290), China (320), United Kingdom (195), Israel (90), Pakistan (160), India (150), North Korea (35).

Beyond the nine nuclear-armed states, Belgium, Germany, Italy, the Netherlands and Turkey each host American nuclear weapons. The United States has operational control of those weapons, which are basically nuclear bombs waiting at air bases in those nations.

Of the 3,800 U.S. warheads, 1,750 are ready to go, and 2,050 are held in reserve. Of those that are armed and ready, 400 are on land-based intercontinental ballistic missiles, 900 are on submarine-launched ballistic missiles, and 300 are at bomber bases, where they can be quickly loaded onto planes. Another 150 are deployed at European air bases. These are short-range nuclear bombs, intended for battlefield use. The combination of land, sea, and air-based nuclear weapons is referred to as the nation's "nuclear triad."

U.S. nuclear weapons are stored at about 24 locations across 11 states and five European countries. The largest U.S. location is also the largest such complex in the world. The Kirtland Underground Munitions Maintenance and Storage Complex, in Albuquerque, New Mexico has a capacity of 301,000 square feet. Most of the weapons there are "retired" and waiting to be shipped to Texas for dismantlement. This transfer is done using large, unmarked trucks accompanied by State Police.

Washington State also has large numbers of weapons at the Strategic Weapons Facility Pacific (SWFPAC) in Silverdale. In 2016, the U.S. Navy built a $294 million underground storage complex where they keep the ballistic missiles and warheads for the Pacific submarine fleet operating in the Pacific Ocean. The adjacent Naval Submarine Base Kitsap is 20 miles from downtown Seattle. The SWFPAC and Kitsap store approximately 1,300 nuclear warheads with a combined explosive power of 14,000 Hiroshima bombs.

U.S. land-based intercontinental ballistic missiles were labeled by former Secretary of Defense William Perry as "some of the most dangerous weapons in the world" because they could set off an accidental nuclear war. These ICBMs are located in 400 hardened, underground massive cylinders, or "silos," scattered across three sites—F.E. Warren Air Force Base, Wyoming, Malmstrom Air Force Base, Montana, and Minot Air Force Base, North Dakota. The Wyoming site extends into northern Colorado and western Nebraska.

Each silo contains one Minuteman III missile carrying one nuclear warhead. The Minuteman system has been in use since 1968, with repeated upgrades. Each silo site covers up to three acres. A silo is 80 feet deep and 12 feet in diameter. The missile itself is sixty feet long and 5½ feet in diameter. When launched, its solid fuel propellant can carry the missile for up to 8,000 miles at a top speed of 15,000 mph. These missiles are intended to arc over the North Pole and strike Russia in about one-half hour. Each silo is operated through an underground launch control center. There are five of these centers for the 400 silos.

Once fired, the missiles cannot be controlled or destroyed. Each warhead has the explosive power of 300-475 kilotons (kt) of TNT, that is, 300,000 to 475,000 tons of TNT. The bomb that destroyed Hiroshima was the equivalent of 15,000 tons.

The Minuteman III missiles, now resting in their silos, are on hair-trigger alert. The Pentagon has a launch-on-warning policy. If an incoming attack is detected, the missiles are to be launched before the attack arrives. Any defect in the warning system could result in a tragic, lethal mistake. In September 2020, the defense contractor Northrup Grumman was awarded a $13.3 billion award in the Ground Based Strategic Deterrent (GBSD) competition to build the next generation of the U.S. Air Force's ICBMs. These will start to replace the Minuteman III missiles in 2029. The Air Force describes these new missiles as offering "strategic nuclear options to address the threats of today and tomorrow." Their greater range will make it possible to target not only Russia but also China, North Korea and Iran. The cost of making these missiles is estimated to be about $100 billion.

The U.S. Navy has a fleet of 14 Ohio-class ballistic missile submarines (SSBNs). Eight of these operate in the Pacific out of Naval Base Kitsap near Bangor, Washington. The others cruise in the Atlantic from Naval Submarine Base Kings Bay, Georgia. They are considered virtually undetectable. Eight to 10 of these 560-foot-long submarines are on 24-hour, year-round patrol, each carrying a crew of 150. Each of the 14 submarines can carry up to 20 Trident II D5 ballistic missiles. These are being upgraded to the Trident D5LE, which has a range of more than 7,400 miles. Each missile can carry up to eight nuclear warheads. The subs are typically loaded with approximately 90 warheads, each of which has the force of at least 32 Hiroshima bombs. Each of these submarines carries the equivalent of the explosive power of seven World

War IIs. Submarine patrols last about 77 days. Most of the patrols occur in the Pacific, due to the increased war planning against China and North Korea.

Planning for a new generation of ballistic missile submarines is well underway, with the Columbia-class replacing the current Ohio-class in the late 2020s at a projected cost of $103 billion.

In 2019, Congress approved the development of the first new nuclear weapon since the end of the Cold War (1991). This "low-yield" warhead has been installed on some of the Trident missiles. The W76-2 has the blast power of eight kilotons—about half that of the Hiroshima bomb. These warheads are considered by many to be "destabilizing" because they lower the threshold between conventional and nuclear war. In one possible scenario, if the Russians, for example, used one of their low-yield weapons in a conflict over Eastern Europe, a response by the U.S. would not only increase the devastation, but Russia might not be able to distinguish the oncoming low-yield missile from a more powerful one, and a large-scale nuclear exchange could follow.

Both the U.S. and Russia have other variable yield nuclear weapons, often referred to as "tactical." These are intended for so-called "limited" conflicts. Former Secretary of Defense James Mattis, in his 2018 testimony before the House Armed Services Committee, said he does not believe that "there is any such thing as a tactical nuclear weapon. Any nuclear weapon used any time is a strategic game changer." Russia has around 2,000 of these, which can be delivered by artillery, missiles, or air dropped. The U.S. maintains an arsenal of 230 air-dropped tactical nuclear bombs. One hundred and fifty of these are deployed at six bases in five European countries, and shared with selected NATO partners.

In 2019, in defending the U.S. deployment of tactical nuclear weapons, Rep. Adam Smith (D-Wash) commented, "We don't care about a fair fight. We're going to kick their ass if they take us on ... So, why we're obsessing about a proportional response, I don't know."

The U.S. Air Force can deliver nuclear weapons from several types of planes. Eighteen B-2A and 42 B-52H bombers are organized into nine bomb squadrons at three bases—Minot Air Force base in North Dakota, Barksdale Air Force Base in Louisiana, and Whiteman Air Force Base in Missouri. The B2s each can carry up to 16 nuclear bombs, and each B52 can carry up to 20 air-launched cruise missiles. The bombs fall by gravity, while the cruise missiles can travel at least 1,500 miles.

The U.S. is developing new and improved nuclear weapons—the B61-12 bomb and the Long Range Standoff Weapon (LRSO). The latter is a nuclear-armed air-launched cruise missile. The prime contractor for the LRSO is Raytheon. The B61-12 bomb can be adjusted to deliver an 0.3 to 50 kiloton warhead, giving the bomb a "strategic" version for city-size targets and a "tactical" type for battlefield use. It has a new guidance system to improve its accuracy. Five hundred of these will be available by 2024 at a cost of $28 million each.

The B-21 Raider will be the new plane. It will enter service in the mid-2020s. One hundred and seventy-five B-21s will be built at a cost of $550 million per plane.

In terms of future developments in nuclear weaponry, the sky's the limit. At a White House ceremony in May 2020 celebrating the founding of the U.S. Space Force—the first new military service since the U.S. Air Force was established in 1947—the president announced that the U.S. is building a "super-duper missile" that can travel "seventeen times faster than what we have right now." He was referring to the development of "hypersonic" missiles—those that travel at least five times the speed of sound. The U.S. is far behind the Russians in this particular facet of arms competition.

In April 2020, the Russians announced the debut of their Avangard hypersonic glide weapon. It sits atop an intercontinental ballistic missile. When released, it can fly 27 times quicker than the speed of sound. It carries a warhead of up to two megatons force (equivalent to 2 million tons of TNT).

Russia also has a new generation of nuclear torpedoes. At 65 feet in length, and capable of moving at a speed of 115 miles per hour at a depth of up to 3,300 feet, the "Poseidon" torpedo is armed with a massive 100 megaton warhead (equivalent to 100 million tons of TNT). A nuclear explosion of this magnitude could create a massive radioactive tsunami.

CHAPTER 3

The monsignor's gleaming black Escalade, bearing on its license plate the word "PRIEST," moved silently and majestically along the river road that hugged the western bank of the Merrimack. Saint Oliver College was barely a mile from Saint James, almost within that parish's borders. To the chagrin of Monsignor O'Malley, several dozen of his parishioners elected to attend Sunday Mass at the college. They reasoned that it was just as good as any Mass they could attend at their drafty old church. They also enjoyed the better brand of music at the college and the fact that there were no collections.

The Escalade turned into the college entrance and passed under a wrought iron arch spanning two granite columns. One column was inscribed with the word "Fiat" and the other with "Lux." Careful planning had situated the entrance so that, upon entering, one proceeded along a wide road lined with graceful linden trees. Beyond the trees one was immediately met by a view of the imposing facade of the red brick, six-story Administration building, covered with the requisite covering of green ivy. The campus itself formed a perfect square of a dozen buildings surrounding a spacious, grassy quadrangle situated directly behind the "Ad" building. Three flags stood in the center of the "quad," numbering an enormous American flag, flanked by the much smaller flags of the state of New Hampshire and the Vatican. In front of these stood a large, flat granite rock, the so-called "pulpit," where generations of faculty had lectured during summer school classes, and on balmy fall or spring days. The previous and current years had seen this podium put to frequent use due to the dangers of the Virus, which had fortunately abated to the point that some students and professors were now shedding their masks.

The appearance of each of the buildings reflected a consistent theme—that of a brick rectangle whose windows were arched in what the designers had hoped created a "monastic" theme. The monastery itself was hidden from view behind the massive church, built in response to the new liturgical demands of the Second Vatican Council in the 1960s, in which the Catholic Church fashioned an adaptation to the modern world.

The monastery had been constructed much earlier, in the days when it was assumed that 50 or 60 men, at least, would be drawn to a life of prayer and work in its confines. Now, as Father Jim pulled into the monastery parking lot, several floors of the monastery were empty, requiring only a periodic dusting by the few novices. The Prior preferred to have the monks park the college's Honda and Toyota sedans in scrupulously even rows. Father Jim made a few attempts to fit the behemoth into a slot, but gave up, wary of creating a blemish on the monsignor's prize vehicle. He turned to Father John with an apologetic look. The monk grinned and opened his door, suitcase in hand.

"No problem, old boy, I'll just hop off here. I think I know the way. And listen, let's keep in touch. We should talk about all this in the college pub over a beer."

"Of course, well, really, although I don't really indulge, I mean …"

"Don't worry, Jimmy Sullivan, we'll have you sipping on one, just one Guinness in short order. Remember, 'Est modus in rebus.' I interpret that to mean just a little bit of almost everything good."

Father Jim was relieved as John closed his door, waved goodbye, and strolled towards the monastery enclosure. He did have to admit to himself that he had rather enjoyed the unaccustomed banter. Smiling, he slid back the cover of the sunroof for the short drive back. Why not, he thought, the monsignor will never know.

Father John slowed as he walked towards the home where he had taken a vow to remain for the rest of his life. He stopped and sat on a broad wooden bench flanked by flagrantly blooming blue hydrangea bushes. He and Brother Isaac had planted them—was it five years ago, six? He chuckled as he thought of Isaac, the big, bearded, gentle giant of a man who was responsible for the college greenhouse, and who cared for all the trees on the campus as though they were the children he would never have.

He sat, basking in the warm sun, thinking of the men he had come to know and respect over the years. Many were now resting in the monastery graveyard in the grove behind the chapel. A few of the elders were still here, struggling against the effects of age. New men had entered during his years there. Some discovered that the religious life was not for them, while others prayerfully accepted its demands, and dedicated themselves to their vocation. He remembered his own prayer as a novice in which he would recite to himself a poem by George Herbert:

Throw away thy rod,
Throw away thy wrath:
O my God,
Take the gentle path.

For my heart's desire
Unto thine is bent:
I aspire
To a full consent.

Yes, he mused, I have happily given full consent to this life, measured in the daily, predictable rhythms of the Benedictine monastery, a discipline honed for over fifteen hundred years as a balance between prayer and work. He stood up, but paused and sat down again on the hard bench. And now here I am, years later, a professed monk and a professor, facing a different kind of challenge. I don't have any doubts about my priestly vocation or my dedication to my students' well-being. I love teaching. But haven't I been putting off the ultimate question? Shouldn't I be actively following the nonviolent Jesus who I discovered back at Notre Dame? My Church has spent centuries not only making war respectable, but blessing war making. But now that the threat of nuclear destruction is all around us, some bishops and even the pope are beginning to publicly condemn those horrific weapons. Even that is not enough. It is just not possible to wage war in conformity with the teachings of Jesus. How can we follow Jesus, and love as he taught us to love, and simultaneously kill our fellow humans? I've known this for a long time, but I have been too quiet, too comfortable.

My homilies at Saint James must have come to me out of this silent struggle I've been having for years. It looks like it's time for a new commitment. And how does all that translate to where I lead my students, and how I live my life here in my beloved monastery?

It's looking like Francis Thompson's good old "Hound of Heaven" is after me, but not to give me faith in God. I've already got that. This time it's the nonviolent Jesus who is speaking to me again. It looks like He is not all that popular out there in the world if my last couple of weeks are any example. I wonder if that Mrs. McIlroy's pistol was loaded? Well, I'm back. Time to face the abbot.

He suddenly realized that even his brief sojourn away from the monastery walls had given him a deeper appreciation for his community, a world of Christian brotherhood unlike any other. Sure, he said, smiling to himself as he stood up from the bench, I can't say that I necessarily like all these guys, but we do all love each other as fellow followers of Jesus. He headed inside, just in time for the noon meal.

He entered the cool, dim interior of the monastic enclosure and walked down the corridor towards his room, careful to walk sedately near the wall on his left, head down. He donned his familiar black tunic and scapula once again, picked up the borrowed suitcase, and headed for the Prior's office. His progress was halted by the Prior himself, Father Lucas, who informed him, in a low, serious voice, that the abbot would see him in his office at one p.m. John was quite familiar with the Prior's various tones of address. He hoped his lunch would fortify him for the scene.

Father John entered the abbot's spacious office at exactly one o'clock, in keeping with Abbot Richard's insistence on punctuality. True to its surroundings, the office was suitably austere. On the beige wall behind the abbot's simple, cherry wood desk there was a small brass crucifix. Two chairs, both cherry wood as well, faced the desk. Off to the right, across the dark green carpeted floor, there was a matching sideboard on which there was an empty crystal pitcher and three glasses. Father John had never seen that particular service put to use. To the left, the wall featured a large oil painting depicting Saint Oliver Plunkett. It was said that his features were quite accurate, having been based on his severed head, which resides in a gold shrine in a church just north of Dublin.

As John advanced towards the desk, the abbot rose and motioned the monk to sit down. He was quite tall, perhaps six feet eight or nine, at least according to Father Padraig, the infirmarian. It had long been acceptable for the abbot's flock to grow facial hair, because it no longer symbolized liberal tendencies. However, the abbot insisted on himself being clean shaven, and he had managed to discipline his surprisingly dense supply of hair into what amounted to a white buzz cut. Abbot Richard had attained his elected post after serving forty-two years as the college librarian. He was a scholar as well, and his writings, mainly centered around the study of canon law, had been published frequently in theology journals. Knowing all this, Father John was ready for what his fellow monks called "an AA meeting," a deluge of references to Aristotle and Aquinas.

Abbot Richard took the other chair and faced Father John, smiling. Despite the diminution of the Virus threat, it seemed natural to maintain the familiar six feet of separation between the two.

"Well, Father John," he began in his deep baritone, "It seems that your mission to help out my friend Monsignor O'Malley has not worked out the way the both of us—by that I mean the monsignor and I—had hoped. He was kind enough to send me videos of your two homilies, or should I say your performances, at two Sunday Masses in Saint James. He also filled me in on several pained reactions from certain parishioners who he considers to be pillars of the church, if you will pardon that old expression. After all, I am seventy-eight years old, so these sayings tend to creep into my vocabulary."

John couldn't help but remember how he once had to remind his mother that it was "pillars" and not "pillows."

The abbot continued, "Toward the end of last semester, it was clear to me that you were showing signs of getting back into that whole 'lefty' business that you had picked up at Notre Dame some years ago. We never had a serious talk about that problem because when you got back here you seemed to have quickly recovered your senses. We have a tradition here at Saint Oliver of avoiding any entanglements in the earthly and often nasty business of politics. I am sure that you remember the several faculty members who pushed for establishing some sort of 'Political Science' Institute to do God knows what. Even the name was upsetting. And Father, you also know that a central theme of our mission here is to teach the young men and women who are entrusted to our care *sentire cum Ecclesia*—how to 'think with the Church.'"

"Well, Abbot," Father John began to reply before being cut off.

"Now, Father," the abbot continued, "it seems from these homilies—although I am more inclined to call them some sort of panegyrics to Gandhi—you are treading in dangerous territory. We need to resolve this before it goes too far. What you are calling for is nothing but a repudiation of the delicate balance that the Church has established and maintained for literally hundreds of years between its Godly mission and the secular demands of a pluralistic society. Now, I know that you probably think that I'm exaggerating, but hear me out. Catholics in this country, along with those who follow other faith traditions, pledge allegiance to this great nation, and to its duly elected leaders. There is no area to which that commitment applies any more important than the loyalty to the armed defense of our borders and our people and our way of life."

"However, abbot, we also" John interjected.

What appeared to be an oncoming objection caused the abbot to raise his hand for silence. He rose slowly out of his chair and begin pacing back and forth, his hands tucked into his broad cincture.

"Please bear with me. This is an important moment in your spiritual development. Tell me—I don't mean that literally—why do you think we have an active Army ROTC program on our campus? Do you think it's a strange coincidence that the young men and women who are preparing for service to this country through ROTC also happen to be well represented in the group of students who attend Mass on a regular basis, including each weekday at noon? All of them have taken seriously the precepts presented to them in their Freshman Humanities seminars—excuse me, their 'First-Year'

Humanities seminars. They understand Aquinas' teaching on how war can be just, and how human reason can, in good conscience, apply the notion of *justum* to *bellum*. Their theology professors introduce them to Ambrose and Augustine as well as the relevant Hebrew and Christian scriptures. Now, the reason I am reminding you of all this is that the homilies you delivered over at Saint James call upon the listeners—the faithful—to call into question the duly elected authorities of our country in their capacity to defend America from its numerous and powerful enemies, nations, may I remind you, who are not simply political foes, but are Godless, and have the very Devil at their side. Would you have had the Crusaders give up their swords and shields as they faced the infidels? Would you have America give up their most powerful weapons, the armaments that have kept us from global conflict for decades? Catholics have been defending their lawful governments since the time of the Emperor Constantine, who by the grace of God was baptized in 337."

"But the pope and the bishops have recently ..."

Again, the abbot raised his hand. "Please, Father John, this is not the time for a discussion. What I want from you now is your commitment to a period of prayer and reflection, a time of discernment in which you ponder this troubling direction you seem to be taking. Remember, you are a teacher and a priest. The souls under your charge can either benefit from your instructions, or they can be led astray from the path leading to right thinking, which is vital to their very salvation."

He returned to his chair and sat down. "Now I know that you originally had planned to use your working hours during this summer to prepare for your fall semester classes. You were interrupted by a brief appearance at Saint James that was intended to last for two months, that is, until you imagined yourself to be Thomas Merton, or maybe John Dear. We know how that turned out. Well, as our current situation turns out, we suddenly, perhaps by the grace of God, have a predicament for which you can offer an answer. Professor Jim Maloney, whom you know well as the Chairperson of the English department, has been struck down by the Virus, that fiendish enemy that has been such a scourge to all of us, but which we hoped had wreaked its last vengeance on this campus. He now resides in Sacred Heart Hospital, and is expected to recover, but slowly, as is typically the case. You, of course, remember what our president went through earlier this year."

"Oh, poor Jim. Looks like he will not be playing golf soon."

"Excuse me, Father, let me finish. It so happens that we have a very busy summer school operating here this season for a variety of reasons, and Professor Maloney, in addition to teaching a course on existential literature, also took on the burden of another course—Introduction to Poetry. Of course, I would not expect you to take on the challenge of the former. Joe Spiel has graciously volunteered to do that, thereby giving up a trip to the Greek Isles with his wife. However, you are just the man to take over the poetry course. Now, let me be clear. While I have always been outspoken in my support of academic freedom, I must insist that you remain circumspect in your choices of poets. My advice is to stick to the old favorites—Robert Frost, Emily Dickinson, Tennyson and the like. And what about that Gerard Manley Hopkins?

He was a Jesuit, you may remember. So off with you now. Check with Father Bede, the Registrar, for the class schedule. I know you will do a fine job, as always."

Father John knew enough to remain silent. As he left the abbot's office, all he could think of was trying to please the abbot by talking to his students about Hopkins, of all people! He needed to talk to someone about all this. Of course, that was it. He headed across the quad, towards the DeFelino Library, a two-story, spreading building featuring a large, colorful, circular stained-glass window above the main entrance. The window was divided into four wedge-shaped segments by a central cross. Clockwise, gold lettering in each section read: *In Hoc Signo Vinces*. The first floor of the building's facade was hidden by a long walkway with twelve arched openings, suggesting the classic appearance of a Benedictine abbey.

He welcomed the comforting sensation of the afternoon sun gently warming his black habit. As he walked over the rim of gravel bordering the quad, he suddenly remembered his shoes. I really could use a new pair, he thought. I'll talk to the Prior about that tomorrow. But no sandals, please. They make my feet cold. If I was into sandals, I would have entered the Franciscans. But I can't even grow a decent beard.

CHAPTER 4

Most classes were over for the day, and DeFelino was humming. The Saint Oliver DeFelino Memorial Faculty Lounge was located on the second floor of the library, directly behind the stained-glass window, giving the room some interesting lighting effects, depending on the time of day. The lounge was unusually populated for a summer day. However, this was by no means a typical summer. The entire previous academic year had been turned upside down by the ravages of the Virus. It had arrived unannounced in early August, just as students were preparing to return to campus. Instead, the entire student body was forced to remain at home, where they were urged to hunker down by their local health authorities.

Initially, there was a good deal of confusion caused by the Federal Government's reluctance to support their own Center for Disease Control's guidelines intended to control the spread of what was quickly recognized as a highly contagious, and sometimes deadly disease. The president feared that closing businesses and shuttering stores, restaurants, and bars would trigger a recession, and harm his political future and that of his allies. However, it did not take him long to understand the ramifications of neglecting the common principles of public health.

He contracted the Virus, no doubt because he disregarded any of the reasonable precautions. In the press conference when he announced his positive Virus test, he made light of the situation, calling himself the "unmasked man." Within a week, however, he found himself lying in a bed, heavily medicated and kept alive with a ventilator.

He managed to survive the trauma and came out the other side of the experience a shaken man. His brush with death, which he insisted included a near death experience in which he met both Lincoln and Herbert Hoover, and which revitalized his religious faith, forced him to recognize the danger that the Virus posed and the necessity to employ stringent precautions to minimize its spread. In the case of educational institutions, all schools were closed, and instruction from the lowest grades to graduate school became a virtual process. At Saint Oliver, no expense was spared in equipping the faculty with all the digital equipment required to teach remotely, and students who were unable to afford devices up to the task were supplied with whatever they needed. Tuition charges were adjusted to reflect the additional funding.

Amazingly, by the time the second semester arrived, the control measures enforced by the local and federal authorities had reduced the incidence of the Virus beyond expectations. As well, in early January, a China-based pharmaceutical firm announced that they had developed an effective vaccine that was administered in a simple nasal spray. The company amassed a labor force that, by February, turned out sufficient amounts of the vaccine to administer massive numbers of doses of their "Novirion" at a relatively modest price.

The students came back to the college and resumed their familiar routine. Because of an occasional new case of the Virus on campus, some students and faculty continued the practice of wearing a mask. Fortunately, the city of Manchester did not offer many temptations for entertainment, so there was little exposure to any afflicted locals. By the end of the second semester, mask use had pretty much faded away except among the nursing students and science majors. However, the uncertainty that had prevailed during the fall semester had caused a severe disruption in the academic schedule.

Many students either had contracted the Virus and could not continue their classes or were simply unable to meet the demands of spending several hours a day battling balky WiFi coverage. As a result, the number of summer school students was far higher than usual. That was the topic of discussion in the library's lounge, a large, comfortably appointed room. There were usually only about four or five summer classes underway at this point in late July, but now there were twelve in session. Students who had missed the opportunity during the academic year needed to complete the requirements of their majors, as well as take the courses necessary to fulfill the college's core curriculum, or as the students expressed it, they wanted to "get them out of the way."

As it turned out, all this was a boon to the faculty, especially the younger members. The contest to gain a teaching position in a summer school class was highly competitive, given the meager faculty salaries at Saint

Oliver. The college President, Father Brandon O'Connell, had only recently pointed out during the annual end of the year dinner for faculty and staff, "Man cannot serve two masters, so while we do the work of God as we instruct the youth, and maintain a healthy respect for the dignity of work, the exigencies of operating this complex enterprise, along with the humble needs of the monastic community, require some prudent restraint on the annual remuneration of our dedicated faculty. Always remember, you are in good hands with the Benedictines."

The professors were expected to supplement their incomes with "outside" employment during the summer. The familiar adage, "I went into teaching for three reasons: June, July, and August" was sometimes said in jest, but at many institutions of higher education it typically referred to a period set aside for scholarly research along with some time for physical and mental rejuvenation, rather than for part-time employment. Fortunately, especially for those faculty members with large families, the State University offered some attractive possibilities for summer teaching. These openings were limited, however, and although the professors had earned Ph.D.s in a variety of fields, they were considered unskilled labor and were not considered competitive for most jobs outside academia.

The eight professors seated on the comfortable chairs and sofas arranged around a central table, featuring a Keurig coffee maker, paper mugs, and scattered newspapers and journals, were about to have at a box of Dunkin Munchkins, when Father John walked in, this time without his usual happy countenance.

"What ho! John approaches!"

"Father, forgive me, just in case I have sinned."

"Catechism got your tongue?"

"Hey, like the bartender said to the horse, why the long face?"

John was used to friendly ribbing from this bunch, and it forced him to give up a reluctant smile. He was one of the few monks who visited the faculty lair, despite the fact that they were always welcome. He loved the good-natured back and forth among the profs. The conversations could get mighty intense, but always with enough mutual respect to keep the temperature down. No appeal to authority here, just a requirement to adhere to the facts. He sat down and grabbed a glazed Munchkin.

"Hello, all. Good to see everybody. Sorry, I don't want to be a downer to your happy hour, but ..." He gave them a quick summary of his adventure at Saint James and the abbot's reaction. "So, I'm back and ready to join the ranks of summer school professors. I hope I won't taint you or my students with my radical ideas. Not that you are all exactly moderates."

"Wait a second, John, are you telling us that you went and gave a no-nukes homily to the assembled blue collars at Saint James, and you escaped with your life?" asked Bill Johnson, the young physics professor. He looked around, knowing that someone would be willing to take up the rhetorical challenge.

"Hold everything, Bill, with all due respect for my friend Padre John, are you assuming that being against the very weapons that have kept our world at peace for decades, and against the technology that supplies us with clean energy, is a position that is defensible?"

This question came from what seemed to be the depths of a large, yellow Naugahyde recliner. One of the older faculty was fond of repeating the claim that the last of the Naugas had been killed to supply them with chairs. The questioner, Mary Shea, stood up to demand more attention. At exactly five feet in height, with fiery red hair, and a fighting weight of one hundred and eleven pounds, Mary, a Notre Dame Ph.D., had developed a reputation for her intimate knowledge of early Church history and her stubborn defense of whatever question had a conservative answer. Her rhetorical opponents joked that there were not many facts about the Church in its first few hundred years for which there was overwhelming evidence, but Mary disagreed and held her own whenever she defended a position.

Dr. Johnson was happy to reply. He declined to stand. His slender height of six-five was topped off by an impressive Afro, which earned him the nickname "Shaft" after the 70's movie hero. Bill's physics degree was from Stanford, but despite more prestigious offers, chose a job Saint Oliver because his parents and siblings lived in Goffstown, a small bedroom town just outside Manchester.

"Well now, Mary, that was quite a mouthful. So, nukes are not only defenders of peace, that is, they deter war among nations while, at the same time, they are ready at a moment's notice to assure mutual destruction if they are unleashed? Oh, yes, and human beings are in charge of all this? Where's our psych prof?"

Mary answered by pointing at Father John. "Father, before we get all sidetracked here with psychology and politics and who knows what else, you are probably the only other egghead here besides me who has a background in theology, so I think you can support me on this. Back when I was in grad school, I wrote a paper on the theological implications of atomic research, so this is a topic I take very seriously, although I must say I differ rather radically—although I dislike using that term—with the current pope's errant stand on this. Now, we know that God gave each of us an intellect in order to uncover and discover the details of His wondrous creation. Right?"

She looked around the room. No one said a word, knowing what was coming next. It was one of Mary's favorite themes.

"So," she continued, undeterred, "We can apply that well-known principle to the atom. Just think, the atom, that tiny building block of nature, has been an indecipherable mystery for almost all of human history, until a few brilliant humans unlocked its innermost secrets within the lifetime of some of us." She paused, and nodded towards Professor Austin, who was dozing on a recliner next to the bookshelves. "During our parents' time, God allowed us to understand the atom through the agency of the inspired intellect, and not simply to assuage our curiosity. No! God allows this, as He allows other insights to emerge through our academic endeavors, so that humanity, His flock if you will, can employ that knowledge as useful instruments as we work out our salvation."

The usual practice, after Mary had delivered her familiar theory, was to murmur polite and insincere agreement, followed by a switch to another subject. However, Bill Johnson had inadvertently consumed a caffeinated K-cup, and could not restrain himself.

"Just a moment friends. It just so happens that the lecture I was diligently preparing yesterday on the golf course, and which I will deliver tomorrow at eight a.m. to fifteen half-awake biology majors, speaks to these issues. These young men and women need my vital physics course in order to apply for admission to graduate schools of medicine, or osteopathy, or even dentistry, depending on the grades they earn with their God-given intellects. Well, my lecture on the morrow just so happens to center around the atom. I am happy to summarize said lecture to those who may be interested."

Professor Austin woke up with a start and waved his cane. "Yes, of course, William."

"Thank you, Professor. We can set aside for now the thorny question of whether or not God created atoms and has finally allowed us to peek inside. We can start with Albert Einstein's momentous insight that mass and energy are interchangeable. So, mass can be converted to energy. Voila! Although there was much more digging to be done on how exactly to do that, we now had the basis for nuclear weapons and nuclear power, those 'blessings' referred to by Ms. Shea. So, let me note that there are a great many more details about the atom that have yet to be unwrapped. We do know that, put simply, an atom is made up of a central nucleus, where particles called protons and neutrons are jammed in together. This is surrounded by a cloud of electrons. And what are they? Don't even get me started."

"I'm afraid it's too late for that," someone said, to general laughter.

Bill grinned. "I'll be brief. By the way, these protons and neutrons are made up of subatomic particles called quarks, but let's not go there, either. Anyway, most of the mass of the atom comes from the protons and neutrons. Now, any two atoms that have the same number of protons belong to the same chemical element. Even if those have equal numbers of protons, they can have a different number of neutrons. If that happens, now you have different isotopes of the same element. These are what is called 'unstable,' which makes some of them radioactive. That just means they slowly fall apart in a process called decay. As they do, they emit particles, alpha and beta, as well as gamma rays—high energy, dangerous radiation. There's plenty of naturally occurring radiation all around us, including the cosmic rays coming from the Sun. We just have to put up with all that radiation, but I suspect you would all prefer not to want to be exposed to the radiation coming from a nuclear explosion or maybe the melting down of a nuclear power plant. Now, a good example of this isotope business is uranium, a very common element. There are two isotopes of this, uranium two hundred thirty-eight and uranium two hundred thirty-five. The two hundred thirty-five form is the one used to make a bomb."

"Is it safe to tell this stuff to our students?" asked someone.

"Absolutely, because while the principle is simple, it took years and thousands of workers and an enormous amount of money to make the first atomic bomb. First, you need to work with uranium two hundred thirty-five. You've got to get huge amounts of uranium ore and extract that fraction. If you want to make a bomb, that stuff has got to be eighty or ninety percent pure, although for a nuclear power plant it can be around four percent.

Even our best chemistry majors probably couldn't handle that. OK, we've got some useful uranium. But speaking of nuclear power plants, the reactions going on there create another isotope, plutonium two hundred thirty-nine. That's the radioactive isotope used in today's nukes—the really big ones. So, here's the recipe: Take some uranium two hundred thirty-five, shoot some more of the same stuff at it, breaking up some of the atoms. That releases neutrons, which knock into other uranium atoms, and the whole thing keeps on going in a so-called chain reaction. What happens when you break apart atoms like that? That's the key. You release the energy that was holding those atoms together. That energy comes out as light and heat. If you use plutonium, the same thing happens. We, and I am talking about the United States of America, dropped a uranium bomb on Hiroshima and a plutonium bomb on Nagasaki. Our victims may not have appreciated the distinction, but they certainly were the first witnesses to feel the effects of that light and heat."

"Hold on, now, Bill." Mary Shea had been sitting during his monologue but was back up on her feet. "That was a clever rhetorical device, but you can't bomb shame us. To begin with, none of us were even alive then. But that's not the point. It was a question of the lesser of two evils. Those bombs were dropped to save lives. The Japanese would have fought to the last person, and we, I mean the U.S., would have had to invade Japan, and who knows the carnage that would have resulted? But again, to get back to my original point here. We need to see the big picture. Certain humans were given the intellectual powers to unlock one of God's deepest secrets—that the energy holding the very universe together can be released to serve us all—provided, of course, that we do this according to His will."

"Hey. Mary, what about the incredible achievement of figuring out DNA and genetics?"

"And germs?"

"Anesthesia and antibiotics?"

"I vote for figuring out that if you attach a leech to your arm, it might not help."

Mary merely smiled and looked around at her colleagues after their questions stopped. "Of course, all those are important discoveries. You are just helping me make my point. Just remember, discovery does not always imply direction, that is, there is no guarantee that new knowledge will assure that right reason will prevail. Don't forget, DNA research might lead to new medicines, for example, but it can also end up in genetic engineering where humans presume to alter God's creative plans, and not just in plants and animals, the very sustenance of humanity—but in humans themselves! As I try to impress upon my students, it seems that God is constantly guiding His creation towards what Teilhard called the Omega Point. He ..."

Mary was interrupted, to the relief of her listeners, who were quite familiar with her championing of that Jesuit's unique ideas, by the persistent tapping of Professor Austin's cane against the side of the wooden bookshelf. He was held in great respect by the faculty for the depth and breadth of his scientific publications and his reputation among generations of students for his fascinating lectures, despite the fact that his use of technology did not extend beyond the use of yellow chalk on a blackboard.

"Now, Mary," he said softly, "we are quite familiar with your fondness for that quirky charlatan of a fellow, and we respect your opinion on the subject. But, being a biologist, I bear the difficult burden of requiring at least a modicum of evidence before I can come to any conclusions. In fact, being a scientist, I regard any conclusion I reach to be open to change, should good evidence to the contrary appear. I do suspect that the fellows who were instrumental in uncovering those secrets of Nature—pardon me, Mary, of God—like Einstein, or Leo Szilard, or Richard Feynman, would be somewhat put off by your theocentric interpretation of their accomplishments. As for your championing of the bombs that 'ended the war,' well, there is a good deal of evidence that negotiations were already underway for that finale before the bombers took off. Mary, those kind of cold calculations about war leave out the human element, as so many theology discussions do. I can only assure you that a massive chain reaction involving uranium or plutonium will produce temperatures higher than the interior of the Sun, light that will blind, and a terrible blast wave, all of which combine to immediately vaporize anyone unfortunate to be near the explosion, and burn humans and everything else for miles around. Did you know that thousands of health care workers perished after those blasts, leaving few to care for the wounded and burned? I won't go on, but really, Mary, if Hiroshima and Nagasaki were the reason why God let Einstein in on his secrets, then it's not the God with which my sainted Irish mother was familiar."

Professor Austin raised his cane and pointed it toward Father John. "Well, now, Father, what would Saint Benedict think of all this business?"

John had been busying himself with making himself a cup of coffee and eating three glazed Munchkins, comfortable in the knowledge that this sort of enjoyable badinage could go on for hours. Suddenly, all eyes turned toward him.

"Oops, sorry, it's not that I wasn't paying attention," he answered, trying to discreetly wipe a crumb from the corner of his mouth, "I'm just hungry, but I have been listening. You know, Benedict tells us in the Rule, 'And let them first pray together, that so they may associate in peace.' Oh, yes, he also says, 'He should first show them in deeds rather than words all that is good and holy.' OK, OK," he added, looking around. "Just kidding, in a way, but Professor Austin, let me get to the first question that Bill asked that set off the scrum here. Yes, I did give a couple of no-nuke homilies, as Bill so eloquently put it. I'm going to make a public confession to you all right now. My need to make moral decisions about the subject of war, and in particular, even the mere prospect of nuclear war, has been weighing on my conscience for a long time. That fact that none of you have ever heard me speak up about it is embarrassing, but there you are. I have been putting it aside, and I can only blame myself for that."

The sudden uncomfortable silence in the room was broken by the low, shy voice of Dr. Georgio, the college's only remaining Classics professor. "Ignoscimus, Pater."

The general laughter was enough to lighten the mood. "Gratias, David," John answered with a slight bow. He had always felt sorry for Dr. Georgio, the sole remnant of the once thriving Classics department, gone now to make room for additional Business and Economics classes.

"That's kind of you. But really, friends, I have to agree with Bill's somber assessment of the nuclear dangers we all face. My challenge now is how to 'show them in deeds rather than words.' I tried to make a start with my pair of homilies, but I learned pretty quickly that I had picked a pretty tough audience to get my message across—Catholic parishioners. Now, Mary, my friend and colleague and fellow Celtic, I am not theologian enough to refute your intriguing theory about scientific discoveries or Teilhard, but I can come to a firm conclusion with major moral implications. Our world is awash in nuclear weapons, the most terrifying weapons ever made. The U.S., that is, all of us, has thousands of these savage destructive devices waiting to be unleashed at a moment's notice from the air, under the ground, or from under the beautiful oceans, and sent to kill and maim untold thousands, possibly millions of our fellow humans, created in the image and likeness of God. And who is considered to have the authority to wreak this havoc? It takes only the decision of one individual, the president, even though he may be sleepy, or ill, or drunk, or under the influence of drugs. Imagine, for a moment, our current president, in a foul mood after being picked on by the news media. He could decide to turn the living Earth into smoldering ruins. Oh, and of course, nuclear war may be set off merely by an accident—a mistaken signal of an attack, or some mechanical or electronic malfunction. So, truthfully, we are faced with a moral dilemma. Can we reject the evil against humanity that results from our using nuclear weapons, while at the same time accepting that evil? And why? Because we remain willing, at the very least, to retaliate against an attack. That's the mutually assured destruction, or MAD, that's supposed to be the basis for the deterrence Mary referenced. Let's face it. What we are saying when we depend on that kind of protection is the following: If you dare to send nuclear weapons towards us, it will be too late for us to prevent them from destroying our cities and murdering our people, so we will fire off our nuclear arsenal and do the same to you. That will be an act of pure revenge—both their assault on us and our angry retaliation—and would be immoral, evil, unjustified. You can come to that conclusion through a belief that each and every person is precious in God's sight, or you can simply arrive at the same place as a secular humanist. You don't necessarily have to believe in the Christian God to conclude that perhaps we should support each other in this vale of tears, rather than waste our creative talents and resources to devise increasingly sophisticated ways of killing each other."

Mary Shea broke the awkward silence that followed the monk's remarks. "Now, Father, I respect your right to your strong opinion, but I have a feeling that you are about to break out the old 'swords to plowshares' argument. You really can't be cherry picking Scripture to make it seem unchristian to defend one's country by whatever means God inspires us to devise. We're not used to you being such a lefty, Father. I've heard enough of this sort of thing before—not often around here, but when I was teaching three years ago at Trinity. The students had a club called 'Pax Christi.' Those kids, and a few faculty by the way, were all about ideas like disarmament, nonviolence, and all that sort of thing. Imagine, co-opting the name of the Lord to justify abandoning civilization's defenses against the barbarians of today! Sorry, Father, but I know you are heading there, so I'm just trying to head you off at the pass."

The priest laughed out loud. "Wow, Mary, that is such a blast from the past. And thanks for adding to my collection of military metaphors. You are taking me back to my grad school days when I was on the streets in South Bend, and a couple of times in Chicago, waving around a Pax Christi sign. Actually, Mary, I wasn't going to go on and on with another homily. I've already talked too much for a lounge conversation, but when Bill asked me about my homilies, I really wanted to let you all where I'm at right now. Oh, wait a minute, Mary. When you have a minute, check out the recent statement from the U.S. Conference of Catholic Bishops. That's a pretty conservative bunch, wouldn't you say? Well, I remember this part of their statement. They said, 'the Catholic bishops of the United States remain firmly committed to global nuclear disarmament.' How about that, Mary, looks like a bunch of lefty bishops, eh?"

"Well, looks like we agree, Father. They are dangerously left, but don't despair. I've got another Church voice for you to listen to. Archbishop Carlo Vigano, who is a former papal nuncio to the U.S., wrote to our president just last month to tell him that he and the president were united in a cosmic battle between the forces of good and evil. Now, he was talking mainly about abortion and the right to life struggle, but I think we can apply his concern to the president's plan to upgrade and improve our nuclear weapons defenses. That is certainly a way to protect life, isn't it? And by the way, the priest in my parish read parts of the letter to us at Mass a couple of weeks ago."

He stood up and said with a grin, "Ite Missa est. Go and sin no more, or 'pecca fortiter,' depending where you are coming from. As for myself, my boss, Abbot Richard, would not be happy if I missed prayers because I was dueling in DeFelino. Oh, wait, that's another one of those terms, isn't it? Thanks for listening, guys. Let's continue this friendly debate next time. I'm counting on you people who are living out there in the world to bring the donuts."

After Mass, during the evening meal, John felt extra gratitude for the silence, unbroken except for the gentle baritone voice of Brother Ambrose reading sayings from the Desert Fathers. Each time he heard the words of those long-ago monks, he had to admit to himself that he never would have survived in a monastery back in the third century. It was just too darn hard back then. Then again, how would those men handle this crazy world we are living in right now? At least our food is better.

He was hoping to get onto one of the two old computers available to the professed monks in the recreation room. When he arrived, both computers were available, and the four monks there were engrossed in a game of Scrabble. He logged on, hoping that there would be some word from the Nashua nuns. He wasn't optimistic about the possibility, however, because when they gave him their contact information back at Saint James, he had neglected to give them his email address. But there it was, an email from ehealy, sent to jfain@oliver.edu. Well, I guess that was pretty obvious. He opened the email. It read:

Hi Father. You met Mary and me at Saint James. I'm sure you remember those two saintly nuns who invited you to join them and other rabble rousers in a peace action over at BAE Systems in Nashua. Well, we are still planning that, but something else has come up. It looks like some Massachusetts folks are trying to get bodies over to Waltham this Saturday at one o'clock—in the afternoon, of course, although you monks are probably up in the a.m. that early. Turns out that Raytheon recently nabbed a $900 million contract with the U.S. government to make a new air-launched, nuclear-armed cruise missile. It's called the Long Range Standoff missile (LRSO). This thing can carry incredibly powerful warheads that can be delivered from planes to targets over a thousand miles away. Plenty to think about there, eh?

Of course, a handful, even a whole fistful, of peaceniks won't shut down a company as big and rich as Raytheon. But, Father, you know the old principle—people of conscience need to take a public stand for what is right and moral. In this case it's clear. This company is creating weapons of mass destruction.

Please let us know if you can make it. If you can get down to Nashua around eleven, we can go together in our Camry. Two hundred twenty thousand miles and still going strong. The Waltham group is hoping to get at least fifty brave souls there. Don't worry, you don't have to do anything heroic. We'll do a sit down at the entrance, and only a few of us will 'cross the line,' if you know what I mean. Mary and I will probably hold off this time. Our probation is not up until next month and we have too much work to do here to go back to the hoosegow. Just let us know and I will give you directions on how to get here.

It would be great if you wore your clericals, but in mufti is OK. It's up to you. Peace, Eileen.

In 1945, President Harry Truman, realizing the devastation wrought by the atomic bombs dropped on Hiroshima and Nagasaki—on his orders—resolved not to use these weapons again. He declared that the sole authority to do so would reside in the president alone. The decision to unleash the atomic bombs of that era, and all their subsequent vastly more powerful permutations, was kept out of the hands of the military and handed to the governing president.

This sole authority comes with grave consequences. Could he or she make the decision, after a few minutes of reflection, based on what was presumed to be valid evidence, to release perhaps hundreds of nuclear weapons that would kill millions? Responding to a faulty report of a nuclear attack by firing missiles, for example, from the silos housing intercontinental ballistic missiles, would be irreversible. Missiles cannot be recalled or destroyed. As those ICBMs streaked towards their targets, others would be rushing toward the U.S. in response.

The president is always accompanied by a nearby military aide who carries the "nuclear football" containing the launch codes for the nation's nuclear weapons. Upon warning of a nuclear attack, the president can initiate a response immediately.

A president's character flaws might contribute to the dangers of the moment. He/she might be impulsive, be suffering from a psychological issue, under the influence of alcohol or medications, or distracted by any number of other pressing issues. In 1969, President Nixon was said to have been drunk when he suggested bombing North Vietnam with nuclear weapons, so was ignored. He did the same thing on more than one occasion in 1972. Or more simply, might a president be awoken in the middle of the night with the warning?

Threatening to use nuclear weapons has not been confined to the U.S. president. In 1951, during the Cold War, Winston Churchill told The New York Times general manager Julius Ochs Adler that he would suggest to the Prime Minister that he lay down strict conditions for the Russian government. If Russia refused, Churchill would recommend telling them that Great Britain would atom bomb a Russian city, "and if necessary, additional ones." This was in keeping with the general planning by both the British government and the U.S. Pentagon in the late 1940s to dismantle the USSR by massive nuclear strikes.

The first American nuclear war plan was adopted in 1948, under the codename "Halfmoon." It called for 50 atomic bombs, later raised to 133, to be dropped on numerous Soviet cities. By the mid-1950s the emphasis moved from targeting cities to military facilities. In December,1960, the U.S. and UK approved an integrated targeting and bombing plan that would stay in effect for more than 30 years. If provoked, the combined forces could unleash 3,423 nuclear weapons on targets located in China, the Soviet Union, North Korea and eastern Europe. Perhaps 220 million people would be killed, while millions more would die due to the aftereffects, including radiation poisoning. The Soviets had nuclear war plans as well, which included about 3,000 nuclear weapons aimed at UK cities.

By the early twenty-first century, the number of nuclear weapons was dramatically decreased, while their explosive power and speed of delivery far exceeded that of earlier weapons. Certain safeguards had been developed, including warning systems. Earlier, in 1968, The U.S. Air Force had ended its policy of keeping planes aloft around the clock, loaded with nuclear bombs. The weapons would be kept at their bases, ready to be loaded onto planes quickly.

However, the world had entered another phase of nuclear-associated danger. The military became more dependent on sophisticated computer systems, opening up the possibility of hackers, viruses, or even artificial intelligence bots triggering a nuclear exchange accidentally or deliberately. In addition, new categories of weapons, strategic planning and risk assessment presented new and dangerous possibilities. For example, weapon systems that were capable of carrying nuclear or conventional warheads risked ambiguity in detection and response. And what of a nation's attitude towards employing nuclear weapons only in response to an attack, and not as a "first use?" What follows below is a partial accounting of the reported "close calls" that flirted with nuclear disaster. Many other similar incidents are still shrouded in secrecy.

Over the years since Truman's decision to vest the president with the sole authority over the U.S. nuclear response, there have been numerous incidents that show the risks that arise from this practice—a long list of false alarms. Despite the pleas by many of the scientists who contributed to the development of the first atomic bomb, and the knowledge of carnage that such weapons deliver, over the years since 1945 there has been a steady increase in their destructive power. In addition, the mere presence of thousands of nuclear weapons scattered across the country and other parts of the world have inevitably created conditions that allow human and mechanical errors to occur that have the potential for enormous devastation.

These weapons and the complex network of facilities where they are manufactured, upgraded, and recycled offer opportunities for the theft and sabotage of nuclear material by terrorist groups. In addition, there are 440 nuclear power plants around the world, with 96 of them in the United States. Despite the safeguards maintained for their safe operation, one only need recall the disasters at Three Mile Island, Pennsylvania, in 1979, Chernobyl, Ukraine, in 1986, and Fukushima, Japan, in 2011, to realize the potential for nuclear disaster beyond the realm of weaponry.

The following are notable examples of how mere chance could determine our future. These near disasters involving nuclear weapons are called "Broken Arrows." Historians differ on how many of these have occurred, but the reported incidents number in the dozens.

July 27, 1956: An American B-47 bomber was practicing touch-and-go landings at the Lakenheath Air base in Suffolk, England. The plane veered off the runway and slammed into a storage facility housing three Mark 6 atomic bombs, which failed to detonate despite being damaged. The crew was killed.

March 11, 1958: A B47E military aircraft loaded with nuclear bombs was on a training mission over South Carolina. Responding to a warning light, an airman accidentally engaged a manual release. A bomb dropped, fell 15,000 feet, and smashed into a child's empty playhouse. The bomb detonated, demolishing a nearby house and injuring the inhabitants. On this flight, the nuclear bomb component had been stored separately on the plane, so this was a conventional explosion. The bomb left a 70-foot-wide crater that can still be seen.

October 5, 1960: Early warning radar detected what was interpreted as numerous Soviet missiles heading for the U.S. The North American Aerospace Defense Command (NORAD) went to the highest alert level and prepared to retaliate. It was soon determined that the rising moon had reflected radar waves and caused the mistaken reaction.

January 24, 1961: A B-52 bomber caught fire and exploded in the air over Goldsboro, North Carolina. Two Mark 39 hydrogen bombs dropped to the ground. One landed relatively undamaged, while the second buried itself 20 feet deep in the soil. Fortunately, a safety switch prevented a detonation. The Air Force disarmed both bombs but could not recover the uranium in the sunken weapon.

November 24, 1961: Early warning systems failed, and nuclear-loaded planes were about to take off, when contact was re-established, and the retaliatory attack was halted. Later investigation traced the problem to a single AT&T switch in Colorado, where they had failed to install a backup system.

October 25, 1962: A guard at a military base in Duluth, Minnesota shot at an intruder attempting to scale a security fence. This triggered an alarm at adjoining military installations, including Volk Field. There, an incorrectly wired system turned on a siren directing nuclear-armed planes to take off. This event occurred at the height of the Cuban Missile Crisis, so everyone was primed for action. The planes were on the runway, ready to go, when a notice came that the intruder had probably been a black bear, not a Soviet agent.

October 27, 1962: During the Cuban Missile Crisis, the Soviet ships approaching Cuba, blockaded by the U.S., were accompanied by submarines armed with nuclear torpedoes. Because it was difficult to contact the submarines, their commanders were given permission to fire the torpedoes without authorization from Moscow. Vasili Alexandrovich Arkhipov was the chief of staff aboard a submarine that was being harassed by depth charges in order to get it to surface. Two other officers thought that a nuclear war could have already begun. They elected to fire a nuclear torpedo at the American ship. All three officers were required to give permission before firing.

Only Arkhipov refused to turn his third and final firing key, thus averting a nuclear catastrophe.

December 5, 1965: An A-4E Skyhawk attack aircraft carrying a B43 nuclear weapon fell off the deck of the USS Ticonderoga as it cruised off the coast of Japan. The pilot, bomb and plane were never recovered.

January 17, 1966: A B-52 carrying four nuclear bombs collided with a refueling tanker over Palomares, Spain. The bombs were released and both planes crashed. These bombs contained conventional explosives designed to detonate the nuclear component. In two, the explosives detonated, but the warheads were not triggered. This scattered radioactive and toxic plutonium over a wide area. Over 1,000 U.S. military personnel worked for three months to gather 1,400 tons of contaminated soil and crops, which were transported back to the Department of Energy's Savannah River site in South Carolina for burial. Another bomb landed intact and was recovered. The fourth landed in the sea. It was recovered after the search, in what was then the most expensive salvage operation in U.S. history.

November 9, 1979: At the NORAD headquarters, operators were shocked to see an unmistakable warning that a large-scale Soviet missile attack was underway. The signals denoted the launches were from Soviet missile silos and submarines off the West Coast. Preparations for response began immediately, but soon were called off when U.S. radar and satellites did not detect any attack. Later, investigators found that a technician had run a training exercise tape which inadvertently had gotten onto U.S. missile warning systems.

June 3, 1980: At 3 a.m., the National Security Adviser Zbigniew Brzezinski received a call notifying him that the U.S. early warning system had detected a massive Soviet missile attack in progress. Before he could wake President Carter, the warning turned out to be a false alarm. Had the call come directly to the president, he would have had about five minutes to respond. ICBM silos had been notified, and nuclear-armed bombers were prepared for takeoff. The problem was caused by a faulty $0.46 computer chip.

September 18, 1980: Workers were performing routine maintenance at a missile silo at Little Rock Air Force Base. The silo housed a Titan II ICBM, a nine-stories high missile, carrying a warhead with a yield of nine megatons, three times the explosive power of all the bombs dropped during World War II, including the atomic bomb. One of the workers accidentally dropped a nine-pound socket that fell 80 feet. It punctured the wall of the rocket's fuel tank, which began to leak. While most personnel were evacuated because the leak could not be stopped, two workers entered the silo area to assess the situation. The fuel exploded, killing one of them—David Livingston—and caused the ICBM warhead to be tossed out of the silo. It landed about 100 feet away.

September 26, 1983: A Soviet early warning system satellite appeared to detect a launch of one U.S. ICBM, and soon afterward, four more. The officer on duty, Lt. Colonel Stanislav Petrov, hesitated. He reasoned that if this was a genuine attack, the U.S. would be launching many more missiles than only the five. He told his superiors it was a false alarm. It turned out that satellites mistook sunlight bouncing off clouds for incoming missiles. A 1979 report by the U.S. Congressional Office of Technology Assessment estimated that a major Soviet nuclear attack at that time would kill between 82 million and 180 million American people. After the Cold War, Petrov would be honored at the United Nations.

October 3, 1986: A Soviet ballistic missile submarine carrying 16 nuclear missiles, while cruising 700 miles off the coast of Bermuda, developed a leak in a hatch cover. Seawater entered, mixed with fuel, and an explosion followed. The sub began to sink, and a Soviet freighter started to tow it. The tow failed, and the captain ordered the crew to abandon ship. The submarine sank. The missiles were never recovered.

January 7, 1987: In Wiltshire, in southwest England, Royal Air Force trucks swerved on an icy road to avoid a collision. In the accident, two trucks went off the road and one of them tipped over. Each was carrying two hydrogen bombs.

April 7, 1989: A Soviet submarine, the Komsomolets, built to dive very deep in order to avoid detection, was on a training mission in the Barents Sea. A fire broke out which could not be controlled. Some of the crew escaped to lifeboats, but 42 were lost as the sub sank. The vessel still rests on the bottom at a depth of 5,512 feet. Two torpedoes are in the wreck, each carrying a nuclear warhead.

January 25, 1995: A group of American and Norwegian scientists notified the U.S., Russia and 28 other countries that they were planning to launch a rocket from an Arctic Circle island in order to study the northern lights. Russian radar observers, unaware of this warning, notified Moscow when the launch occurred, suggesting an American attack. The then-Russia President Boris Yeltsin was given the satchel containing the information necessary to order a retaliatory strike. After a few minute's consultation, Yeltsin and his advisers were informed that the rocket had gone out to sea and was not a threat.

August 29, 2007: Airmen at Minot Air Force Base, North Dakota loaded six AGM-129 nuclear-armed cruise missiles onto a B-52 bomber. The missiles were thought to be armed with inert instead of active nuclear warheads. They sat unguarded overnight. The next day they were flown to Barksdale Air Force Base, Louisiana. There, a maintenance crew discovered that the warheads were active.

October 2010: A launch control center at Warren Air Force Base could not contact 50 missile silos for nearly an hour. During that time, the center lost its ability to detect and cancel an unauthorized launch attempt. The problem was later traced to a circuit card that had been incorrectly placed in a computer.

January 2014: Ninety-two launch officers at Malmstrom Air Force Base in Montana were suspended and had their security clearances revoked for cheating on their monthly proficiency exams. The officers were responsible for the missiles waiting on "hair-trigger" alert in silos, meaning that they were to be launched within minutes of receiving a legitimate order to do so. The Air Force admitted that the cheating problem was "systemic."

March 2016: Investigators broke up a drug ring involving LSD use on and off F.E. Warren Air Force Base in Wyoming. Fourteen airmen were "disciplined," and six others ended up in court. The service members were from the group that controls one-third of the 400 Minuteman III ICBM missile silos. According to news sources, the nuclear missile corps "has struggled with misbehavior, mismanagement and low morale."

President Ronald Reagan admitted "I can't believe that this world can go on beyond our generation and on down to succeeding generations with this kind of weapon on both sides poised at each other without someday some fool or some maniac or some accident triggering the kind of war that is the end of the line for all of us."

In Albert Camus' famous 1947 novel, "The Plague," he observes how the citizens of a town decimated by a rodent-borne plague rejoiced when the pestilence seemed to have disappeared. They were unaware, he writes, "that ... the plague bacillus never dies or vanishes entirely ... it remains dormant for dozens of years ... it waits patiently ... the day will come when the plague will once again rouse its rats and send them to die in some new well-contented city."

Nuclear weapons, more deadly than any plague, wait patiently in silos, airplane hangars, and submarines, for the moment they may be sent on their way by chance or on purpose.

CHAPTER 5

Later that evening in his room, Father John sat down at his small desk and faced the stack of books piled perilously next to the lamp. "Two roads diverged in a yellow wood," he thought, and I don't have much time to decide which one to take. Well, at least I'm thinking about it in poetic terms. Tomorrow morning I'll be facing twenty-three students, according to Brother Philip, the registrar, and not only am I woefully unprepared to teach someone else's English course, I've got to answer an email from a woman who thinks I'm quite willing to upend my life to play David against some corporate Goliath.

He stood up quickly and grabbed the books as they began to topple over. He put a few on the floor and sat down again, laughing to himself. Maybe that's a sign, he thought—but of what? Let's make it simple. First, I've got to use some of that discipline that I am supposed to have developed by following the Rule, and at least put together a syllabus for this course that will interest my students. Of course, the point of the contents of a syllabus is to inform, not to entertain, but I've been in this game long enough to know that educators are in the entertainment business, so I had better be funny as well as philosophical.

Retrieving it from the floor, he opened up his dog-eared copy of Coffin's *The Major Poets*. OK, let's start right here, he reasoned. Who could not love any of these poems? And why don't I introduce my young audience to Billy Collins—a good Catholic college graduate and Poet Laureate—and get them to think about how to read a poem, how to actually listen to it and react to it, and not just surgically take it apart and write about it as though they were composing an autopsy report? What are those lines in his *Introduction to Poets*? Oh, yeah, "all they want to do / is tie the poem to a chair with rope / and torture a confession out of it." And I don't like the idea of having students read and listen to gifted poets, and then spend time writing their own poems about whatever—maybe their feelings. And to be perfectly honest, I don't want to have to parse that pile of poesy.

The monk reached over to the shelf next to his desk and picked up a blank yellow legal pad. He grabbed a pen from the collection of his favored black Paper Mates. Two hours later, he was as ready as he could be under the circumstances. It was not until he was falling off to sleep that he realized his absorption in planning a course syllabus had made him neglect an even bigger challenge—his invitation to use "deeds rather than words" in an act of civil disobedience that he was sure would never be approved by the abbot.

The next morning, after prayers in private and with his community, and fortified by a bowl of oatmeal and two cups of strong coffee, John headed across the quad to Gary, the colorful building housing the English department. What he remembered had been rather staid surroundings three years earlier had livened considerably when the Art department moved in and began covering the beige corridor walls with murals and positioning a rotating series of sculptures along the inside of the portico facing the quad. Unlike John, who shuddered at having his students try their hand at poetry writing, Professor Joe Hammel, the gifted painter who led the department, had no such compunction in encouraging his students to express themselves in a variety of media.

As Father John walked into his classroom through a door covered with brilliantly colored depictions of dragonflies and sunflowers, he knew that he was surprising the students sitting there in various levels of early morning stupor. They were not yet aware that Professor Maloney was being replaced by a monk. Most of them were taking the course to fulfill a first-year student requirement, and were anticipating a real "gut" course based on what they had been hearing about Dr. Maloney and his aversion to handing out any grades lower than a "gentleman's C." They now faced the prospect of not only having to exert themselves in a summer school course, but also being forced to listen to someone who probably was intent on questioning and elevating their moral lives—and with poems, no less.

John's experience allowed him to see all this angst at a glance. He placed his briefcase on the desk, slowly removed its contents, placing them carefully on the desk. He turned and faced the students, his hands folded. "Let us pray," he said, in a solemn voice. There was stunned silence.

He paused for a moment, then laughed. He put his hands into his belt, and said, still chuckling, "OK, never mind. You can do that on your own. Let's get started so you can learn how to love poetry while getting rid of this requirement. Right now, Professor Maloney is lying in a hospital bed, coughing up Virus particles. They say he will recover, but it will take some time. Hence, I have been asked to take over. Don't worry, I have a Ph.D. and a happy disposition as well as a fascinating syllabus that I will ask you—pointing to a student who had just woken up in the front row—to pass out. You appear to be experienced in that category."

Back in the saddle, John thought. I had almost forgotten how much fun this is. Now, let's get started. One class a day for the next four weeks. But what about Raytheon? I'll have to decide today. Or maybe tomorrow.

That evening, Father John found that both computers were occupied in the recreation room. He had time to sit and compose his reply to Sister Eileen. There were plenty of computers over in the library, but he often felt more comfortable writing emails here in the privacy of the monastery, unless they were too time consuming. The moment he read the email from the nun, he realized that her invitation implied far more than just a friendly request to join some sort of gaggle of sign wavers standing next to a road where the passing cars could see them. Most drivers and passengers would simply ignore them, a few would honk either in agreement or derision, and a few would offer the universal single digital expression. He had done plenty of that back at Notre Dame. I have no problem with that kind of sincere witness, he thought, it needs to happen as a part of the big picture of raising consciousness about important issues. But he had a feeling that this action at Raytheon was going to be a whole new ball game. Those companies tended not to like peaceniks questioning their activities or upsetting their faithful employees. Well, tough. It's time I spoke out in some way beyond giving homilies, given what's going on in those buildings just down the road.

After the first meeting with his summer school students, a class that his experience told him would be productive and a whole lot of fun despite the difficulties in harnessing the attention of young students, he had headed back to the library. He had a general impression of the Raytheon company. He knew it was a "defense contractor" among other things, and there was an office down near the southern part of the state, near the Massachusetts border. It was one of those companies that showed up in the news once in a while. He had a dim memory of Raytheon getting some heat about their Patriot missile that didn't work very well. That was always one of those word plays that impressed him as an English professor. A missile that didn't "work well" sounded like it was a car that had problems with a starter or alternator. In reality, it meant that this death-dealing complicated machine may have ended up far from its intended target, and perhaps killed children in their school instead of killing soldiers while they slept in their barracks.

Missiles were indeed complex devices that required the advanced skills of many talented people, particularly engineers. Companies like Raytheon and those other names one heard about now and then like Boeing, or Northrop Grumman, and Lockheed Martin, seemed to have a fixed place in the economy of the country, creating lots of jobs as key players in supplying the military. He remembered vaguely some headlines during the early days of the current U.S. presidency about Raytheon and some big contract. And now, Eileen Healy was telling him about a new multimillion dollar deal to make a new missile type to carry nuclear warheads hundreds of miles? Better learn more about this, he realized, and I have an hour to use before prayers.

It took less than that hour of reading to leave the monk stunned and shocked. Had he been living in an alternate universe? A few simple Google searches were all he needed to learn the bitter truth. Of course, information offered by Raytheon itself did not offer the perspective gained from reading sources such as the Raytheon Anti-War Campaign, or the American Friends Service Committee. But the Raytheon website did announce the news of their recent merger with United Technologies to form a conglomerate, Raytheon Technologies, an "aerospace and defense company that provides advanced systems and services for commercial, military and government customers worldwide." They boasted of having 195,000 employees, including 60,000 engineers, and a combined annual revenue of $74 billion.

As John read about the basic details of this giant, he couldn't help but be reminded of a reference that he had on his bookshelf. The book, which he considered a modern classic in rhetoric, was *Battlebabble*. It was basically a dictionary, translating words and expressions used by the military and the government to cover and mask the stark truths behind their comfortable euphemisms. If one were to be brutally honest, John realized, a "defense" company simply means a company that makes deadly weapons that are used by the U.S. military, or the military of any country who buys those weapons, to destroy buildings, roads, bridges, water supply facilities, hospitals, schools, nursing homes, etc., and burn, maim, and kill whoever the government decides is the enemy. Raytheon Technologies makes "precision weapons." These do the same, but with better aim—except when they miss.

He almost had to stop when he began to read about Yemen. It was almost too much to bear, especially because he was learning the story in stark detail for the first time. Saudi Arabia, one of the world's richest countries, had been bombing Yemen for the previous five years, with U.S. support. The people in Yemen are mostly Shiite Muslims, while the Saudis are Sunnis. He read the UN study reporting that more than 200,000 Yemenis had perished in this conflict, many from starvation and disease. He learned that Raytheon is a major supplier of weapons to Saudi Arabia. One of their products, a laser-guided bomb, was instrumental in wreaking destruction and death in that poverty-stricken country. How could all this continue almost without notice, and with our assent? And what the heck did it have to do with "defense?"

His reluctance to get back in the streets as a protestor was now an embarrassment. He thought back to that statement delivered by one of his heroes, the Jesuit Daniel Berrigan, during his trial along with eight others for burning draft records to protest the Vietnam War: "Our apologies, good friends, for the fracture of good order, the burning of paper instead of children, the angering of the orderlies in the front parlor of the charnel house. We could not, so help us God, do otherwise." It was time to be a witness.

Brother Francis gave up his attempt to finish The New York Times online crossword with a sigh of resignation, and the computer became available. Father John wrote:

> Hi Eileen, I want you to know that I will be happy to join you two intrepid souls in your participation in the Raytheon action. It only took a few minutes of reading to get a better understanding beyond what you already told me of why you want to be a witness against that company. I have to admit I used to think about Raytheon as a kind of local company that makes some sort of vaguely sinister military products, but now I see the bigger picture, and it's horrific. Now, it will be tricky for me to get down there on Saturday, given the fact that I can't exactly tell the abbot that I am off to break the law in the Bay State. I'll just have to sign out a car to do "errands." I'll see you two around eleven at the address you gave me on that card. Best, John OSB

For the next few days, John's routine was comfortably back to the familiar prayer and work, although he had always regarded teaching as anything but work. That was supplied by Brother Isaac, who enlisted his help in pruning the colorful array of flowering shrubs lining the quad. The campus typically looked its best when most of the students were not there, although this year's summer school population provided a sizeable audience. The labor in the warming sun gave John plenty of time to think. Thinking, he knew, was very different from meditation, and in this case, not as helpful. On the one hand, he was convinced that he could no longer stay on the sidelines. Making weapons of mass destruction for profit—immense profit—while much of the world struggled with poverty and disease—amounted to larceny from the poor.

To add to the absurdity, nuclear weapons could never be used. Releasing even one or a few of these new LRSO missiles, for example, could trigger an eruption of retaliatory violence that would reduce whole countries into smoking ruins. This was a moral absurdity, and yet the looming presence of the thousands of nuclear weapons in our midst, ready at a moment's notice to erupt by command or accident, was barely noticed. Surely, it was not a subject dealt with in Sunday homilies, even though the pope, along with many bishops, had condemned even the possession of these instruments of death. That thought made him recall Joseph Stalin's famous question regarding the pope, "How many divisions does he have?" John used to laugh at the absurdity of that question, until he realized how many divisions do serve with the pope's tacit approval. That would continue as long as chaplains blessed troops and armaments. Militarism was alive and well in his Church, a far cry from any dedication to the Prince of Peace.

On the other hand, John thought, as he reached deep into an azalea bush and felt a sharp twinge in his lower back, I am a professed monk at Saint Oliver College in

Manchester, New Hampshire, and I have taken a vow of obedience to my abbot. I'm going to be heading to Nashua on Saturday under false pretenses. Shouldn't I stop pretending to be an itinerant preacher and concentrate on my vocation? I can certainly pray a lot more. But it is going to take people of faith, and lots of others, to make a public witness against legitimizing this moral outrage.

He stood up slowly, grateful that his back seemed to be still in the proper alignment. Looks like I will be headed for the Gate City on Saturday. Maybe best I stick to jeans and a work shirt. No need to give Abbot Richard an ulcer. I'd better not leave that good Irishman Oliver Plunkett out of my prayers. He was a victim of vicious persecution and violence. Thank God they didn't have nukes in those days.

Classes went well for the remainder of the week. He decided to roam through various genres of poetry rather than take a strictly chronological approach. Nothing worse than that with a class or a congregation. Once they knew that you were heading for the twenty-first century, but were only on the sixteenth, or there were six more epistles ahead to be dissected, you had lost half of them to discreet glances at those ubiquitous phones. The day had passed when the students obediently left their phones outside the classroom. Too many phones went missing. Now, potential quiz answers jotted down on palms were replaced with subtle Google searches.

At week's end, after the class in which he had managed to get his students to emerge from the lassitude that always developed on Fridays by giving them a chance to write haikus, John bumped into Bill Johnson just as he emerged from his Introduction to Physics lecture.

"Hey, Bill," John said with a smile. "I didn't know you were laboring in the same vineyard as myself."

"Hello, John, good to see you. I have been wanting to talk to you since that, shall we say, spirited repartee in the lounge. You know, as a physics guy, the whole thing about the Manhattan Project creating 'The Bomb' was really a conundrum for lots of scientists. The sheer brilliance of that undertaking was such beautiful science that it drew some of the best minds into it. Just think, unlimited money, getting whatever resources you needed, working on a set of intriguing physics, math and engineering problems. How could you say no that not, even the ones who worried that if they could split those atoms, they would create a monster? After Trinity, some of them got cold feet, but it was too late. I really liked what you had to say, and from my remarks, you can probably tell that you and I are pretty much simpatico when it comes to nukes. We should talk some more about this some time."

John nodded. "Absolutely. Please keep this under your hat, but you might remember I was musing back in the lounge about Benedict's challenge to use 'deeds rather than words to show all that is good and holy.' Well, it's clear to me that being good and holy is incompatible with giving assent to use nuclear weapons of mass destruction against God's creation."

"I hear you, Father, although I have to admit, as a confirmed atheist, my objections end up in the same anti-nuke position as yours without recourse to your God's rules, although I certainly respect where you're coming from. In fact, I'd better, since I'm up for tenure next year. But seriously, we need to turn more attention to these weapons. I mean, it's OK to have academic discussions about MAD and then go home to supper, but we need to go further."

They had migrated to the shaded portico during their conversation. John stopped and looked up at the scientist. "Bill, I wasn't going to bring this up when we started talking, but I have a proposition for you. I am going to go down to Nashua on Saturday to meet up with a couple of nuns—older women who have literally spent their lives in service to others. We're planning to join a nonviolent demo down at the Raytheon headquarters in Waltham. Of course, we won't change the world on Saturday. But we can only hope that the accumulated weight of testimonies like ours might at least contribute to raising the public's awareness of the death-dealing weapons coming out of those peaceful looking buildings down there in Waltham. Can you make it? I can pick you up around ten."

The physicist hesitated before answering. "Well," he answered, slowly, "that is really interesting, I mean, that people are putting themselves on the line for this. I guess sometimes they even get arrested and such at these things. So, I support the effort but, actually, my kids have got soccer games on Saturday and I'm this week's designated driver. Look, why don't I take a rain check on this one—you know, kind of a late notice thing? Listen, be careful down there and if they are collecting money let me know. I'm good for some cash. Gotta run, Father, I've got a lab coming up. It's on energy—coincidentally, I guess. Good luck."

☢

Saturday morning arrived. The day promised to be clear and warm. Headed down the Everett Turnpike, Father John remembered his conversation with Bill Johnson. The poor guy, he thought, I didn't mean to make it sound like I was asking him to go to jail with a bunch of law-breakers. I shouldn't have even mentioned it. I mean, he's up for tenure. I wonder if he tells his students he's an atheist. His attention switched suddenly to the toll booth looming ahead. He glided slowly through the E-Z Pass lane. Each of the cars in the monastery fleet of vehicles bore an E-Z Pass transponder, eliminating the need for the driver to have cash, and also allowing the Prior to keep track of where the car had been.

Fifteen minutes later, he pulled up in front of a faded yellow three-decker in the south end of the city. The two Sisters emerged immediately through the front door and motioned for him to pull in behind the building. He parked, and the trio were soon heading back to the turnpike, with John squeezed into the back seat, which was protected by a blanket covered with dog hair.

"Sorry," Mary said with a laugh. "That mess is from our Lab, Benedict. We've had him so long he's named after the last pope. We've thought about changing him into a Francis for obvious reasons, but he's used to his name, so ..."

"No problem, I always had dogs growing up. So, what's on the agenda? I'm a bit rusty for this stuff. To be perfectly honest, I've done a lot of sign carrying and waving, but nothing ever involved going on to a property. Or is that not going to happen?"

"Well," Mary replied, "the way this is planned, we are supposed to meet up around the corner from the main entrance, and then march over there and stand along the road leading up to the guard shack. There's a line that designates where the Raytheon property starts, so I think the consensus is that we go up to the line but not beyond—maybe. You know, I don't think the organizers have a permit for that brief march in the street, so that could be messy. We'll see."

Eileen spoke up. "Anyway, thanks for coming, Father. This merger that these companies have pulled off, and all the fanfare about Raytheon developing this new long range nuclear missile—we certainly can't match this giant in the public relations department, but we've got to at least get our objections somewhere in the papers—maybe next to the obituaries would be a good spot. It's funny, our landlord's kid laughs when I talk about making the newspapers. People her age—high schoolers—hardly ever see a paper. She says it's all about Facebook and Twitter. I gave her a list of my favorite sites on the Web from the Federation of American Scientists to the Nuclear Resister to show her all the voices out there sounding the alarm about nuclear weapons. She was impressed, but I kind of blew it by handing her the list written on a piece of paper."

"Don't worry, Eileen, at least she knows where you stand. So, what's your advice for a rusty peacenik like me?"

"The usual. We are going into a situation where the security people at Raytheon and the local police are geared up for trouble, given the advance publicity about this demo. They know the drill. I don't think the organizers are going to do a full-scale CD. We probably should have warned you, though, about a few things. In case there are arrests you probably want to have some cash on you to bail out. We're ready to help you out with that. And we're assuming you are not carrying any drugs. But don't worry, I think we'll be OK today. Of course, we always aim to be nonviolent and respectful. As far as Mary and I are concerned, we'll be holding signs. We've got one for you in the trunk, and our beautiful voices are ready to sing."

The nuns' faded blue Toyota groaned to a stop in a Target parking lot, plenty big and busy enough to absorb lots of cars driven by non-shoppers without drawing notice. They picked up their signs and headed across the street to a small public park. Within fifteen minutes, a surprisingly large crowd of demonstrators had gathered on the green grass surrounding a white wooden gazebo. At least a dozen or so were wearing masks. The specter of the Virus was not easily shaken.

A tall, slender, grey-haired women wearing jeans and a blue cotton shirt topped by the white collar of an Episcopal priest climbed the steps of the bandstand and addressed the group, using a megaphone.

"Good morning! Thank you all for coming. I have a question for you. If any of you were walking down the street and saw a house on fire, and there was a little girl inside screaming for help, would you hesitate to break down the door to try to rescue her? Would you worry about being charged with property damage or trespassing? I think you would be more concerned about that innocent child being burned up in the flames. Sure, you'd be taking a risk, but I bet you'd try it. Maybe you would have religious motives for the rescue, maybe you would think that it was a moral obligation under God to save a life. Or maybe you wouldn't think about that at all, but you'd know that you just had to help a little child in danger of death. Think about Yemen on this beautiful, sunny summer day. Think about the children, maybe lying in a hospital bed, recovering from cholera caused because the local water supply had been bombed. Think of the ten-foot-long bomb guided by Raytheon's laser system streaking towards where the children are sleeping fitfully. Think of the explosion, spewing shards of metal that tear them apart. Think of the sobbing parents, sifting through the wreckage in the vain hope that their child might have survived.

We are around the corner from a complex of innocent looking buildings, where each day, hundreds of employees, many of whom have children, settle in to work for one of America's biggest war profiteers. These are our friends and neighbors and parishioners. How has it come to this, that the business of war—the business of killing—has become so ingrained in our national fabric that participating in this military-industrial complex has become a job like any other, as though this company were making widgets and not weapons? Why has the Secretary of Defense in our government been recruited from Raytheon, and the one before him from Boeing?

We are not here to condemn any of our fellow Americans who work here and are caught up in this dilemma. But we are here to make our voices heard, and to declare to them and to all who will listen, that this immensely profitable business represents larceny from the poor, and that making the tools of war, nuclear or otherwise, while they may be marvels of technology, destroys human lives, and as such is profoundly immoral.

We will be marching towards a kind of shrine in which our fellow citizens can be said to worship weapons, false idols standing in the place of compassion, brother and sisterhood, and love for all creation. You all know of another sort of shrine not far from here—Walden Pond. Thoreau asked of the American government, 'Why does it not cherish its wise minority? Why does it not encourage its citizens to point out its faults, and do better than it would have them?' That same government in our day, subsidizing the most massive buildup of lethal weaponry in the history of the world, needs to hear from us, the vocal minority. Let us speak together today in nonviolence and take a stand for peace."

The group, now numbering about seventy, applauded, and began to move together along the sidewalk. They soon spilled out into the street as they surged around the corner, moving toward the company's entrance. As they moved along slowly, most carried colorful signs, and out in front, a half-dozen grey-haired men and women held a long, white banner that read in large, red letters, "SAY NO TO NUKES." A few steps beyond the banner, two Buddhist monks in saffron robes set the pace by slowly beating large, circular drums with wooden mallets. Here and there, specific organizations identified themselves with tall posters—"Granite State Peace Action," "Waltham Concerned Citizens."

John, swept along near the rear of the marchers, suddenly felt a strong sense of déjà vu. He had been with a strikingly similar group in Chicago years earlier. There was the same eclectic mix of young and old, the signs demanding and yearning for peace—even the drumming monks. As he looked around for Eileen and Mary, he realized that he was feeling the same unsettling mix of idealism and optimism, frustrated by the realization of the odds against swaying the opinions of the massive weapons industry, so interwoven into the economy of America.

He saw two dark blue police vans parked conspicuously just beyond the steel barriers situated at the guard's enclosure, now lowered to block the entrance. The Episcopal priest who had addressed the group raised her megaphone and announced: "OK, everybody up on the grass along the drive. Hold up those signs and let's hear your voices." She began a chant, "No nukes, save the children."

As soon as the protestors begun to follow her lead, the barriers abruptly lifted, and the police vans drove out and advanced slowly toward them. The vehicles stopped, and six officers in riot gear got out of each van and lined up in the middle of the road. One of them stepped forward and shouted, "We are warning you that you are violating the law. You are standing on private property, and the owners do not wish you to be here. Unless you move off that property you will be guilty of criminal trespass and subject to arrest. Is that clear?"

A man, somewhere in his eighties, supported by a cane and wearing a purple T-shirt featuring a bleeding peace sign, stepped out of the crowd. "Mike, is that you?" he shouted. "Are you guys getting some overtime? Come on, you're usually driving the beat in my neighborhood." The protestors erupted in laughter and held their ground. The police officer who had issued the warning, giving away his identity answered, "Now look, Walter, I'm tired of arresting you for this stuff. Besides, you have enough money to bail all these people out. Now why don't you all just cooperate and move along. It's a beautiful day and the Sox are playing this afternoon. What do you say? The good people that work here are paying the taxes that make this community a great place to live."

As he kept talking, the sound of his voice was drowned out by the familiar sound of "We Shall Overcome" sung by the marchers, standing resolutely on Raytheon's carefully manicured grass. Where are my fellow travelers? John thought, looking around for Eileen and Mary. Oh, brother, this could be big trouble. I came down here to be a sign waver, but it looks like the long arm of the law is about to reach out and get us in a world of trouble.

He realized that he could not simply walk away. Besides, what kind of commitment did he have if he was afraid of nothing more than a possible fine? That would at least make the point. But a monk wandering around Nashua waving a sign that says, "Nuclear Weapons = Omnicide" alongside a bunch of radical Episcopalians, Buddhists, and probably Unitarians to boot, and all this without the abbot's permission?

John had little time to think about possible alternatives as an officer walked past a gaggle of protestors and approached, grabbed him by the arm, and propelled him toward a clump of bushes. They stopped, and the policeman took off his face shield and turned toward John.

"Father, don't you recognize me? I'm Angelo Catanese. I was a Criminal Justice major and I had you for Freshman English. You got me turned on to James Joyce, remember?"

"Of course, Angelo. How's it going?"

"Not bad, I've read *Ulysses* three times, and I'm working on *Finnegan's Wake* right now, but it's hard. Listen,

Father, what are you doing with this bunch? And out of uniform, if you know what I mean."

"Angelo, I guess the simplest answer is that I am following my conscience. You took Intro to Theology the same year I had you in class. Remember what you learned about making sure you had an 'informed' conscience? Well, my friends and I joined these protestors because we're informed by what we know about how Raytheon and companies like it are making weapons and weapon systems that have only one purpose—to kill. We can't support this. I know you are just doing your job, but what do you think about all this?"

"Look, Father, I always thought you were a really good teacher, but you know, you can't just force your opinions on everybody else. Listen, this is a huge company, and they make lots of good stuff, not just bombs. Besides, we need all them—if we didn't have them the Russians would take us over in a minute. But look, we should talk about this some other time. Right now, I've got to get you out of here. Where are your friends?"

John looked around and spotted the two nuns heading towards where the police officer was standing with him. "Angelo," he said hurriedly, "be cool with these two. They're both nuns, and they probably think you are getting ready to beat me up."

"You're kidding! What is this, a religious convention? Good morning, Sisters! My name is Angelo and I graduated from Saint O's, and before that from Bishop Guertin. Listen, I am going to get you guys out of here now. Hold it, Sister, that look tells me that you want to get arrested. Not on my watch—so just walk out that side exit over there behind that maple tree, or whatever it is, and you can do your thing another day. Now give me a break and get out of here. And say a prayer for me, will you? I've got a one-year-old with heart problems."

Back on campus, John slipped back into his robes and his routine. The whole affair seemed unreal, some kind of time warp that he had escaped from with an unsettling feeling of guilt and satisfaction. Nothing about his commitment to nonviolence and his opposition to nuclear weapons, or for that matter, to all weapons of war and to the spirit of militarism that seemed to have permeated American society at every level, was lessened by his experience in Nashua. That whole scene had re-invigorated his conviction that his work and vocation somehow had to bend towards peace. Should he have stayed and let himself be arrested with all the others? Who do I think I am, some kind of hero? Eileen and Mary wanted to go back, but I told them I was scheduled to say four o'clock Mass. How heroic!

But he had deceived his abbot. He pictured himself telling Abbot Richard how inspired he had been that morning by the words of an Episcopal priest—and a woman, at that! Well, I don't have to worry about that scene, he thought, this incident will remain in the vault, for the greater good, of course. No more chapter of faults around here, thank goodness.

CHAPTER 6

The first thoughts John had when he awoke on Sunday morning and headed to the chapel, along with his fellow groggy monastic brethren, were not spiritual in nature, nor were they marked with concern over having his Waltham adventure discovered. He realized that he had made a mistake with his syllabus, particularly for a summer school class filled with students who also were working full-time jobs. He had been far too ambitious in his expectations, planning on having eighteen-year-olds share his interest in the chronological evolution of poetic styles dating back to Virgil, Ovid, Chaucer, Petrarch, Spenser, or John Donne. Sure, his job was to introduce these kids to the beauty and inspiration of poetry, but he had better leave those "dead white guys," as one of his students had put it that morning, to senior seminars. After he joined in concelebrating Mass, where once again he was comforted and inspired by his prayerful community, he headed for the library. His mental syllabus was filling up with names like Langston Hughes, Maya Angelou, Wilfred Owen—maybe even Ferlinghetti? Better get this organized, and fashion some common thread to follow.

He began to pull on the library door just as Brother Edwin was pushing it open from the other side. The young novice stopped abruptly, with a worried look on his cherubic face. John had been following Edwin's frustrating experiment with growing a beard. It looked like he had failed in the attempt.

"Oh, Father John. I was hoping to find you here. The abbot wants to see you right away, in his office. He said something about the 'papers,' but that's all I know."

"Do you know what he meant?"

"Oh, no, not really," the novice answered, his voice quavering. He turned and sped off into the library. John suddenly thought of the lines in the E.E. Cummings poem about Olaf, a conscientious objector to World War II: "straightway the silver bird looked grave / (departing hurriedly to shave)." Probably not going to shave, but he sure is nervous about something. I'm pretty sure the abbot doesn't want to talk to me about Raytheon, but I had better be armed before I see him. Darn it, there I go again.

John went back to his room, shuffled through the papers littering his desk, and selected a couple of articles he had photocopied from the National Catholic Reporter, just in case. He walked slowly towards the abbot's office and knocked. The abbot's voice said, "Enter," in what John hoped was a friendly tone.

As John entered and headed for a chair facing Abbot Richard's desk, the abbot abruptly stood up and advanced towards him, waving a newspaper. John recognized the familiar Manchester Union Leader.

"What is this business all about? What in the world were you thinking? I knew you were trafficking with some pretty radical notions from what Monsignor O'Malley told me, but here you were, dressed up like you were going out to mow the lawn, cavorting around the streets of some town down in Massachusetts with what looks like a bunch of hoodlums! Take a look!"

He handed the paper to John. There, below the fold, was a picture of the assembled protestors gathered at Raytheon, In the center of the scene, John could be seen holding a sign that read, "Nuclear Weapons = Omnicide." The headline said, "Local priest seen at protest."

"For the love of all that's good and holy," the abbot shouted, "what is going on here? I don't recall you asking my permission to join this pitchfork brigade. I've already had three phone calls from our trustees, one of whom was about to sign over his estate to us—and he's a retired Navy Captain! He spent his career defending this country, and now this? Back in the day, when Bill Loeb was running this newspaper, he would have quashed this story, but these people now are happy to splash this all over the front page. Do you see that logo up on the top of the page next to the Flag? It says, 'There is nothing so powerful as truth.' We try to teach the truth around here and you go off and run around carrying a cockamamie sign with a bunch of trespassers! Those people were arrested, for heaven sakes. The paper says you 'slipped away with two unidentified women.' Mother of God, what was that all about?"

John, still holding the paper, answered quietly, "Abbot, please, can we talk about this?"

"Fine, Father, that's very kind of you to offer to converse about this. Your story had better be good."

"Well, Abbot Richard, I am as surprised at this newspaper story as you are. I thought I was in the clear. I am truly sorry that this has been so upsetting. I had no intention to go this public, so to speak, with my opposition to nuclear weapons and war in general, although I admit, I did get pretty open with my objections in my homilies at Saint James. The thing is, after I met these two women at that church—who by the way are both Sisters of Mercy from Nashua—I accepted their invitation to join a nonviolent protest down in Waltham. I didn't know it would end up with people getting arrested, although to tell you the truth I felt guilty about kind of sneaking away with the Sisters." He recounted his surprise meeting with Angelo Catanese, the Saint O's graduate who whisked the trio out the side gate.

"Angelo was trying to avoid just this kind of publicity for the College. It looks like he hadn't counted on the press photographer being there. On our way back, Sister Eileen told me that they always notified the papers about their demos, but I never thought the Union Leader would be down there."

"Well, isn't that interesting. You thought you could get away with it? Would you mind telling me what you were doing there in the first place? And by the way, not only do I have two nephews who are still in the Armed Services, but my best friend from college was also an Army chaplain for many years. Now there's a fine vocation for a priest."

John looked at the abbot. "Abbot Richard, you know that I have the greatest respect for you. You have known me ever since I was an undergraduate here, and all through my years in this monastery studying for the priesthood, and then as a professor after graduate school. You have never known me to be rebellious, or disrespectful towards others, including those with whom I disagreed. When you apparently were concerned about what you may have considered to be my 'liberal leanings,' and told me to put in some time this summer at Saint James, I went there out of obedience. It turns out that you were correct about those 'tendencies,' and your sending me to that parish was a blessing. It gave me time to face a moral issue that had been dormant in me since I came back here from grad school at Notre Dame. How do I live as a Catholic priest and professed monk, teaching college students in a Catholic college, and not speak out about one of the most pressing dilemmas facing our country and the world?"

The abbot interrupted. "Wait a minute, are you talking about abortion? Your sign said omnicide, not infanticide. You were protesting against Raytheon, which I am told is a major, important business. Why were you shouting at them? Do they have anything to do with right to life?"

"Abbot Richard, it's interesting that you bring up the abortion issue. We went to Raytheon to highlight what is very much a right to life issue. Each and every human being, Christian or otherwise, has an inalienable right to a life free from the real fear that, at any moment, their life and the lives of possibly millions of others can be snuffed out. And why? Because Raytheon and other giant corporations like them are engaged, for enormous profits, in improving and modernizing nuclear weapons. Many thousands of these killing machines are poised to attack, especially here in the United States and in Russia, and their use will not only destroy life and property on an unimaginable scale, but also will create conditions that can defile and injure our environment. So, yes, this was truly a right to life protest. So, my dilemma is, I am convinced that it's not possible to wage war in keeping with the teachings of Jesus. How can we follow Jesus, and love as he taught us to love, and at the same time kill our fellow humans?"

The abbot sighed. "All right, now we are getting somewhere. No wonder Monsignor O'Malley and his confused parishioners were so upset with your homilies. Have you forgotten the basics that you learned in the seminary? Remember, we know from Augustine and Aquinas and other wise minds that there is such a thing as a 'just war.' There are certain conditions that must be met, but the Church can confidently bless the efforts of nations to defend themselves if those criteria are met."

"Certainly, abbot, I am painfully aware of that theory and the criteria you are talking about. They include the warning that a war is immoral if the resulting destruction would outweigh the good achieved, and if more force is used than is necessary to achieve just objectives. Think about a nuclear war. What is the good accomplished? No one would 'win,' and there would be a profound lack of any proportionality. There would simply be destruction almost beyond imagining. I am afraid that once you begin to think about justifying any war at all, but especially a nuclear war, we are all in trouble. Don't forget, our government is saying, in our name, not only are we willing to make these weapons by the thousands and point them at the enemy, but we are also willing to use these weapons, and have every intention of using them if that decision is made, perhaps within the space of a few minutes. I want to follow the nonviolent Jesus, and given the challenge, follow my God and not my government."

"Father, you are wandering down a dangerous path. First, you need to remember that as a Catholic priest, and especially as a monk, you must avoid getting involved in politics. Now that you seem to be taking a stand against your own government, let me remind you of a recent letter to our very own president from an official high up in the Vatican. In fact, Archbishop Carlo Vigano is a former Papal nuncio to the U.S. He told the president that they were both united in a 'cosmic battle against good and evil.' He assured the president that the 'deep state' opposing him at every turn was matched by a 'deep church,' fighting against the Church's 'good shepherds.' If you want to start talking about political issues, you might want to listen to that message instead of tilting at windmills down in Massachusetts. Father John, don't you know that we need all our powerful weapons to keep us safe? It's called deterrence, and it's why the nations of the world are able to remain at peace with each other."

"My apologies, abbot, but I have to remind you that the situation you just described is called MAD, or mutual assured destruction. It is a balance of terror. Deterrence is a moral issue, abbot. We possess thousands of nuclear weapons, many times more powerful than the bombs our country used to incinerate Hiroshima and Nagasaki. We are saying, in effect, to our adversaries, 'If you dare to attack us, or even if we simply think you are about to attack, we will unleash devastation all across your nation.' It's time to get rid of these weapons before they get rid of us. The Vatican, under Pope Francis, is committed to working toward nuclear disarmament. In fact, the Holy See signed a treaty a couple of years ago, sponsored by the UN, that called for a universal ban on making and using any nuclear explosive devices. Over one hundred countries have already signed on. Abbot, the world is crying out for protection from these terrible weapons. I went to Raytheon to join this struggle for peace. You mentioned Cardinal Vigano's letter. I'm not quite sure how that is an example of non-interference in politics, but if I may, I can quote a higher authority than the Cardinal."

The abbot began to pace the floor, hands behind his back. "Now, Father John, I can assure you that I am aware of the latest comments by our current pope about this business. You may or may not have noticed that we have every edition of *The Pope Speaks* on our library shelves. It's been a long time since I perused that document without a sense of foreboding. I didn't hear about that pie in the sky treaty, but it's clear that this pope has gone rogue. All the wisdom of Pope Benedict seems to have gone in one ear and out the other. Since you are quoting popes here let me remind you that other popes—and quite influential ones—have been very clear about keeping nuclear weapons, even if it is reluctantly, to keep us safe. I mean, John Paul —you might remember him because he was just canonized—said that this deterrence thing was 'morally acceptable.' He did say that we needed at the same time to work toward disarmament. But Pope Francis has gone around the bend. Now he's going on about civil unions and …"

The abbot's voice had grown louder and more agitated. He stopped in front of Saint Plunkett's image, then turned to face Father John.

"Well, that's for another day. I'm anticipating you using the pope's recent comment again that not only the use, but the very possession of nuclear weapons is immoral. He's gone way overboard on that subject along with quite a few others. And don't forget, when he goes on about these things in some interview with the press he is not speaking 'ex cathedra.' It's just his personal opinion."

He returned to his seat behind the desk.

"Look, Father John. This is all new, coming from you, all of a sudden. Are you trying to make yourself into a combination of Thomas Merton and that renegade Jesuit—what's his name—Berrigan? There were two of them. Anyway, you are a monk, and from what I hear you are a pretty good professor when it comes to your poems and such. But I can't have you gallivanting around with nuns and who knows who else trying to stop our duly elected government from making weapons—cruel though they may be, I will admit—that our military needs to give them the upper hand. You are here to pray for peace, and to live a life of sacrifice. A monastery is like a spiritual battery charging the community with graces. Now please, I don't want to read any more headlines featuring anyone from this college or monastery unless they are bringing us good publicity, not scandal."

"I understand, Abbot Richard," John answered, as he stood up to leave. "May I just mention a word about Archbishop Takami before I go?"

The abbot closed his eyes and said, "Go ahead, but be brief, please."

"The Archbishop of Nagasaki is Joseph Takami. That city, which was devastated by an atomic bomb dropped by our government seventy-five years ago, was the center of Catholicism in Japan. The Archbishop was present at that bombing as a fetus in his mother's womb. He has been traveling the world with the remains of a wooden statue of Mary that had been in Nagasaki's destroyed cathedral. He shows the scorched head of the Blessed Mother to underline his message that war cannot be compatible with the Gospel of peace as lived by Jesus. Abbot Richard, I will do my best to enhance the reputation of Saint Oliver. Thank you, abbot."

The abbot kept his eyes closed, nodded, and pointed toward the door.

As a nuclear warhead reaches a specific position and altitude, poised above its target, it answers to its sophisticated guidance and control systems, and begins to undergo the process of fission. This is triggered when a relatively small chemical explosion inside the warhead compresses a special form of plutonium formed into a spherical "pit." The pit is squeezed under tremendous pressure, bringing its atoms closer together. Neutrons are injected, causing an explosion. The energy from this "fission" explosion causes certain forms of hydrogen to fuse together to form helium. In this "fusion" reaction, the hydrogen loses some of its mass, which releases enormous amounts of energy.

The two atomic bombs dropped in 1945 used only fission reactions to create the fierce explosions that lit up the skies over the heads of the citizens of Hiroshima and Nagasaki in the last moments of their lives. Today's far more sophisticated nuclear weapons combine fission and fusion in vastly more powerful thermonuclear reactions.

For example, one 750 kiloton warhead will erupt within one second with a force of up to 750,000 tons of TNT. The bomb dropped on Hiroshima was equivalent to 15,000 tons of TNT. As a point of reference, an explosion of one million tons of TNT can destroy 80 square miles. Such disturbing results can be visualized by referring to the NUKEMAP website, an interactive map which enables users to model the explosions of nuclear weapons on any location of their choice.

A major cause of devastation in a nuclear detonation is due to the explosive blast. It sends a shock wave of air in all directions moving at several times the speed of sound. The magnitude of the blast effect depends on the height of the explosion above ground level. The warhead can be programmed to detonate at a height that will maximize the spread of the destruction. The point immediately below the explosion is "ground zero." Anyone at ground zero will be killed instantaneously. Beyond that point, survivors may incur internal injuries such as crushed lungs and internal bleeding. A major cause of injury and death will be the severe damage caused to structures. Victims will be buried under falling buildings or hurled against hard surfaces. Flying shards of metal, masonry, wood and glass splinters pierce and shred bodies. In Hiroshima and Nagasaki, about 30 percent of all fatalities were caused by falling and flying debris.

Those two Japanese cities are, fortunately, the only examples of where nuclear weapons have been directed at humans. Because of the vast differences in the power of today's thermonuclear weapons compared to those much smaller atomic bombs, the effects described here for the latter must be multiplied many times over for any nuclear war using modern weapons.

Approximately 35 percent of the energy released in a nuclear explosion is an enormous burst of heat. In a Hiroshima-type bomb, the fireball expands immediately to 1,200 feet in diameter with an external temperature of 10,800 degrees Fahrenheit. Humans a half-mile from ground zero are vaporized. This thermal radiation moves at almost the speed of light. A blinding flash of light and heat comes just before the blast wave, like lightening is seen before the thunder is heard. Anyone who sees this visible light is blinded, either permanently or temporarily, depending upon the distance from ground zero. This light and heat inflict severe burns on human skin even miles away from the source. Fires ignite over a wide area, which are whipped into a giant firestorm in the powerful winds, which reach over 7,000 miles per hour, consuming everything combustible. Even people sheltered in basements die from lack of oxygen consumed by the fires.

Even as the initial fireball begins to dim, at five miles away the glare is 10 times that of daylight. As the famous mushroom cloud begins to rise several thousands of feet above the city, it sucks up superheated air, adding to the raging fires. The city is demolished, ablaze, and thousands are dead, while thousands more are terribly burned and injured. Medical personnel and hospitals have vanished, and the injured have no recourse.

In addition to the blast and heat, an insidious and long-lasting result of a nuclear explosion is radiation. The most lethal forms of radiation here are gamma rays and neutrons. High doses of this radiation destroy cells in living tissues, breaking chemical bonds and damaging DNA, leading to an agonizing death within hours. Nonlethal doses can cause immediate symptoms such as intestinal injury, fevers, hair loss, and years later, cancers. In Hiroshima, children that had been exposed to radiation in the womb suffered intellectual disabilities, impaired growth, and had an increased risk of developing cancer.

The mushroom cloud of dust and debris rising out of the carnage is filled with radioactive particles. It may take days for the heavier particles to fall out of the cloud, spreading contamination to areas downwind from the explosion. The radioactive material can eventually enter the food chain and be consumed by humans or animals. Larger warheads can elevate radioactive particles into the stratosphere, where they may remain for several years before descending somewhere on the Earth's surface as fallout. This commonly includes radioactive substances such as Iodine-13, a cause of thyroid cancer, and Strontium-90, injurious to bones, teeth and bone marrow.

Gamma radiation has another effect, particularly relevant to our modern civilization, so dependent on electronic communication. A nuclear explosion forms a strong pulse of electric current which generates an electromagnetic field that can severely damage electronic equipment. Computers, electrical systems, and telecommunications stop functioning. One thermonuclear bomb detonated at a high altitude can knock out all electronics systems for hundreds of square miles.

The long-term effects of radiation poisoning would be outdone by another phenomenon in the case of a major nuclear conflagration. According to the International Campaign to Abolish Nuclear Weapons (ICAN), in a war which involved five percent of the world's nuclear arsenal, the planet would "become uninhabitable." Even a more limited conflict of around 100 Hiroshima-sized weapons could alter the global climate and agricultural production so much that more than a billion people could face famine.

Although exact predictions cannot be made, it is clear that the enormous amounts of smoke and dust resulting from nuclear explosions would rise into the stratosphere and be carried around the globe. This would reflect enough sunlight to lower air temperatures, severely affecting harvests, even in areas far from the conflict zones. In one simulation, global harvests were reduced between 20 to 40 percent for at least 10 years. The climate shift triggered widespread drought. The worldwide famine led to the death of millions. The scenario predicting that this deadly phenomenon would occur is the "nuclear winter" hypothesis introduced by Carl Sagan in 1983. The deadly details depend on variables such as the amount of smoke and dust released, but the dire consequences of nuclear war are unquestionable.

Even beyond destruction and famine would be the prolonged and severe disruption of the protective ozone layer surrounding the planet. The intensity of ultraviolet light reaching us would increase, causing skin cancers and damaging crops and marine life.

The first nuclear bomb test in New Mexico in July 1945 proved the feasibility of the atomic bomb design and gave some indication of the damage this weapon could cause. It provided little insight into the extent of the radioactive nuclear fallout that would ensue, and it would take years before the insidious effects would be understood. Immediately after World War II came to a close, an all-out arms race began between the two emerging superpowers, the United States and the Soviet Union. The U.S. conducted six nuclear tests between 1946 and 1949. The Soviet Union followed with its first test in August 1949. The "Cold War" was underway, with each party vying for nuclear superiority. In 1951, the U.S. established a dedicated test site in Nevada, where there would eventually be over 900 tests. They also tested extensively in the Pacific Proving Grounds at the Marshall Islands in the Central Pacific. The Soviets began testing in Kazakhstan. The United Kingdom joined in with tests in 1952 in Australia.

In 1952 the U.S. tested the first thermonuclear bomb on the Bikini Atoll in the Marshall Islands. The explosion had a force of 15 megatons, and was the largest nuclear weapon ever detonated by the U.S. Radioactive fallout spread over more than 4,200 square miles. A Japanese fishing vessel 90 miles downwind was heavily contaminated, and one crew member soon died from radiation poisoning. International criticism grew over nuclear testing. Bikini residents were moved away from the island, and were brought back again in 1972, only to be forced to abandon the area in 1978 because of high levels of radiation.

It was not until 1996, when the Comprehensive Nuclear Test Ban Treaty (CNTBT) went into effect, that nuclear testing ceased. By that time, there had been over 2,000 tests carried out at over 60 locations all over the world, the majority by the U.S. Since 1996, at least 10 tests have been conducted, by India, Pakistan, and North Korea. The nuclear "club" testing weapons expanded to eight nations, including China and France.

Before the CNTBT went into effect, a 1963 Partial Test Ban Treaty prohibited testing in the atmosphere, underwater, in space, but not underground. This curbed radioactive fallout, especially from atmospheric tests, but widespread underground testing had remained until 1996. North Korea is the only country to have conducted nuclear tests in this century. However, although 183 countries have signed the CNTBT, only 166 have ratified it. The U.S. has not. In 2020, the U.S. president proposed resuming testing as a show of might to improve the U.S. negotiating position towards regulating China and Russia's nuclear arsenals.

We have only estimates of the illnesses and deaths caused by the decades of nuclear testing. According to the respected Arms Control Association, "millions of people ... have died and suffered from illnesses directly related to the radioactive fallout from [nuclear] tests." In their study of global fallout, the U.S. Centers for Disease Control and Prevention (CDC) found that "any person living in the contiguous United States since 1951 has been exposed to some radioactive fallout, and all of a person's organs and tissues have received some exposure."

CHAPTER 7

"Two roads diverged in a yellow wood/and sorry I could not travel both."

Father John muttered those familiar lines to himself as he trudged over the quad towards his waiting class. I suppose I am sorry, but really, "both" is not an option. It looks like I have taken the one "less traveled." But how much difference will it make? I haven't exactly swayed the abbot.

Halfway across the quad, he stopped suddenly. Wait a minute, he realized, the Union Leader! My Irish mug was on the front page of the Sunday paper! Here I am worried about my syllabus, and my students will have read all about my "coming out" as a radical. What will they think of all that business? I'd better be ready with some answers.

When he entered the classroom, almost all the students were there. The usual buzz of conversation stopped abruptly as he entered. Usually, the chatter would not cease until he put his briefcase down on the lecture table and began to speak. Not today. Instead, there was an eerie silence, until Kathleen spoke up. She had emerged as the most vocal of the class, to the consternation of some, who wished she would shut up, and to the relief of others, who lived in fear of being called on. Kathleen said, "Good morning, Father. That was an interesting picture. We have been wondering if it will be alright if we talk about it."

John threw his head back and laughed. The tension in the room relaxed immediately.

"Why, thanks Kathleen. I do have to admit that they got my best side. I never expected to end up on the Leader's front page. Wait just a minute. How many of you actually read Sunday's paper?"

Three hands went up, slowly.

"Hah, just as I thought. You guys don't read much that's not on a screen. Don't be offended, though, you have access to way more information than people who are looking at newspapers featuring yesterday's news. But to get more serious about this, the attention that this whole affair is getting speaks to the point of why I and lots of others were there in Waltham on Saturday. Unless you have objections, and I will respect them, I think it's probably OK to talk about this in a poetry class. After all, poets look at life from many different angles and with insights that can surprise their readers. To be more blunt, poetry can be a shining light that represents the best of a civilization—and right now, the continued existence of our global civilization and the accumulated learning of centuries of human thought and creativity is in danger of being wiped out of existence. I know that may sound like hyperbole, but I'm talking about the sword of Damocles hanging over our heads in the form of the thousands of nuclear weapons poised to attack at a moment's notice. And after class, please check out Chaucer's reference to that sword. This is not a political issue, or some fine point of military tactics. It is an existential crisis, and crucially, it's a moral question that we all have to face whether or not we have a commitment to any specific religion, or to any at all. Sorry, I'd better stop and ask what questions you have about what I just said."

After a slight pause, a young man in the front row asked, "Father, with all due respect, do you think that, as a priest, you ought to be giving a better example of Christianity than breaking the law by protesting against a company that our own government is using to build arms that defend our country?"

The monk looked around the room. "Good question, Leo. How many of you have the same concerns?"

All but four or five raised their hands.

"Well, I'm happy to answer you as best I can. Leo, your question is twofold. What should the Christian attitude be towards war, and especially one using nuclear weapons, and how can a priest like me or anyone else for that matter, break a law to achieve a just end? I suppose we could also talk about whether or not these weapons really do 'defend' our country, but let's put that off for the moment. By the way, for extra reading, you can probably get a Kindle copy of *Civil Disobedience* by Thoreau for about a buck. It's a great essay about this whole business—minus the bombs, of course."

He paused and sat on the desk in the front of the room.

"OK, first point. When it comes to war in general, the Catholic Church, for seventeen hundred years, has made participating in war respectable. I have a real problem with that, because there is no way one can wage war in conformity with the teachings of Jesus Christ. Now, let's be careful. I am not issuing a blanket condemnation of young men and women who join the military. After all, most religions, including Catholicism, are comfortable with war-making, so we are very much conditioned to taking that attitude for granted, and, in fact, are quick to condemn anyone who objects. Take a look at the E.E. Cummings poem, 'I sing of Olaf.' I am saying that every act of aggressive violence against a fellow human being is an act of desecration, and is out of conformity with the teaching, life, and spirit of Jesus."

"What about self-defense, Father?" said a voice from the rear of the room.

"Another good question. I'm not talking about legitimate self-defense for individuals. We can get to that some other time, if you want. The big lie about war is that war is just self-defense on a larger scale and is always somehow justified. All religions espouse brotherhood. All people want peace. It is governments and 'Defense Departments' that issue the call to war, not the citizens. We are urged to follow our political leaders, not our consciences. Can you imagine what would happen if Christians and Muslims and Hindus and all other believers stood up and said no to war? For Christians, the teachings of Jesus demand nonviolence when governments call for warriors. In a future class, we really need to talk about nonviolence as a real and practical alternative to war. I don't have to remind any of you to remember MLK or Gandhi as major examples, or Nelson Mandela.

But right now, let's zero in on the issues at hand. To make matters worse, we are no longer talking about the kinds of wars that have been fought over the centuries. Humans have continuously developed bigger, more powerful, and ingeniously efficient ways of killing each other.

Ironically, there are 'rules of war' that put limits on certain types of weaponry because of their cruelty, as though the admitted weapons are somehow humane.

Now, by the end of World War Two, creative minds had uncovered a previously hidden secret of nature—the enormous power compressed into the atoms of matter itself. Two relatively small atomic bombs were used to destroy Hiroshima and Nagasaki and slaughter its citizens. Those bombs were the beginning of an insane arms race in which the destructive power of these so-called 'nuclear weapons' has grown to the point where the world could become uninhabitable because of an all-out nuclear exchange.

There's lots of angst out there about the effects of climate change and I share those worries. Your generation is facing a climate crisis in your future, but I can assure you that a nuclear war, which might take only a few hours, would make the effects of global warming pale in comparison to the consequences of a burning, ravaged Earth."

Father John stood and walked over to one of the large windows looking out over the green quad. He paused for a moment, then turned and looked at his students. "Yes, I am a priest who engaged in an act of civil disobedience. And here I am, two days later in a comfortable classroom. There's another priest I want you to think about. How many of you have heard of the Kings Bay Plowshares Seven?"

Three students raised their hand.

"I'm not surprised. These things don't get a lot of press. Well, here's what happened. Two years ago, a group of seven Catholic peace activists broke into the Kings Bay military facility in Georgia. That's where our government stores lots of the nuclear missiles that are carried on U.S. submarines. They did some minor symbolic damage—spray painted messages on walls, spilled small bottles of their own blood, and hammered on monuments to nuclear weapons. They waited there to be arrested. Some were held in jail for more than a year afterward, and several have since been given prison sentences. One of the sentenced activists is a Jesuit priest, Father Steve Kelly, who has spent a lifetime living and working with impoverished people. Martha Hennessy, by the way, another of the imprisoned activists, is the granddaughter of Dorothy Day, the founder of the Catholic Worker Movement. I'm kind of afraid to ask you this, but how many of you have heard of Catholic Worker communities?"

One hand went up.

"Sheryl, looks like you win. What do you know about the Catholic Worker?"

"Well, Father, there is one of those places down in Nashua near where I live. Lots of people objected to them putting it there because lots of street people hang around there. I think they're just looking for food, though. And my grandfather, who died from the Virus, used to tell us that the Catholic Workers are communists."

"Thanks, Sheryl. Wrong, but I appreciate your input. OK, class, one more assignment. Get a copy of Peter Maurin's *Easy Essays*. Peter was a co-founder of the Catholic Worker Movement, and his brief poems will tell you what you need to know about what's behind the almost two hundred communities serving the poor. Wait a second, I'm neglecting our high-tech facilities, here—if I can just find an extension cord."

He went over to the desk, tapped a few points on a display built into the desktop, and projected an image on the large screen that had lowered in front of the whiteboard. The screen displayed one of Peter Maurin's brief poems:

"Theodore Roosevelt used to say: If you want peace / prepare for war. // So everybody prepared for war / but war preparations / did not bring peace; / they brought war. // Since war preparations brought war, / why not quit preparing for war."

He shut off the display, and the screen rose, noiselessly.

"Sorry, I love playing with that. So, there you are, a deceptively simple suggestion. Humans can live quite comfortably with attitudes and behaviors that now seem to us to be almost incomprehensible. Does your family have slaves? Have you seen twelve-year-olds working six days a week in factories? Does the government prohibit your mother from voting because she is a woman? So, why is the insanity of war any less susceptible to new insights? By the way, I just showed you a piece of that Maurin poem. Later on, it says: 'The best kind of disarmament / is the disarmament of the heart.'

And that was our goal in Waltham—the same goal that the Kings Bay protestors had—waking up a world that is complacent while giant corporations profit from making weapons that threaten all life on this beautiful planet. Believe me, what I did is a pale imitation of Father Steve Kelly's and his companions' brave resistance to the immorality of nuclear weapons. I remember him saying, 'We cannot be fully human while one nuclear weapon exists.' I agree.

I broke a simple trespassing law and was not arrested. Father Kelly and his six fellow resisters were charged with destruction of federal property. When they went to trial, they were not allowed to defend their actions based on their religious objections to nuclear weapons. Oh, by the way, I didn't mention that Plowshares activists have been courageously speaking out and acting out against nukes since 1980.

I went to Waltham to add my voice to the call for the abolition of nuclear weapons, and I did that knowing that the might of our government, both local and national, was against our cause. I certainly had religious motives, but not everyone did, and that was not a requirement. We all spoke out for justice and peace."

The students were silent for a moment. Then a tall young man with close cropped blond hair stood up, his hands held behind his back as though he had been commanded to stand "at ease."

"Father, my name is Roger Goodman. I want to say that I admire your courage for putting your convictions on display so publicly, although I should say that facing enemy fire on a battlefield probably is a bit tougher. But look. I am in ROTC here, and we have been reviewing all the amazing armaments that the U.S. military has at our disposal. We've got nukes that can take out anybody, twenty times over, and we've got them in silos, on submarines like the ones those plowshare people were objecting to, and they can be dropped or fired from planes that can pretty much get to anywhere on this planet.

So, you want us to get rid of those nukes, and open us up to nuclear blackmail? To let Russia or China threaten us because they know we can't respond? I'm sorry, I don't mean to be disrespectful, but we need to let our enemies know that we can wipe them off the face of the Earth if it just looks like they are getting ready to attack us. That is what is keeping us safe. And to tell you the truth, I don't think any country would want to give up such powerful weapons. They probably are trying to get their own so they can be protected just like us."

"Whoa, wait a second." Kathleen stood up. "Can I just say a couple of things about all that? First of all, that stuff about 'enemy fire.' My grandfather spent two years fighting in the Vietnam War. I never met him, because five years after he got back, he committed suicide. My grandmother never really recovered from that. I'm sure my grandfather had plenty of courage. But my gramma told us that he had had to do things over there that 'broke his spirit.' That's the way she put it."

Both students sat down.

"Thank you both for sharing, Roger and Kathleen. I'm so sorry to hear about your poor grandfather. His story is not unusual, I'm afraid. War is a social invention. It's not a fixed feature of human existence. Military training is aimed at conditioning young people to commit acts that are against their natural inclinations—killing fellow human beings. War doesn't kill just people, it kills minds.

And Roger, I do have to let you know that there are lots of nations that want nothing at all to do with nuclear weapons. In fact, earlier this summer, a leading UN official said that the total abolition of nuclear weapons was, and I remember his exact words, 'the UN's highest disarmament priority.' Roger, I'm not singling you out, I'm letting all of you know, because these things don't tend to show up on the daily news or TikTok, about the UN Treaty on the Prohibition of Nuclear Weapons. Fifty nations have ratified it since 2017, and the treaty goes into effect early next year. It prohibits the participating nations from making, keeping, using, or even threatening to use nuclear weapons. And who has signed and ratified the treaty? The Vatican. You can probably guess that the nine countries that have these weapons wanted nothing to do with the treaty. Still, this is a major symbolic step in the right direction.

And strange as it may seem to some of you, back before you were born, the U.S. president, Ronald Reagan, had a summit meeting in 1985 with the leader of the Soviet Union, Mikhail Gorbachev. Both of them wanted to sign an agreement to dismantle all of their nuclear weapons. It didn't happen, but we came that close.

Later on—not now please, I know you are itching to handle your phones—check out the "Back from the Brink" campaign website. This a grassroots movement sweeping across the country that is not calling only for the elimination of nuclear arsenals. It's calling for actions like ending the sole, unchecked authority of the U.S. president to launch a nuclear attack and taking U.S. nukes off hair-trigger alert."

A voice asked, "The Vatican is involved in all this? Never heard about it in church, and our pastor is pretty liberal."

"Good point, wherever you are. Nuclear disarmament is such a pressing moral issue that you might expect to hear about it in homilies, but that's pretty rare. That seems strange, given that the Catholic bishops, at least many of them, and some popes, have been urging nuclear disarmament for years."

The same voice identified herself.

"Father, I'm Maureen, over here. I know there's a lot

of issues flying around here, but they're all pretty much about war, and my prof. in Theology, Dr. Shea, seems pretty confident that if we follow the criteria for fighting a just war, then we can feel confident that God will give his blessings on our decision. Is that right?"

"Lots to unravel, Maureen, but let's talk about those criteria. If you follow those 'rules,' which come out of a fourth century C.E. rejection of the traditional practice of pacifism, you are met with the requirement that the war has to be fought with 'proportional means.' In other words, the evil of the destruction cannot outweigh the evil of not going to war. I hope that makes sense to you. Plus, these 'just war' criteria include a warning that civilians—non-combatants—are never to be attacked. Well, when you have a war featuring the purposeful slaughter of civilians by mass aerial bombardment and the newly invented atomic bomb, you can only conclude that World War Two was an unjust war. I'll add to that the deaths of over one hundred million people, the maiming and dislocation of millions of others, the birth of two new superpowers, and the beginnings of the age of nuclear terror in which we all now live. War has become obsolete and unjustified."

"Father, would you do it again?" a voice asked.

"Well, I'm sure you can understand how that might be a dilemma for me. I know I've been sounding pretty idealistic this morning, but I know I'm no Father Kelly, that's for sure. I guess I'll have to balance the consequences of what I might do against the good that it might accomplish."

John could hear the usual shuffling that signaled the students sensing the class was coming to a close.

"One second please, ladies and gentlemen. Next time we are going to get into William Stafford's poetry. He was a conscientious objector during World War Two, along with Robert Lowell, who we'll be reading as well. Oh, yes, Stafford was also the American Poet Laureate in nineteen-seventy—although then they called it the Consultant in Poetry to the Library of Congress. One more thing, take a look at Wilfred Owen. We'll talk about him, too. He was no CO, but perhaps he would have become one if he had not been killed in action in nineteen-eighteen at the age of twenty-five. OK, see you tomorrow. Thanks for your questions."

As John walked back across the quad after class, he immediately regretted what he had said in response to that last question, "Will you do it again?" What was I thinking? They can easily interpret my answer to mean, "If I won't suffer too much from my actions, then it's OK to go ahead." That's pretty embarrassing. But is that what I meant? I believe in the cause of speaking out against nuclear weapons—not just possessing an enormous arsenal of the things but being willing to use them against fellow humans. The enormity of that crime against humanity surpasses any so-called justification of war. It's not like I can stop Raytheon from doing what it does, although none of those protestors thought that would happen. They wanted to educate people to raise their voices as well. These companies will only rethink what they are doing if their nuclear business somehow becomes unprofitable. Not likely while capitalism reigns. Uh-oh, there go my socialist thoughts. I really need a coffee. Better head over to the lounge and catch some more grief over my Union Leader exposé. Well, it's not like going to prison.

As John walked into the lounge, he was met with silence. There were six professors seated in various locations, seemingly engrossed in reading newspapers and journals. He hesitated, puzzled, and walked slowly over to the coffee maker. He added a paper cup, inserted a Dunkin' Donuts Original Blend K-Cup, tapped and waited. He took his filled cup and added just a bit of powdered milk. After selecting two chocolate, glazed Munchkins, he walked over to a chair and sat down, not sure what to do next. The silent faculty could not hold out any longer. They dropped their props and let out whoops of laughter.

Professor Austin stood up slowly, an unusual posture for him in the lounge. He said, gravely, "Sir, we are honored to have you in our presence. We saw your picture in Sunday's rotogravure and noted that you had partaken in some sort of protest against a prominent company that is affording many locals with employment and developing advanced technologies for America's defense. Apparently, you and your fellow rabble stormed the barricades but were repulsed by the local authorities. It seems that, as an afficionado of poets, you have forgotten the famous advice of Frost, 'Good defenses make good neighbors.' What do you have to say for yourself?"

John joined in the general laughter that followed.

"Oh, brother, I have to admit you had me there. I wasn't sure what kind of reaction to my new-found fame I was going to get from this crowd. Sorry if that seems like a criticism."

"Oh, don't worry, Father," answered Mary Shea, "our little surprise doesn't mean we all agree with what you did. We were just worried about you. Looks like you didn't get hauled off to the clink, at least, and you seem to be your old self, considering the coffee and the donuts. You know, you remind me a bit of Thomas More. He dreamed of a society where everyone could live peacefully and there were no wars or military. Just think of all the failed utopias ever since. Of course, he is a saint, so ..."

"Why thanks, Mary. I must say, though, we were not looking to establish a utopia. That's a pretty big ask, and I don't think humanity will ever get there. Our aim was to raise awareness of the existential threat and sheer immorality of nuclear weapons. We were standing up for disarmament, nuclear at the very least."

"Wow, that sounds utopian to me, with just as many chances for success."

"Well ..."

"Hold everything, now, let's not disparage wild optimism here." Ruth Conerly, a young woman with long, straight black hair and impossibly large glasses spoke up from the couch. She smiled at Mary and continued. "I have been living with Immanuel Kant for the last four years while I was finishing my thesis, and I can tell you that optimism can lead to results, although it may take a few centuries—but what's a few hundred years, right, David?" She turned to look over at David Georgio, who had recently published an article on Stoicism, a paper which his colleagues predicted would earn him tenure. He nodded, politely.

Ruth went on. "Kant held that perpetual peace can be achieved through universal democracy and international cooperation. Sound familiar? Sure, that was back in the eighteenth century, but there is a clear thread from there to the founding of the United Nations in nineteen forty-five. Of course, the military in Kant's day was a bit less lethal compared to today—he was concerned about using assassins and poison. So, Father, your quest might not succeed right now, but you might be planting the seeds of peace for the future. I have to admit, though, I don't like the idea of breaking laws to get new ones that you prefer. In the end, Father, these nuclear weapons are so powerful that they keep the peace because nations are rightly afraid to use them, knowing the consequences."

Before the monk could reply, a deep baritone emanated from the corner of the room next to the coffee maker. A bald, middle-aged man with a neatly trimmed black beard said in a low, but penetrating voice, "Mary, perhaps you might want to reconsider your opinion."

Dennis Perodi, the Chairperson of the Psychology department, was a universally respected professor. Ten years earlier, he had been recruited by Saint Oliver to form the department after many failed attempts by the faculty and trustees to add psychology studies to the curriculum. The administration had a sudden change of heart when the Association of New England Colleges informed them that without that course of studies the college would lose its accreditation. "Only God sees into our hearts," the college president wrote to the faculty when announcing the change, seemingly in defense of his opposition, "and while we acknowledge the strides made by the behavioral sciences, we must always be vigilant in acknowledging our guilt before Him and trust in His care for our welfare, if only we ask for His assistance.

God gives us strength adequate to bear the yoke He places on our shoulders."

"With all due respect, Mary, remember the specific and general circumstances in which we find ourselves in these troubled times," Dr. Perodi replied. "Our nuclear weapons, that is to say, the nuclear weapons at the disposal of our government, are literally in the unsure hands of a president who is clearly a disturbed individual. Yes, I know that I am not supposed to diagnose from afar, but my fifteen years as a clinical psychologist tell me all I need to know about this guy. He is a bucket of insecurities. You can reassure us that those nukes are scaring off our adversaries from attacking us because of fear of recrimination, but in reality, to put it in technical terms, we are damn lucky that between our so-called 'leader' and the dictators in North Korea or Russia, for example, there has not been some repressed anger, resentment, or delusion that has boiled up and triggered an all-out war. Kissinger, that famous war criminal, once observed that the concept of deterrence 'is as much a psychological as a military problem.' Of course, that does not even take into account the very real possibility of an accident or miscommunication that sets off the beginning of the end of our world. And don't forget, Mary, we are approaching an election in November. If the president loses that election, we are at risk of having a man who does not have the mental tools to accept defeat. Would he distract us with what he might think can be confined to a 'local nuclear conflict?' You might recall this is the president who recently suggested exploding a nuclear bomb to break up a hurricane. I am only a recovering Catholic, but I agree with the pope on this one. Even possessing nukes with the clear intent to use them is wrong. For the pope that 'wrong' is a moral judgement. I'll add that it is also a military mistake for our safety to depend on 'mutual assured destruction' when humans are in charge."

John smiled at the psychologist.

"Dennis, I hear you. And I 'll throw in for good measure that the multibillion-dollar effort underway to upgrade those nukes and develop even bigger and more deadly ones makes us less, not more, safe. We become an even bigger threat and adds fuel to a constant arms race. That's one reason I was at Raytheon for what turned out to be my photo opportunity. You know, this is not about me or a small bunch of disgruntled citizens here and there. Sure, street protests can make headlines, fortunately, but in the big picture, the growing movement to abolish nuclear weapons has gone global. Don't forget, by the way, South Africa dismantled its nuclear program towards the end of the apartheid regime, so it has been done once already. In class earlier this morning I told my students about the latest move in the United Nations—the Treaty on the Prohibition of Nuclear Weapons. The UN General Assembly established that treaty in two thousand seventeen, and just recently it got the necessary fifty signatures to ensure that it goes into effect next January. The UN is even planning on hosting an International Day for the Total Elimination of Nuclear Weapons."

Mary Shea, smiling, spoke up.

"Well, I guess that takes care of the problem. Wait, Father, that sounded nasty. I didn't mean it that way. What I am saying is that after seventy-five years of devising, producing and deploying a vast complex of nuclear weapons, at enormous expense, and basing mutual defensive systems on threatening each other with these unbelievably powerful things, everyone should somehow mutually agree to trash them and trust that no one would ever start the race all over again?"

"Good question, Mary, and don't worry about sounding nasty. We all know you better than that. Your concern is a valid one, and that's precisely why it's encouraging that the nuclear disarmament effort is so prominent at the United Nations. Just to give you one other example of the scope of this movement, there's Global Zero. Even the name sounds idealistic, right? Well, it's an international organization with over half a million members worldwide, and at least three hundred world leaders dedicated to spreading the word about their detailed strategy to influence the nine nuclear-armed nations to remove all their nuclear weapons from service by two thousand thirty and ensure that they are permanently dismantled by two thousand forty-five. There are even twenty-nine campus chapters in twenty-nine countries. Maybe I should start one here if I can be more convincing than I was with my class this morning. It's funny, you know, we do have an Environmental Club with lots of students all riled up about the dangers of climate change, and I certainly agree with them. But the possibility of a nuclear war is the biggest threat to the Earth's climate than anything else. You're the theologian, Mary, you know we are supposed to be exercising stewardship over God's creation. That's a whole new homily, so I'd better finish these donuts I wandered over here to find and let you guys do the talking."

John looked over at a bearded figure sitting nearby, who appeared to be poring over what looked like a racing form. "Art, I don't think you were here last week when we got into all this stuff. You're the money guy—what about divestment—you know, withdrawing investments? I don't think we've mentioned that angle."

Professor Art Roman, the Chairperson of the Business and Economics department, looked up at that question and said in a startlingly loud voice, "I think Blaze looks good in the third. Sorry, Father, I was just going over some notes for my statistics class later on. I like giving the students real world experience. I have a proven ability to multitask, so I was listening with one attentive ear to your conversation. That word 'divestment' can be a real nasty one on a college or university campus, let alone in the corporate world. We're talking about the bottom line, folks, and if you're good capitalists, as I know we all are, that can be a line in the sand."

Professor Georgio interjected in his usual quiet, serious tone, "I was just reading a review article in the Times about that warning by Eisenhower back in the Fifties about a developing 'military-industrial complex.' You know, that cozy relationship where big corporations enrich themselves with government contracts for devising and manufacturing war-making products."

Mary Shea quickly interjected, "You mean defense products, don't you, David?"

"No, I generally mean what I say, Mary. Art, elaborate on that divestment story. It's an interesting angle."

"Sure, it's really pretty simple, in a way. There is an important group in the divestment movement called Don't Bank on the Bomb (DBOBT). They put out an annual report on the financing of nuclear weapons manufacturers. I should add that they are assisted by another really big organization, the International Campaign to Abolish Nuclear Weapons (ICAN). Anyway, to give you some perspective here, last year's report showed that three hundred twenty-five financial institutions invested over nine hundred billion in twenty-eight manufacturers associated with nuclear weapons. I have my students use the DBOTB website to look up how specific financial institutions play a role in the nuclear weapons industry. That's really useful if you are, let's say, a college or a university whose conscience has been bothering you about supporting the nuclear arms race. How you manage to get them to that point is another question. But, as I tell my students, anybody with a bank account has a voice on this issue. Of course, the bigger the chorus of voices that financial institutions hear, the more pressure can be applied."

Professor Austin raised his arm. "May I interject a thought here? We are purportedly a Catholic, Christian college, so one ought to keep in mind an incontrovertible fact that should be instrumental in any investment decision we make. I recall that when Pope Francis was speaking in Hiroshima last year, he referred to the fact that enormous profits are made in making destructive weapons while millions live in inhuman conditions of poverty. What about that, Art?"

Art Roman paused for a moment, and looked down at the floor, shaking his head slowly.

"You're getting at a classic dilemma which is one of the challenges we all face in a Catholic educational institution like this. We have got to go beyond facts and figures and approach this question with our students. How should we live? How do we balance our own needs and wants with our obligations to others who may not be as fortunate as us? That question always has to be in the background. In this case, we have a Pentagon with a budget of over half a trillion dollars annually, and that in a nation in which over twenty percent of children live in poverty. Oh, and the current plans for modernizing and upgrading our nuclear arsenal will cost over a trillion dollars. If you pay taxes, over half goes to the military. So, if we are talking about taking a stand against this kind of obscene exploitation of your money, there are things individuals and institutions can do. You ..."

"Please, Art," Mary Shea said, "don't tell us to only pay half our taxes—maybe the president can get away with that, but the Feds will put us in jail for such a high-minded act."

"Mary, I agree that's a lot to ask. Of course, there are people who go even further—they limit their income to the point where they don't need to pay federal income taxes at all. One of our graduates, for example, and his family do just that in their peace community down in Massachusetts. But to get back to what individuals and institutions can do, we do an exercise in class where we use information provided by the Future of Life Institute. Their website has a divestment/investment tool that shows, for example, which mutual funds are nuclear-free. We tend to forget about the details of where our money is—you know, pension funds, mutual funds and so on. Back in two thousand sixteen, the city council in Cambridge, MA voted to divest their one-billion-dollar pension fund from companies producing nuclear weapons. That's some serious cash, but it pales in comparison to a couple of the largest pension funds in the world, ABP and the Norwegian Government Pension Fund. They recently withdrew from financing nuclear weapons producers to the tune of billions. When we talk about investment and divestment, remember, we are talking about a global movement. If you want to think about local actors, when you head down to the Mall in Nashua, you drive by a modest sign for a company hidden back off the road—BAE Systems. They are involved in the nuclear weapons programs in France and the UK as well as the U.S. They make key components for the Trident missiles. Those are the ones carried on submarines. They also produce Minuteman intercontinental ballistic missile systems, and components for France's nuclear-armed air-to-surface missiles."

Professor Austin spoke up.

"Thanks, Art. That last point is something I didn't know about. Now, while I appreciate getting down in the weeds with you, let's ask Father John, our mild mannered, photogenic rabble rouser. Has the college examined its investments with any regard to their moral implications, and in particular, the military-industrial complex?"

As soon as he had turned the conversation to divestment, John realized this question was probably coming, and he was totally unprepared for it. His recommitment to peace activism had made him painfully aware that this national and international effort had not made its way to Saint Oliver. Before he could decide where to begin, Art Roman answered for him.

"I can speak to that, Professor. Occasionally, and infrequently, the college asks my opinion on some aspects of the college's finances. I do appreciate their recognition of my expertise, but they have not been particularly impressed with my input on socially responsible investing. Over the last couple of years, I have managed to get the treasurer, Father Edmund, to at least consider divestment from fossil fuels, but when I mention anything that has to do with the military, he balks. I tried to press the point that the employees of this Catholic college might not want their retirement security to be tied up with maintaining or enlarging the weapons industry. However, I haven't pressed the issue lately because of his heart condition. I think he's somewhere north of eighty, and I don't want to be the one to deprive Saint O's of the only monk who seems to know much about business. Not that that is their vocation."

Before John could speak, Dennis Perodi said, "It's not even my avocation. Maybe that's why I'm still driving my old Chevy. But there is another aspect of this that I happen to know something about only because I have a bad habit of reading the Washington Post. A while back there was an article about the fifty or so college and university campuses that contribute to the nuclear weapons complex by supplying scientific, technical and human capital that offer vital assistance to the development and production of weapons of mass destruction. Places like the University of California, Johns Hopkins, and Texas A&M have signed agreements in the many millions of dollars to manage or partner with nuclear weapons development and production. It struck me because I wonder about the psychological conflicts that people must be facing at all levels of this damnable business."

"Not so fast, Dennis," Mary Shea almost shouted, "That is a judgement that you should not be making. These people and schools and companies are supplying all of us with the means of defending ourselves. I just hope that our president is re-elected, because the Democrats are so far left that they will be trying to disarm this country to the point that we will be in mortal danger. And you know, I am perfectly willing to let the government decide where it wants to spend my tax dollars, especially when they want to use some of them to defend us. So, Father it looks like you and I agree to disagree, like good Episcopalians."

"Mary, I agree. Or is that redundant? I think we can all agree on at least two points. One—we will not resolve these issues this morning, and two—most of you probably have class in about five minutes. I appreciate the fact that I have not been voted out of the club, at least not yet. Enjoy your day, everybody."

Professor Austin spoke up. "Just a moment, please, as you depart this cozy caffeine-infused gathering. Please take your K-Cups with you. With all this talk of stewardship this morning, you might be interested in knowing that our local transfer station, formerly the dump, does not accept those lovely little devices for recycling. The company suggests that you mail them back so they can incinerate them. You might want to think about employing the classic thermos in the future. With all due respect, of course."

Ten minutes after leaving the lounge, Father John sat down in one of the hard wooden choir stalls in the college church. He was alone in the cavernous, domed interior. Sunlight filtered through the tall, slender stained-glass windows along the wall facing his seat.

I should be praying more and talking less, he thought. Maybe I should have been a Trappist. The thought brought a smile to his face immediately. No, they get up way too early and never get enough to eat. And the silence! I love to gab too much. God, have mercy on me. I have been living a comfortable life. This monastery is my home. I am immersed in a steady rhythm of work and prayer. That is how I have been working out my salvation, as my old confessor used to tell me. Maybe if we were living out in the middle of a desert, I wouldn't be tempted to get involved in all this business and aggravate my abbot. After all, he is my second father. I wonder what own father would say about my gallivanting around with all sorts of people in the streets when I should be minding my own business? I wish he were here right now; may he rest in peace. Brian Fain, country lawyer who came over from Galway as a young man and found my mother and new opportunities. Well, God love him, we never talked much about things. He was too Irish for that. All right then, I need time to think and pray about this.

That evening, Father John sat in the recreation room, staring at the two computers. Neither was occupied. He had not lost his resolve to stop, think and pray, but was it wrong to check his email, just in case his nun co-conspirators wanted to get in touch? Probably, he thought to himself, smiling, but after all, it wouldn't be polite not to keep tabs on them.

He sat down and opened his email account. There were two messages from ehealy. The first offered him a temptation, politely. The second had been sent a few hours after the first, simply asking if he had seen the earlier email.

The temptation read:

> Hi Father, Eileen here. Remember me and my sidekick, Mary? We are back in Nashua, safe and sound. Which is more than we can say for lots of poor, suffering people, like in Yemen. Anyway, we are sorry that you ended up in the Leader on Sunday. That probably didn't go down well with your boss. But let's face it, our message got across louder and more clearly than just a written account buried somewhere in the paper. The message is the point, right?
>
> Well, it looks like Raytheon hasn't closed its doors yet, but that may take a bit longer and a lot more uproar. Speaking of which, do you remember, when we asked you to join us in Waltham, I mentioned that there would be a protest at BAE Systems in Nashua? Well, it is coming up one week from Saturday. We have been itching to yell something publicly about our Nashua neighbor for a long time. Granite State Peace Action has been recruiting volunteers since April to demonstrate at the Nashua site to raise awareness about BAE's involvement in nuclear weapons development. Maybe you didn't know because of that low profile you have been keeping (until last weekend), but BAE has over six thousand employees in New Hampshire.
>
> So, here's the deal. Despite the fact that BAE does a lot of work that has plenty of non-military

applications, they certainly are deeply involved in nuclear weapons systems. I was just looking over one of their websites and the word 'stewardship' caught my eye. They say they want to 'maintain and enhance the integrity of our products ... in particular their safety, quality ... and environmental footprint.' Wow! Just one of their ICBMs or Trident missiles exploding would create quite a devastating 'footprint' all right. So, if you think you are up for it, can you get down to our place on that Saturday at ten? Father, if you want to hold off on this, that's OK. Please let me know your decision so we can make more or less peanut butter sandwiches for our lunch—just in case the cops don't arrive until afternoon.

We know this is a crucial decision for you. If you think it is not for you, we will respect your decision. Please pray for us and the others that our message will be heard.

Peace, Eileen

P.S. Roman collars optional but suggested.

Until all nuclear weapons are dismantled and destroyed in keeping with multilateral, verifiable agreements, the danger of their use will exist. This "disarmament" is distinguished from "arms control." The former requires destruction of the weapons leading to their elimination. The latter does not necessarily lead to a reduction in the numbers of weapons involved. For example, the 1970 Non-Proliferation Treaty (NPT) tries to prevent other states from obtaining nuclear weapons but does not block existing nuclear states from increasing their nuclear stockpiles.

Those states—the United States, Russia, the United Kingdom, France and China—possess nuclear weapons. They signed the NPT. Four others did not sign, but have nuclear weapons—India, Pakistan, North Korea, and Israel. Those nine states assume that these weapons of mass destruction are necessary for their defense and should be ready and available for immediate use.

During the Cold War, the United States and the Soviet Union amassed a staggering stockpile of nuclear weapons. By 1986 the combined total was 64,000 warheads. These numbers have since been reduced through a number of agreements. However, neither the U.S. nor Russia have met the commitment stated in the NPT to "achieve at the earliest possible date the cessation of the nuclear arms race and to undertake effective measures in the direction of nuclear disarmament."

In spite of 50 years of failure of these states to achieve the stated goal of nuclear elimination, in October 2020, the United Nations General Assembly held a special meeting on the "International Day for the Total Elimination of Nuclear Weapons." The UN Secretary-General Antonio Guterres, in his keynote address, said, "Nuclear disarmament has been a priority of the United Nations since the very beginning of the Organization's existence." In the face of this lofty ideal, almost every proposal for multilateral disarmament proposed at the UN has been met with determined opposition from several or more of the nuclear weapons states.

Idealism has survived, at least in some quarters. In an address given by the then President Obama in Prague, on April 5, 2009, he said, "So today, I state clearly and with conviction, America's commitment to seek the peace and security of a world without nuclear weapons. I'm not naïve. This goal will not be reached quickly—perhaps not in my lifetime. It will take patience and persistence. But now, we, too, must ignore the voices who tell us that the world cannot change. We have to insist, 'Yes, we can.'" The White House report that quotes these lofty aims later states, "Reducing the number and role of nuclear weapons in U.S. security policy, while maintaining a nuclear arsenal that is safe, secure, and effective for as long as nuclear weapons exist, is a key driver toward a world without nuclear weapons ... DOD and DOE are working diligently to modernize our nuclear arsenal and develop a responsive nuclear infrastructure."

Chris Ford, the Assistant Secretary of State for International Security and Non-Proliferation, serving in the administration following that of President Obama, went far beyond this ambivalence. He regarded advocates of nuclear disarmament as having "bad habits" and making "bad choices." Ford preferred "arms control for adults" emphasizing security, believing that nuclear weapons offer security rather than risks.

While he excoriated nuclear disarmament advocates, numerous experts, including prominent civil servants and military officials disagree. Many have signed on to the Global Zero initiative. Begun in 2008, this is an international movement for the elimination of all nuclear weapons. This effort has spread rapidly, and by 2020 included 300 world leaders and a half-million citizens. Global Zero combines policy development, direct dialogue with governments, and public outreach "to make the elimination of nuclear weapons an urgent global imperative." Their stated aim is to foster a "treaty among the world's nine nuclear-armed nations that will remove all nuclear weapons from service by 2030 and ensure they are permanently dismantled by 2045."

Only a few months after the U.S. destroyed Hiroshima and Nagasaki with two atomic bombs, prominent scientists including Albert Einstein, Robert Oppenheimer and Leo Szilard, who had helped create those terrifying weapons, published a book of essays: *One World or None: A Report to the Public on the Full Meaning of the Atomic Bomb.* They warned the public about the serious implications of the nuclear age they had unleashed. Over 100,000 copies were sold. Since then, there have been a series of attempts to control the spread of nuclear weapons, accompanied by a constant evolution in their destructive power. Below is a brief chronology of those agreements, some of which are no longer in force.

DECEMBER 1, 1959
THE ANTARCTIC TREATY

The vast Antarctic continent embraces the South Pole. All but two percent of the area is covered with snow and ice. By the early twentieth century, improved technology allowed increasing exploration and establishment of permanent research stations. The 12 nations active in Antarctica held meetings during the International Geophysical Year in 1957-58 that led to agreement that peaceful scientific cooperation should continue indefinitely.

This led to the Antarctic Treaty, signed on December 1, 1959 by Argentina, Australia, Belgium, Chile, France, Japan, New Zealand, Norway, South Africa, the United Kingdom, the United States and the USSR. By 2020, 48 nations had agreed to the treaty. Major sections of the agreement stipulate that the continent should be used exclusively for peaceful purposes. Military activities, such as the establishment of military bases or weapons testing, are specifically prohibited. This ban includes nuclear testing and the disposal of radioactive waste.

This treaty is recognized as one of the most successful international agreements.

AUGUST 5, 1963
LIMITED TEST BAN TREATY

Concern had grown for years over the effects of radioactive fallout from testing atomic bombs and, later, thermonuclear devices. The fears centered around what this contamination of the environment might do to nature and to the genetics of humans. Negotiations began in 1955 among the United States, the United Kingdom, Canada, France, and the Soviet Union. Talks dragged on for years, mainly due to an impasse over the issue of verification. In late 1961, the Soviet Union conducted 31 nuclear tests, including the largest nuclear bomb in history—an astonishing 50 megatons. The 1962 Cuban missile crisis occurred during the period of negotiations, triggering fears that the world was on the brink of nuclear war. Negotiations resumed in 1963, and on August 5, 1963, the Limited Nuclear Test Ban Treaty was signed in Moscow. France and China were invited to join the agreement, but they declined.

The treaty was ratified by the United States Senate on September 24, 1963. It banned nuclear weapons tests "in the atmosphere, in outer space, and underwater." It did not prohibit tests underground, unless they caused "radioactive debris" to spread beyond the "territorial limits of the State." This modification eliminated the need for on-site inspections, a major sticking point for the Kremlin. President John F. Kennedy, who had urged the Senate to support the treaty, signed the ratified treaty less than three months before his assassination.

THE COMPREHENSIVE NUCLEAR TEST BAN TREATY (CNTBT)

The UN Conference on Disarmament began formal negotiations on a multilateral agreement to prohibit the explosive testing of nuclear weapons. These talks lasted until 1996, when a treaty was agreed upon. It opened for signatures on September 24, 1996, but it still awaits ratification by 44 of the 183 signatories. The U.S. has not ratified the treaty. As soon as President George H.W. Bush had signed the treaty, the Senate objected. Later, in 2009, President Obama indicated his interest in ratification, but ultimately this did not occur. Three nations have neither signed nor ratified the treaty—India, Pakistan, and North Korea. However, the U.S. has exercised a unilateral moratorium on nuclear weapons testing since 1992, using computer simulations instead.

In summary, the treaty bans states from exploding nuclear material regardless of whether the purposes are weapons-related or peaceful. It establishes a global system of monitors, including 170 seismic stations. It establishes a Comprehensive Nuclear Test Ban Treaty Organization that promotes the ratification of the treaty and prepares the verification regime.

In August 2020, Msgr. Frederik Hansen, chargé d'affaires at the Permanent Observer Mission of the Holy See to the United Nations, urged the completion of the ratification of the CTBT.

He told the United Nations, "Further nuclear testing, which would add to current nuclear weapon capabilities, can only diminish global security, and thus the peace, security and stability of all members of this body and that of the peoples whom they represent."

During a 2020 meeting with senior officials representing top national security agencies, the president's administration indicated that it was considering a single nuclear test explosion to demonstrate to Russia and China the U.S. capabilities—a show of might to put the U.S. in a better negotiating position to regulate those countries' nuclear arsenals.

JANUARY 27, 1967
OUTER SPACE TREATY

In 1957, the United States, in the face of advancements in rocketry, proposed that space should be used exclusively for "peaceful and scientific purposes." The Soviet Union rejected this principle because it was testing its first intercontinental ballistic missile, and was preparing to launch Sputnik, the world's first satellite.

Between 1959 and 1962, Western nations urged that outer space should be off limits for military purposes, including orbiting and stationing weapons of mass destruction. President Eisenhower suggested that the principles of the Antarctic Treaty be applied to outer space and celestial bodies. The Soviet Union continued to refuse cooperation in these efforts, unless the U.S. remove foreign bases at which short-range and medium-range missiles were located. They relaxed that objection after the signing of the Limited Test Ban Treaty.

The Outer Space Treaty was signed on January 27, 1967. It forbids placing nuclear or any other weapons of mass destruction on the Moon or any other celestial body. It also prohibits such devices from being "stationed" in outer space. There are a number of other provisions, including that space should be accessible to all countries to freely investigate.

TREATY ON THE NON-PROLIFERATION OF NUCLEAR WEAPONS (NPT)

Early postwar attempts to fashion agreements on nuclear disarmament failed. By 1964, the Soviet Union, the United Kingdom, France, and the Peoples Republic of China had joined the United States in becoming nuclear weapon states. Nuclear proliferation had allowed advances in the technology of nuclear reactors for the generation of electric power. By 1966 such reactors were operating in five countries. These reactors, in addition to producing electricity, also make plutonium which can be separated and used in the manufacture of nuclear weapons.

A series of initiatives began in the 1950s to check nuclear proliferation. In 1961, the UN General assembly unanimously approved a resolution by Ireland to develop an international agreement to refrain from transfer or acquisition of nuclear weapons. Years of arduous and complex negotiations followed among the United States and its allies and adversaries.

The NPT was finally agreed to in 1968 by the United States, the United Kingdom, the Soviet Union, and 59 other countries. By 2020, 191 states had joined the treaty, including France and China. In the treaty, the five nuclear weapon states (NWS) agree not to help non-nuclear weapon states (NNWS) develop or acquire nuclear weapons, and the NNWS commit never to pursue such weapons. There are also safeguards against the transfer of materials between the NWS and the NNWS that could be used to make nuclear weapons. The treaty also promotes the peaceful uses of nuclear energy.

Another key provision in the treaty, Article VI, commits participants to "pursue negotiations in good faith on effective measures relating to cessation of the nuclear arms race at an early date and to nuclear disarmament, and on a treaty on general and complete disarmament under strict and effective international control."

The NPT is considered the cornerstone of international efforts over the last half-century to reduce and eliminate nuclear weapons. Only Israel, India and Pakistan have never signed the treaty. North Korea withdrew from the treaty in 2003. Every five years since the signing, there has been a conference to review the NPT operation and provisions. At the 1995 conference, the NPT was extended for an indefinite duration and without conditions. The 2020 conference could not be held because of the global pandemic.

The NPT enabled the enforcement of rules that guard against new nuclear-armed states. The 2015 nuclear deal with Iran was a vital agreement that curtailed that nation's ability to produce material useful for nuclear weapon production. Iran agreed to a very strict verification plan. In 2018, the U.S. president withdrew from the agreement with Iran and reimposed sanctions. Since that time, Iran has increased its production of plutonium.

Despite the fact that in March 2017, Christopher Ford, the National Security Council's Senior Director for Weapons of Mass Destruction and Counterproliferation, said that the administration would examine whether global nuclear disarmament was a "realistic goal." The ideal of a world free of nuclear weapons, more than 50 years after the signing of the NPT, has yet to be fulfilled.

ABM TREATY, STRATEGIC ARMS LIMITATION TREATY
(INTERIM AGREEMENT)

Strategic arms, in this case, are nuclear weapons and the systems designed to deliver them from one continent to another. During the late 1960s, the Soviet Union began a large-scale effort to build up their intercontinental ballistic missile (ICBM) system in order to match that of the United States. In 1966, they began to deploy an antiballistic missile (ABM) system around Moscow. The U.S. began to install its own ABM system. On July 1, 1968, at the signing of the NPT, President Johnson announced that the U.S. and the Soviet Union had agreed to begin talks on limiting and reducing nuclear weapons delivery systems and ballistic missile defenses.

In November 1969, in the early days of the Nixon administration, the Strategic Arms Limitation Talks began in Helsinki. They continued for two and a half years. Soviet ICBM numbers grew from 1,000 to around 1,618. Also, Soviet submarine-based launchers had quadrupled. The U.S. had 1,054 ICBMs and 656 submarine launchers and was undertaking a rapid deployment of missiles with "Multiple Independently-targeted Re-entry Vehicles" (MIRV). These are carried on a missile and can be directed at separate targets.

After prolonged negotiations, the first Strategic Arms Limitation Talks (SALT) reached an agreement on May 26, 1972, when President Nixon and General Secretary Brezhnev signed both the Interim Agreement and the Antiballistic Missile (ABM)Treaty. The former agreement was seen as complementing the ABM Treaty by stalling an arms race and allowing time for further negotiations by halting an increase in the number of ICBM launchers.

The agreement also limited missile launchers on submarines (SLBMs). The U.S. was allowed 710 launchers on 44 submarines, and the Soviet Union could increase their SLBMs to 950. It did not address MIRVs.

The ABM Treaty limited missile defenses to 200 interceptors and allowed both parties to build two missile defense sites, one to protect the national capital, and the other to protect one ICBM field. This stipulation prevented each side from building a nationwide ABM defense. They also agreed to prohibit sea-based, air-based, or space-based ABM systems.

The ABM Treaty was to be of "unlimited duration." Each party had the right to withdraw if it thought its interests were jeopardized by "extraordinary events." On December 13, 2001, President George W. Bush announced that the U.S. was withdrawing from the ABM Treaty. A few days later, construction began in Alaska for the first U.S. missile defense system.

The Interim Agreement was for a five-year span. It was regarded as a temporary agreement, inhibiting some competition in offensive weapons and allowing time for further negotiations. These began in November 1972, as SALT II.

JUNE 17, 1979
STRATEGIC ARMS LIMITATION TREATY II

The first Strategic Arms Limitation Treaty did not forbid either side from focusing on limiting, and then, reducing, the numbers of MIRVs allowed. These talks spanned the Nixon, Ford, and Carter administrations.

At a 1974 summit in Vladivostok, President Ford and General Secretary Brezhnev agreed to a basic outline for an agreement. There would be a limit of 2,400 for nuclear delivery vehicles

(ICBMs, SLBMs, and heavy bombers) and a 1,320 limit on MIRV systems. They could not agree on the number of bombers and the total number of warheads each side could have in their nuclear arsenal.

President Carter and Brezhnev signed the SALT II Treaty on June 17, 1979. In the U.S., a broad coalition of Republicans and conservative Democrats opposed the agreement, centering on their concerns over verification and a general distrust of the Soviet Union. On December 25,1980, the Soviets invaded Afghanistan. A few days later, Carter asked the Senate not to consider SALT II for its consent, and it was never ratified. Ronald Reagan, Carter's successor, had strongly opposed the Treaty, but agreed to abide by its terms while he pursued negotiations that eventually would lead to a Strategic Arms Reduction Treaty in 1991.

On May 26, 1986, President Reagan accused the Soviet Union of not living up to their stated commitments to follow the SALT II restrictions. He declared, "Given this situation ... in the future, the United States must base decisions regarding its strategic force structure on the nature and magnitude of the threat posed by Soviet strategic forces and not on standards contained in the SALT structure ..." He did add that the United States would "continue to exercise the utmost restraint."

DECEMBER 8, 1987
INTERMEDIATE-RANGE NUCLEAR FORCES (INF) TREATY

In the mid-1970s, the Soviet Union began to deploy intermediate-range nuclear missiles. These are missiles that have a range of 500 to 5,500 kilometers (310 to 3,417 miles). NATO asked for negotiations to prevent this, while at the same time it installed nuclear-armed U.S. intermediate-range missiles in

Europe. The negotiations stalled until Mikhail Gorbachev became the Soviet General Secretary in 1985. President Reagan and Gorbachev signed the INF Treaty on December 8, 1987. This agreement marked the first time the two nations had agreed to reduce their nuclear arsenals and eliminate a category of weapons. It set up a thorough on-site inspection system. The U.S. and the Soviets destroyed a total of 2,692 missiles by mid-1991.

In 2011, during the President Obama administration, the U.S. accused Russia of deploying missiles that could violate the INF Treaty. Over the following few years, similar concerns by the U.S. were voiced, followed by Russian denials. Russia then began to raise the possibility of withdrawing from the treaty because it prevented them from having weapons that its neighbor, China, was developing and fielding. They also objected to the U.S. installing anti-ballistic missile systems in Europe. In early 2017, the U.S. declared that Russia had deployed a cruise missile that "violates the spirit and intent" of the INF Treaty. (A cruise missile is one that remains in the atmosphere during its flight.)

Continued talks yielded no agreement, and the U.S. formally withdrew from the treaty on August 2, 2019. Secretary of State Mike Pompeo claimed that "Russia is solely responsible for the treaty's demise." Russia also suspended participation in the treaty. Russia blamed the U.S. for the withdrawal "instead of engaging in a meaningful discussion." The U.S. Defense Department requested nearly $100 million in fiscal year 2020 for three new missile systems that would exceed the range limits of the treaty. In his 2019 State of the Union, the U.S. president said, "Perhaps we can negotiate a different agreement, adding China and others, or perhaps we can't ... in which case, we will outspend and out-innovate all others by far."

STRATEGIC ARMS REDUCTION TREATY

By the mid-1980s, the Soviet Union could not afford continued defense spending, and resumed arms negotiations. Discussions between President Reagan and Soviet leader Mikhail Gorbachev later led to a comprehensive strategic arms reduction treaty (START) signed by President George H.W. Bush and Gorbachev on July 31, 1991. The agreement limited the number of intercontinental ballistic missiles (ICBMs) and nuclear warheads either party could possess. It resulted in the removal of about 80 percent of all strategic nuclear weapons then in existence. The treaty was renamed START 1 after negotiations began on the second START Treaty. START 1 was the first to cause deep reductions in strategic nuclear weapons. It set an aggregate limit of 1,600 delivery vehicles and 6,000 warheads for each party—a reduction from 10-12,000 warheads in 1991. It also banned new ballistic missiles with more than 10 warheads.

Five months after the signing of START 1, the Soviet Union came apart, leaving four independent states in possession of nuclear weapons—Russia, Belarus, Ukraine, and Kazakhstan. On May 23, 1992, the U.S. and those four states signed the Lisbon Protocol, which made all of them party to START 1.

START 1 remained in force until December 5, 2009. During the 1990s, there were attempts to fashion a new treaty that would provide for deeper reductions. The START II Treaty was signed by President George H.W. Bush and Russian President Boris Yeltsin on January 3, 1993. It never entered into force, as Russia formally withdrew from the treaty on June 14, 2002 in response to the U.S. withdrawal from the ABM Treaty. The START 1 Treaty turned out to be expensive, very complicated, and cumbersome, leading to the U.S. and Russia replacing it with a new treaty in 2010.

THE OPEN SKIES TREATY (OST)

In 1955, President Eisenhower proposed mutual overflights among European nations, as well as the U.S., for purposes of observation in order to gather intelligence and build confidence that war preparations were not underway. The Soviets rejected the idea, regarding such flights as espionage. President George H.W. Bush revived the idea in 1989, and he and Secretary of State James Baker negotiated the OST in 1992, after the collapse of the Soviet Union. It was aimed at reducing the chances of an accidental war by exposing troop movements and the positioning of missiles and armaments.

According to the agreement, the 34 member states, including Russia, allow countries to fly unarmed aircraft with cameras and other sensors over the territory of the other members. Each country has two quotas, the number of flights it may take, and the number it may allow. U.S. allies, many of whom do not have satellite imagery available to them, have access to all of the Open Skies data. By 2019, the 34 parties to the treaty had operated more than 1,500 overflights. The U.S. has made 196 flights over Russia and Belarus, while Russia has conducted 71 flights over the U.S. In 2014, U.S. overflights were particularly useful in monitoring activities along the Ukraine-Russian border.

There were some violations by Russia of the treaty provisions, some of which were resolved. It was widely reported that the U.S. president was angered by a Russian flight directly over his New Jersey golf course in 2017. In May 2020, the President announced that the U.S. would officially withdraw from the

OST on November 22 of that year. Nevertheless, European nations still regard the flights as an important source of information and have pledged to continue to implement the treaty, "which has a clear added value for our conventional arms control architecture and cooperative security."

In November 2020, Russian Foreign Minister Sergei Lavrov said that if the treaty remained in effect, Russia would insist that its flights could continue to take pictures of U.S. military bases in the participant's territories.

THE STRATEGIC OFFENSIVE REDUCTIONS TREATY (SORT)

In the same year that the U.S. withdrew from the ABM Treaty and the Russians withdrew from SALT II, those two nations signed the Strategic Offensive Weapons Treaty (SORT), commonly known as the Moscow Treaty.

Both President George W. Bush and Russian President Vladimir Putin expressed their desire to reduce the numbers of deployed nuclear warheads to far lower numbers than their forces held at that time – around 6,000 apiece – close to the 1991 START I limit. A series of summit meetings led to the signings of several documents on May 24, 2002, ranging from arms control to economic, energy and information technology agreements. Among these was a two-page treaty committing both sides to reducing their deployed strategic nuclear forces to 1,700-2,200 warheads apiece. It was to expire on December 31, 2012, after which the parties would be free to increase or decrease their forces. There was to be no limit on how many strategic warheads the U.S. or Russia could keep in storage or reserve. By 2020, both sides had about 4,000 warheads poised for use. There were no provisions for measuring compliance.

THE NEW START TREATY

By time the Soviet Union fell apart in 1991, the three treaties noted above, the ABM Treaty, the INF Treaty, and START 1, had at least helped slow down the arms race. President George W. Bush killed the ABM Treaty, and the president following Barack Obama withdrew from the INF Treaty. On April 8, 2010, the United States, under President Obama, and Russia, signed the successor to START 1, "Measures for the Further Reduction and Limitation of Strategic Offensive Arms," more commonly known as New START. The treaty was due to expire in February 2021, unless both sides agreed to extend it for up to five years. With this treaty, the Obama administration intended to enhance U.S. national security, and to advance the possibility of further reductions.

The basic agreement under the treaty required the U.S. and Russia to meet certain limits on strategic arms by February 5, 2011. In summary, the limits were as follows:

- 700 deployed intercontinental ballistic missiles (ICBMs), deployed submarine-launched ballistic missiles (SLBMs), and deployed heavy bombers equipped for nuclear armaments

- 1,550 nuclear warheads on deployed ICBMs, deployed SLBMs, and deployed heavy bombers equipped for nuclear armaments

- 800 deployed and non-deployed ICBM launchers, SLBM launchers, and heavy bombers equipped for nuclear armaments

The treaty has a thorough verification system, including on-site inspections and an extensive database that identifies the numbers, types, and locations of items limited by the treaty.

New START leaves both sides with incredible firepower. For example, under the treaty, U.S. submarines can carry up to 20 Trident missiles, each of which can carry up to eight nuclear warheads. Each warhead is capable of an explosion with a destructive power 32 times greater than that of the Hiroshima bomb. However, the treaty represented the last remaining agreement on constraint on the U.S. and Russian nuclear arsenals, leading arms control advocates to underline the critical importance of a February 2021 renewal.

However, in 2018 and 2019, the president began voicing concerns over whether the treaty served U.S. national security interests. He and other administration officials suggested that the U.S. replace New START with a "next generation" pact that would include China. In March 2020, a Chinese spokesperson said, "China has repeatedly reiterated that it has no intention of participating in the so-called trilateral arms control negotiations."

Without New START, there would no longer be any nuclear arms control. The treaty provided important verification and transparency measures vital to any hopes for some stability. In September 2020, the administration's new arms control envoy, Marshall Billingslea said, "We will be extremely happy to continue ... without the [New] START restrictions," adding that the U.S. would build up its nuclear arsenal. Earlier that year, he had warned that if Russia and China did not agree to the president's terms for a new agreement, "We know how to spend the adversary into oblivion."

In February 2021, the new Joseph Biden administration renewed the New START Treaty.

THE JOINT COMPREHENSIVE PLAN OF ACTION

In 2003, the International Atomic Energy Agency reported on hidden nuclear facilities in Iran. In October of that year, France, Germany, and the United Kingdom concluded an agreement with Iran which temporarily suspended aspects of its nuclear program. In January 2006, Iran announced that it would resume research and development of uranium enriching centrifuges. This led to Iran engaging in multiple rounds of talks with China, France, Germany, Russia, the United Kingdom, and the United States (collectively known as the P5+1). The UN Security Council adopted several resolutions requiring Iran to not only suspend its nuclear related activities, but also refrain from any research on ballistic missiles capable of delivering nuclear weapons. The resolution also imposed sanctions, including such measures as an arms embargo, inspection of their cargo vessels, and wide-ranging financial restrictions.

On July 14, 2015, the P5+1 and Iran agreed upon a Joint Comprehensive Plan of Action (JPCOA). Iran was to use its nuclear program solely for peaceful purposes in exchange for the lifting of sanctions. The participants, including the Obama administration, agreed that the JCPOA, commonly referred to as the Iran nuclear deal, was an effective means to prevent Iran from developing nuclear weapons. It included provisions for sanctions to be reimposed if Iran violated its commitments.

The administration following the Obama years argued that the JPCOA did not coincide with America's interests, claiming that the sanctions were not strict enough to prohibit Iran from engaging in "malign activities." On May 8, 2018, the president announced that the U.S. would no longer be a participant in the agreement and would reimpose sanctions on Iran. Soon after, the European Commission declared U.S. sanctions to be illegal in Europe and banned its citizens and companies from complying with them. The commission also instructed the European Investment Bank to help European companies invest in Iran. UN Secretary-General Guterres dismissed the U.S. reimposition of sanctions, because the withdrawal from the JCPOA did not entitle it to make such a move.

In response to the U.S. president's decision, Iran began a series of escalations moving Iran further away from compliance with the nuclear deal. For example, in May 2019, Iran announced it would no longer be bound by limits on enriching its nuclear stockpiles. Earlier, they had ignored the bans on uranium enrichment and research and development of advanced centrifuges, both steps that could lead to nuclear weapon production.

On Friday, January 3, 2020, the U.S. killed Qassem Soleimani, the head of the Iranian Revolutionary Guard Corps-Quds Force, in a drone airstrike near Baghdad International Airport. Just days afterward, Iran announced it would no longer comply with the JPCOA.

JULY 7, 2017
TREATY ON THE
PROHIBITION OF NUCLEAR WEAPONS (TPNW)

Also called the Nuclear Weapons Ban Treaty, this is the first binding international agreement to prohibit all aspects of nuclear weapons, with the goal being their ultimate elimination worldwide. It was adopted at the UN on July 7, 2017. With the signing of Honduras on October 24, 2020, the treaty passed the 50-state threshold for entry into force.

For over a decade, a broad coalition of nuclear control advocates had been voicing their serious concerns about the terrible humanitarian consequences of nuclear war. A large coalition, including Japan's Hibakusha, the survivors of the 1945 atomic bombings, formed the International Campaign to Abolish Nuclear Weapons (ICAN). They worked with scientists, UN diplomats, and humanitarian organizations to work toward their goal of nuclear disarmament.

A group of non-nuclear states, the Humanitarian Initiative, tried to get the 2015 Review Conference on the Non-proliferation of Nuclear Weapons (NPT) to adopt a consensus final document. One hundred and sixty states endorsed their efforts, but that was insufficient. However, their efforts led to a 2013 UN General Assembly resolution to develop a working group to advance multilateral nuclear disarmament negotiations. A series of three international conferences took place in 2013 and 2014, coordinated by ICAN. Finally, the TPNW was approved by the UN General Assembly on July 7, 2017 and went into force on January 22, 2021. Negotiations leading to this approval were boycotted by all nuclear weapon possessing states, most NATO countries, and many military allies of nuclear states. The U.S. administration declared the treaty as "dangerous" and urged the signers to withdraw their support.

Ironically, Japan has not signed the treaty. That country is among those who feel that they receive some form of security from states who have nuclear weapons. However, Mayor Kazumi, the Mayor of Hiroshima, encouraged his government to rethink that position, saying, "Hiroshima considers it our duty to build in civil society a consensus that the people must unite to achieve nuclear weapons abolition and lasting world peace."

The TPNW has the status of international law. The proponents of this treaty point out that the treaty will present new norms that will help to stigmatize this class of weapons, the same way that attention given to biological and chemical weapons and landmines caused them to be banned. Military-industrial companies will face increasing pressure to move away from producing nuclear weapons if financial institutions feel pressure to stop investing in them.

ICAN received the Nobel Peace Prize in 2017 for its efforts to draw attention to the disastrous effects of any use of nuclear weapons, and for its work in fostering this ground-breaking treaty to prohibit such weapons.

CHAPTER 8

Father John sat in the gathering darkness of the silent college chapel. He chose the very last row of pews, where he could face the entire peaceful church interior. He was in the habit of stopping there for a quick prayer on his way to class. This time was different, however. Sister Eileen's emails had left John at a crossroads, a position that, despite his new resurgence of strong convictions about the need for public witness against the nuclear weapons industry, left him deeply conflicted.

He had been aware of the BAE Systems facility in Nashua for years, as well as Raytheon in New Hampshire and down in Massachusetts. Only recently however, with what he now admitted, with a keen sense of guilt, was a rebirth of conscience, had those convictions urged him to action. He had gone with the nuns to the Raytheon protest and re-experienced the emotions he had felt back at Notre Dame—especially that heady sense of fellowship and solidarity with kindred souls who felt obliged to declare, in public and open to the possibility of punishment, that any participation in making and supporting nuclear weapons could only lead to irreparable disaster for the world.

But it was not that simple. He had spent hours at the library computers since receiving those still unanswered emails. It had occurred to him that Sister Eileen might have been exaggerating about BAE Systems. However, it turned out that her few remarks were only an introduction to a much bigger story. He found that the company was one of New Hampshire's largest employers. She was right about those 6,000 employees, and that number was getting bigger. BAE Systems, based in the UK, was described as the largest defense contractor in Europe, and the biggest manufacturer in Britain. Its U.S. subsidiary, BAE Systems, Inc., turned out to be one of the six largest suppliers to the U.S. Department of Defense. Beyond the Electronics Systems sector, headquartered in Nashua, the company had employees in 30 states in the U.S. Worldwide, this massive business employed 83,000 people with a wide spectrum of skills from engineering, electronics, and design, to dozens of other qualifications.

John found a good summary of the company's purpose in a remark made by a BAE official— "[We] deliver high-quality products to the warfighter." He shuddered at the thought of the nuclear weapons made possible by New Hampshire workers being used as "warfighting" tools. He thought about the nuclear weapons made with vital input by BAE. Art Roman had listed them to the faculty in the lounge a few days earlier—the Trident II missiles carried on submarines, the ICBMs waiting in silos out West, the missiles carried by the French Air Force ... If these were used in war, the entire planet would be the victim.

Those Trident missiles had been the subjects of the Kings Bay Plowshares 7, the peace activists who were serving sentences for a public display of their courageous dissent, among them a priest and Dorothy Day's granddaughter. Sitting there in the quiet chapel, such a wartime scenario seemed implausible. Who would consent to supplying the weapons for such a devastating war? How could that be possible, if the parties knew the consequences? And who would be a part of the system that literally made such horrific weapons possible? But it had to be more complicated than he imagined. Of course, there was always the argument that the threat those weapons pose is the key has prevented any serious aggression that might lead to them being unleashed. In other words, they were a "deterrent."

And after all, more than six thousand of his New Hampshire neighbors were earning a living every day right here in the Granite State, using their talents to fashion the complex systems that went into the most powerful weapons in the history of humanity, devices that made the atomic bombs that killed hundreds of thousands in Japan in nineteen forty-five seem weak. This was not a cabal of schemers, plotting to endanger everyone—quite the opposite. They were busy providing for their families, using their skills in what was labelled a "defense" industry. He was sure that there must be a few who had second thoughts about their work at BAE Systems, but he had certainly never heard of any organized objections within the company.

Searching across the internet, he had come across remarks by Sir Roger Carr, the chairperson of BAE Systems, who had answered questions from some shareholders at an annual meeting in answer to that very puzzle. They had admitted to having bought some shares of the company so that they could attend the meeting. That handful of shareholders were probing BAE's dealings with Saudi

Arabia. Saudi forces, according to them, had conducted "widespread and systematic" attacks on civilian targets in Yemen.

He responded, in part, "We are not here to judge the way that other governments work, we are here to do a job under the rules and regulations we are given." He went on to say, in response to the peace activists who maintained that lasting peace could only be achieved through negotiations, "… in the world in which we live, [there is] the principle of speaking softly but carrying a big stick—and that very often encourages people to negotiate. We try and provide our people, our government, our allies with the very best weapons, the very best sticks they can have, to encourage peace … [this] allows us to do this work in a proud and positive way."

This notion that weapons sales promote peace—the company leader's basic message—is just that good old deterrence argument, John thought. It usually comes down to that, doesn't it? The essence is this. Our side (the good guys) will arm ourselves to the teeth with missiles and bombs aimed at the bad guys, weapons that can never be used without destroying both sides and assume that their very dangerous presence will prevent a nuclear war, unless it starts and spirals out of control because of an accident, or perhaps simply because an individual—confused, or emotionally disturbed, or simple angry, sets it off. Aren't humans fallible, and haven't there been too many close calls already because of accidents?

The silence of the chapel was suddenly broken by a student swinging open the door and walking down the side corridor to the front pews. She knelt down and put her face in her hands. John recognized her as one of his poetry class students.

Am I right about all this, he asked himself, or am I just being self-righteous? There's my student—and I'm not really sure of her name—I don't know what she's going through right now. How can I know what's in the hearts of thousands of defense workers fashioning the world's most dangerous weapons, even though it makes no sense to me?

He stood up to leave, paused, then sat down again. Wait a minute, he thought, I'm sitting here struggling with myself as though this is some kind of isolated conundrum. Speaking of BAE being headquartered in the UK, what about that statement I came across in the library? It was put out by a group of Anglican bishops urging their government to sign and ratify that UN-backed Treaty on the Prohibition of Nuclear Weapons. They made a great point—that something like eighty-five states from around the world have signed the treaty—which is a pretty radical document. It's the one I mentioned in in my famous homily at Saint James. It obliges the signers to quite literally have nothing to do with nuclear weapons, including every aspect from manufacture to possession. That article made the point that most nations live in peace with their neighbors without having nuclear weapons and oppose their existence elsewhere in the world.

Let's not leave out Rome here, he thought, with a quiet laugh. There's good Pope Francis, making his verdict crystal clear when he spoke about nuclear weapons recently, "... the threat of their use, as well as their very possession, is to be firmly condemned." Can't get much more straightforward than that. But how does that translate to me openly demonstrating with peace activists down in Massachusetts, or this this time, in Nashua? "Activists" is what they call us. Others might label us as a mob of dissidents, interfering with people just trying to do their job.

OK, it's almost time for the five o'clock Mass. He looked up at the candle flame flickering behind the red glass lamp in the sanctuary. Maybe I've been too busy talking to myself. It's time to pray, and then to listen.

It was easy for John to fall back quickly into his daily, familiar routine. Saint Benedict had formulated a Rule under which monks had thrived for 1,500 years, not by accident, but because he understood human nature so well. Certainly, he urged the necessity of asceticism and self-denial, but his Rule succeeded in "setting down nothing harsh, nothing burdensome." The monastic life, with its carefully balanced rhythm of prayer and work, had never seemed a burden to John. Rather, it was a source of strength and fulfillment.

One week passed, and John's Raytheon adventure already seemed to have taken place in the distant past. The conversation in the lounge turned to the weather and the misfortunes of the Red Sox. The presidential election was coming up in November, and the candidates were slated to debate at another local college later that month. Politics was in the air. However, the lounge habitués generally frowned on any extended discussions on that topic. Aristotle, Darwin, Picasso, or Walt Whitman might be fair game, but any mention of either candidate could disturb the genteel jousting among the faculty. Also, the Faculty Dean was a confirmed Republican, and the younger, nontenured faculty, having just completed their doctorates, tended to be Democrats.

By Wednesday evening, three days before the protest at BAE Systems in Nashua was slated to take place, John was finally faced with having to make a decision. He had never had the habit of checking on his email every day, but he was now a daily visitor to the library to do just that. The week before, as soon as he had read Sister Eileen's last email, he wrote back with a somewhat vague promise to give her a definite answer about his possible participation. Now, as he settled down at the library computer, he was almost relieved that she had not pressed him for his answer.

After all, what's the hurry? He thought. I should just sit this one out. I really need to think it over a bit more. I mean, I need to work on getting that "informed conscience" moral theologians talk about. Maybe I could write a letter to the Editor at the Leader and say ...

But there were three emails in his inbox. The first was from ehealy:

> Hi, John, What's up? Don't tell me. Did I ever mention that I have a Master's in psychology? I don't know you that well, but it was pretty clear from your email to me last week that you are struggling with a tough decision. I can empathize, because I've already been through that struggle. The Sisters here and I come down on the side of the greater good, and acting to bring about that good, even

though we seem to be outnumbered. The real and present evil of nuclear weapons literally poised to envelop humanity in a living hell has to be resisted. What else should you and I represent as members of religious orders, followers of Jesus, but His message, which is one of nonviolent love for each and every human and all of Creation? So how is that compatible with remaining silent while we continue to "refine" and "improve" weapons of mass destruction?

And don't forget, Father, that "deterrence" means that we are willing to use those nuclear weapons to answer a nuclear attack—or, more recently, even to use them first if we suspect that an attack may be planned. Silence and acquiescence in the face of that willingness cannot be a justified choice.

We hear so much about the looming dangers of climate change, and the growth of poverty even here in the affluent United States, or, worldwide, the millions of refugees fleeing poverty and oppression and hunger. These are crises that are real and frightening. We can work together as individuals and communities and nations to try to ameliorate these enormous problems. Humans can combine their skills and resources to accomplish so much for the common good, given the will to do so.

But how can we work in our food pantry down here, or gather clothes to donate to those who have so little, and not be vocal witnesses against a nearby industry whose stated purpose is to arm our country and others with weapons of mass destruction? Didn't the U.S. and some of its willing allies go to war because Iraq might be hiding some chemical weapons—paltry dangers compared to a single missile bursting out of a Trident submarine?

Believe me, we will respect whatever you decide about Saturday. We know where your heart lies. If you decide to show up—and we will bring extras for lunch in case you do, you need to know this. We were just informed that the Granite State Peace Action, the group organizing this protest, has announced that the site has been changed from Nashua to Manchester. There's one practical reason—it's tough to find parking near the BAE Nashua location. But beyond that, they realize that there needs to be a public spotlight on the new BAE facility going up in Manchester right now. The place is planning on hiring 800 employees by next year, all focusing on the company's "electronic warfare programs."

The time is the same—10 a.m. on Saturday. The work at the site is behind schedule, so there will be plenty of workers there. You won't need to meet up with us down here, just show up there. Don't worry, we 'll recognize you even if you don't wear that collar. Please email me if you want to let us know your decision.

Oh, wait, one more thing. I never got around to asking if you had ever run into Eddie Egbert, who runs the G.S. Peace Action. He's a Quaker, a great guy who seems to have a hand in every social justice effort in New Hampshire. I was talking with him

a couple of days ago and he told me to have you give him a call if you wanted to talk about Saturday. His number is in our shared phone, and somebody else has it right now, so just look it up—the office is in Concord. May you find peace in your decision.
Eileen

The other two emails were from companies selling shoes. He had been searching the Web to see what was out there for sensible black shoes. So much for privacy, he thought. I'd better leave that purchase up to the Prior.

Luckily, Eddie Egbert's number was for a landline in his office, so it showed up in the phonebook John had tracked down in the library after 15 minutes of frustration trying to find a free phone number online. He walked back to his room in the monastery and used the phone there, a rare occasion for him. A cheerful voice answered the second ring.

"Hi, this is Eddie. How can we help you?"

"Hello, Eddie, this is Father John Fain calling from Saint O's—well, I am calling from there, but this is really a personal call, so I don't mean to imply that I represent the college."

"Great to hear from you, Father, Sister Eileen told me the whole Saint James and Raytheon saga when we talked a couple of days ago. She was hoping you would get in touch with us, and I'm glad you did. There is strength in numbers, as you know. I mean, you guys have the trinity, right? Ok, that was a bad joke, but I've been wanting to use it for a while."

"No problem, Eddie, but I have to warn you that I'm going to use it next chance I get. And hey, so you know Eileen pretty well?"

"Are you kidding? She has been working with us for decades. She probably told you, or maybe not, that the Granite State Peace Action has been insinuating themselves in just about every social justice issue here in the state since the Seventies. Everything from economic justice, immigrant's rights, to what I guess you are calling about—the BAE protest coming up in Manchester. We've also been putting a spotlight on the excessive political influence of corporations that profit from war and militarism. In a real sense, BAE is a good corporate citizen with a billion-dollar annual impact on New Hampshire's economy. For example, they match charitable donations from employees, and one of their executives sits on the board of the local United Way. And BAE's former president was the Republican candidate for Governor of New Hampshire in two thousand fourteen. But their largesse is a product of the war economy. Father, four million of that went to lobbying last year, according to the Center for Responsive Politics. So, do you want to talk about Saturday? We're expecting a good turnout, and we've made sure the press will be there. After all, publicity is the point in this situation. We want to raise the public awareness of these issues and challenge their consciences about the nuclear threat. Looks like you've had a hand in that already based on that your front-page appearance last week. We were happy to see that. So—what questions can I answer for you?"

After his conversation with Eddie, John sat in silence for a long while. The only sound to break the stillness was the occasional, faint tread of a monk passing the doorway. That quiet solitude had always been a comfort to him, a blessing that helped him meditate and pray and work. The monastery was a purposeful oasis.

But what about all those suffering people that Eddie had told him about—the refugees fleeing persecution, ending up in cold New Hampshire with nowhere to stay, with only the clothes on their backs? What about the local homeless, and the minorities facing cruel persecution in subtle and open ways? Eddie had talked about his organization and the volunteers who gave their time and dollars to help the poor and suffering. Those activists numbered Catholics, followers of Jesus, and other Christians, but also Quakers, Unitarians, Jews, atheists, all united to help their fellow humans in their painful struggle against injustice and want in a forceful but always nonviolent voice. And Eddie had been quite clear where the GSPA stood in relation to nuclear weapons, and their plans for Saturday. He had ended with a warm invitation for John to join them if he "felt comfortable about being there."

It's funny, John thought, in the middle of our conversation, Eddie told me that I was beginning to sound like Thomas Merton. Never mind the fact that I was surprised he had read Merton—really very unfair of me—he was way off on that one. Merton was an intellectual, and he managed by sheer effort to influence millions outside his monastery—in "the world" as we like to say, as though we monks are not part of it—with a message of peace and justice. Funny, though, I have been planning to ask my students to read the prose poem Merton wrote back in the '60s. It's called "Original Child Bomb." The Japanese people labelled the atomic bomb that killed those poor souls in Hiroshima "Original Child" because it was the first of its kind. The Trappist monk saw through the rhetoric about how the bombing was the only way to end the war. Well, Merton managed to stay in the monastery right up to the end, although who knows what he would have decided if he had not met that tragic death? Anyway, I'm far from a Tom Merton. I'll email Eileen tomorrow … or maybe Friday.

It was not until he concelebrated the five o'clock Mass that John was certain about his decision. When he heard the words, "Let us pray for peace in the world," and the reply, "Lord, hear our prayer," he knew in his heart, for him, in these circumstances, more than that familiar plea was needed. As a follower of the nonviolent Jesus, he wanted to join people of other faiths and some with none at all, united by their common humanity, to be a public witness against any participation in the nuclear weapons industry.

Earlier that day, he had read a moving message that Eddie had recommended. Two of the authors were from Global Zero. They described people as having become resigned to "crouching before the shadow of a horrifying God-bomb," as though they needed to lead lives of quiet desperation because they needed those weapons to keep us safe. Not true, they emphasized. Most of the world's countries have rejected any notion of needing nuclear weapons. Most chilling of all was their logical conclusion. Human beings are fallible and prone to mistakes. Because humans are involved in all aspects of nuclear "deterrence" it will inevitably fail.

So much for God's creation and any notion of responsible "stewardship" when that moment comes, he realized.

The re-awakening he had experienced at Saint James had moved him to preach that message. He had gone with the Sisters down to Raytheon as a witness to that message, earning the wrath of the abbot.

And now it was time to put his prayers and hopes into action at a site in his adopted city, practically around the corner from Saint O's. Eddie had told him that there had been a training session for the protestors who chose to do a sit-down when the police arrived. I'd better wear jeans and stay on the fringes, he thought. If the abbot sees my mug in the papers again, I might find myself on the way to a monastery in the desert somewhere, or worse. I'll just add my body to the numbers of demonstrators and stay away from the photographers. And no selfies or I'll be all over Facebook. But I'm sure the good abbot doesn't even know what that is.

Saturday arrived, with the promise of it being a hot, humid day. John emerged from the monastery and got into one of the several gray Honda Civics parked nearby. The abbot preferred simplicity, even in automobiles. John was wearing jeans, a blue T-shirt and a faded Red Sox cap. He had wanted to wear the Sox shirt his students had given him a couple of years earlier but decided against it. He didn't want to take a further chance of getting into additional disputes with any Yankee fans who might be working at the site.

The construction site for the new BAE "campus" was only about a 10-minute drive from the college, down along the west side of the river, over the bridge, and a quick jog to the right. There was the usual light

Saturday morning traffic, until he turned on to the road leading up to the site. He found himself in a line of cars, all headed towards an entrance about two hundred yards ahead, marked by a tall sign that stated in large, red letters, "NO ADMITTANCE."

These must be my people, John said to himself with a grin, because they are all ignoring that sign and driving right in. He also could see the familiar plumage of the progressive's car—at least two bumper stickers, usually a faded Obama-Biden one and a newer Biden-Harris, along with a colorful variety of liberal messages guaranteed to annoy fans of the current occupant of the White House.

He turned in past the forbidding sign, and found a spot in the large, paved lot where there were already several hundred cars. He could hear the slow, rhythmic beating of drums, and could see a sizable crowd of people heading toward several tall brick buildings. Many of the demonstrators were carrying signs, and a half-dozen had already positioned themselves out in front of the buildings. Most were wearing the familiar cloth mask. Fear of the Virus, which by then had all but disappeared, except for a brief outbreak here and there, still had a grip on people who knew that the threat was real, and not the hoax described by the president. One group of six held a cloth banner, stretching out 15 feet or so. It proclaimed, "No New Nukes – Remember Hiroshima."

He could see that the protestors were not alone. About twenty men and a couple of women had emerged from the buildings and were standing in a loose cluster in front of what appeared to be the future main entrance. At this point, the only emotion John could read on their faces was confusion and disbelief. The weekend crew was certainly unaccustomed to seeing the spacious parking lot almost filled, and to seeing hundreds of people, from young kids on their parents' shoulders to elderly folks using canes, and a few in wheelchairs, moving towards the renovation site with signs seeming to object to what they were doing. And those drums! What in the world was that about? Just then, as John worked his way toward the workers, he heard a familiar voice hailing him.

"Hi, John, over here!"

He looked to his left and saw Eileen and Mary walking toward him. They each were holding one side of a sign on a white poster board. It read, "Let's Risk Peace, not War."

"So, you're here after all," Mary said, smiling.

"Yup. In the end, I had to do it. And looking around, I'm glad I did. There must be a couple of hundred people here. So, do I look anonymous?"

"I'm not sure," Eileen answered, "I mean, only a priest would wear those old black brogues with jeans. But don't worry, you don't need to be in the front row. You're adding to the numbers and that's important."

The crowd suddenly grew quiet. A lone figure, a short, dark-haired middle-aged man, emerged from near the drummers, who stopped their slow beating when Eddie Egbert walked toward the workers.

One of the laborers moved forward to meet him. He was a tall, heavy-set man who appeared to have graduated from surprise at the gathering to a state bordering on serious irritation.

It was no problem for everyone present to hear him shout at Eddie, "Who the hell are you, and what are you all doing here? Me and my crew have got to renovate two hundred thousand square feet of buildings here. It's called earning an honest living. It looks like you think we're making bombs or something in here, which is a crazy idea. We're framing and putting up dry wall and trying to finish up the plumbing and electric. What the owners do in here is their own damn business. Now, it's a nice Saturday morning, and the cops will be showing up soon. We've let them know that you're all trespassing on private property. Just haul out of here. You've had your fun, you feel good about it, so don't get into the hassle of getting into a legal mess."

Eddie answered in what he hoped was an equally loud voice, which didn't quite work. John was close enough to hear him say, "We're all here with the Granite State Peace Action to shine a light on what will go on in these buildings when you've finished your hard work. About eight hundred workers of another kind will move in and produce sophisticated electronic systems that will go into weapons of war, including nuclear weapons whose very existence is a real threat to life on this planet. Those nukes run on what will be made here, and we are asking you to think about that, along with the company you're working for. We're a group of peace people who are not here to criticize you personally. We're making a public statement against the nuclear weapons industry."

Before there was an answer to Eddie's explanation, a young woman stepped out of the crowd and approached the worker who had confronted him. She held up a microphone bearing the label WMUR 9. She asked him, "May I have your name, sir?"

"Sorry sweetheart, but we've got work to do. We've heard their story and now we're going back to work. One of my boys called our boss a few minutes ago, so he should be arriving real soon, probably followed by the cops. If these people are smart, they'll leave and take those kids with them. They shouldn't have brought them in the first place." He turned and joined the other workers walking under a scaffolding and back into the building.

The reporter scanned the demonstrators for a moment. She stopped and looked straight at John.

"Say, Haven't I seen you before? You look familiar. May I have a few words?"

Before he could answer, the sight of a large, black SUV caught her attention. Heads turned as it approached them, seemingly trying to find a suitably sized parking place in the overcrowded lot. The gleaming vehicle slowed, then pulled into a spot marked by a sign, "Reserved for Manager." The door opened and a slim figure stepped out, dressed in black. Despite the neat, dark suit, he did not have the air of someone with authority.

He stood there for a moment, with a slightly bewildered look on his face. John was stunned. This was not a BAE executive, not even close. It was Father Jim, the curate from Saint James. That black suit was topped by a Roman collar.

Jim saw Father John and walked over to him. The monk asked, "Jim, what are you doing here? In Monsignor's car?"

"Hello. I've been thinking a lot and praying about those homilies, and when one of the Knights told me about this thing today, I thought I would ride over and join up with you all. I didn't expect this many people."

The reporter immediately switched her attention and camera to Father Jim. "So, Father, where are you from, and why have you come here today—and parked in the boss's spot?"

"Oh, uh, I'm from a New Hampshire parish. I came to support all these good people."

"And why would you do that? Is this a religious issue?"

The priest hesitated, then looked around at the gathering for a moment. He answered "Why of course it is. This company is part of the war industry which is making incredibly expensive nuclear weapons that could destroy civilization—God's creation—knowing that those things can never be used. Just think of all the poverty and human suffering right here in New Hampshire that could be relieved with just some of that money. Our pope has condemned nuclear weapons, so what am I supposed to do when parts of them are being made in my neighborhood?"

Before he could elaborate further, the piercing wail of approaching police sirens turned attention away from the two priests and towards the six vehicles that quickly circled the parking lot and pulled up in front of the buildings. There were four squad cars and two large vans—the kind the older people in the crowd might label "paddy wagons." Police officers piled out, with an air of quiet resignation about having to go through all this trouble on a Saturday morning.

One of them lifted a bullhorn to his mouth and shouted, "All right, folks, just to let you know that you are trespassing on private property, and the owners do not want you to be here. So, if you will all leave now there won't be any more problems, and you can go home and have a barbeque and watch the game. Anyone who's still here after ten minutes we're going to have to arrest, and you really don't want that hassle. And listen, we all know

Eddie. He's a good guy. We know why you and Eddie are here. We've already arrested Eddie so often that we know his shoe size—but none of this has anything to do with the real issue—the law. You are not allowed here, and you must leave. That's it, folks."

It was Eddie's turn. His shouted message reached the first half of the group, and they passed it along to the rear. Immediately, most of the crowd drifted back toward their cars. They began to sing, "We shall overcome," at first in scattered voices, and then in one loud chorus. The rest sat down and remained quiet. Eddie joined them.

John turned to the young curate. "Jim, I'm proud of you. That took real courage on your part. But maybe you'd better get back to the parish before the monsignor ..."

Before Father Jim could reply, the WMUR reporter, who had been standing nearby said, "Well, it looks like you two have something in common. I'd like to interview you both on camera. Do you mind? Are you going to stay with the rest?"

John pulled Jim aside, out of the reporter's hearing. She turned away as the cameraman began to capture some of the more colorful posters and banners.

"Listen, do me a favor, Get back to Saint James with that precious Cadillac. They don't know your name yet, and I am probably going to need you later on today to bail me out. The abbot might just let me sit in jail overnight if I ask him for money. OK?"

The priest hesitated but agreed. Before he could climb up into the huge SUV, a police officer hailed him.

"Hey Father, it's Mike, from the Knights. I can't believe you're hanging out with this bunch. Their antics will have you in the slammer, and believe me, if you think they'll turn you into the prison chaplain, you've got another think coming. Better get out of here. Let's talk after Mass tomorrow, if you're still in one piece if your boss finds out. Tell him the TV is out of order."

Meanwhile, John had joined the knot of seated protestors. The police walked among them and stood them up, one at a time, attached plastic cuffs on them, and helped them step up into the vans parked nearby. Most were older, some in their eighties. John, half that age, was about to get in with them when one of the officers took his arm and quickly deposited him into the back of his squad car.

They drove off. The officer looked up at John in the rearview mirror.

"Father, I have a kid who goes to Saint O's, so I know who you are. Mother of God, Father, why are you getting involved with this crowd? You're a monk and all, so I thought you wouldn't be out breaking laws. Let me just drop you off at the school. I hope they didn't get your picture again. What do you say?"

"Thanks, anyway, but I would rather have you take me where everybody else is going. In for a penny, in for a pound, like they say."

"Hey, it's up to you, but it will cost you more than a pound, and somebody will have to pay your bail. You guys don't carry a wallet, do you?"

"Sure, we do, Roger—I think that's what your badge says. We need someplace for an I.D. But you're right, we don't pack much cash. My father used to call it 'ready money.'"

"Roger it is, Father, Officer Roger LeTourneau. So off we go to the station. You're entering another world now, Monsieur le Curé."

It was only a five-minute trip to the station. The others were already there. They greeted him with smiles when he joined the line of protestors waiting patiently to be fingerprinted. After about a half hour of this, an officer spoke up.

"OK, this is the deal. You are now waiting for the bail guy, and you can bail out and head home with a date to appear in court for your arraignment. That's where a judge will decide what to do with you next. We have a huge backlog because of the Virus, so that may be a while. Just take a seat and cool your heels. Please, take my advice, don't get cute and refuse to pay your bail unless you look forward to spending time in a jail cell. From the looks of you, you really don't need that experience. Go home and save the world from your couch. And the food's better."

An hour later, Father Jim walked into the station and pointed at John. He was soon escorting John to a black Toyota Corolla parked nearby. They pulled out and headed across the bridge.

"Thanks, Jim. First question. How did it go with Monsignor O'Malley?"

"Oh, he's taking a nap right now. He wouldn't talk to me, but I got him his little pills and pulled down the shades. I won't have the full report until later. I'll have to say the four o'clock later, so I'll drop you off. Are you OK?"

"Oh, sure, right now. I'm really impressed with you for joining the rebels. I think we were the only clergy there, but my nun friends were right up front. They were both at the station. I'd better give you their contact info. What's your email? Wait, let me guess. It's jsulli@gmail.com"

"That's it. I hardly ever use it for anything, although my mother likes to hear from me every evening, so it's convenient. But listen, never mind the monsignor, what about the abbot? I can always get assigned to another parish, although there are so few of us that's pretty unlikely, but you? You took a vow of stability, right?"

"Well, he is not going to be happy. According to our Rule, if I remember this correctly, my faults have to rise to the level of 'notorious' to make him boot me. But I shouldn't be kidding about this. I need to talk with my abbot and explain where I am in all this and hope he understands, at least to the point of tolerance. But it wouldn't surprise me at all if I am in serious trouble here with the man who I've vowed to obey. Jim, we'd better watch this evening's WMUR news. Maybe, if we're lucky, they won't show us, but just talk about why all those people were there. I mean, that's the point, isn't it? Thanks for everything, Jim. Peace, brother."

Budgets are moral documents. They demonstrate what a country values. The numbers reveal that the U.S. has, for decades, treasured its war-making capabilities. Regardless of the political party in power, the national budget has retained massive military spending as a seemingly sacrosanct expense. Successive administrations have lavished trillions on the Pentagon. This is deemed necessary because the U.S. believes in war as a way to resolve conflict. The tools of modern war, particularly nuclear weapons, are incredibly expensive.

However, the massive U.S. forces, spread across the globe, are powerless against serious threats to national security—dangers that are nonmilitary. These range from raging pandemics and encroaching climate change to the unmet needs of millions of citizens struggling to pay for food, housing and health care, while the air they breathe and the water they drink continues to be contaminated.

The U.S. outrivals all other nations in its military outlays. The Pentagon budget in Fiscal Year 2019 was three times larger than China's and 10 times bigger than Russia's and was 38 percent of military spending worldwide. By 2020, this global investment in war capabilities amounted to almost $2 trillion. In the U.S., military expenditures had grown significantly and increased almost $100 billion beyond President Obama's final budget. The federal deficit soared to almost $4 trillion.

There are many demands on U.S. financial resources. One major category is the mandatory/entitlement spending, including such vital commitments as Social Security, Medicare, and Medicaid, Disability Assistance, and Food and Nutrition Assistance. The other is discretionary spending. This is optional spending that Congress determines each year through

214

an appropriations process. Subcommittees in the House of Representatives and the Senate suggest specific budgets, and the two chambers reconcile their differences.

The latter category includes what is called "defense" spending. (In 1789, the civilian Department of War was founded to organize the U.S. military forces. Between 1947 and 1949, after World War II, the Congress passed a series of laws that reorganized the military establishment. The Secretary of War became the Secretary of Defense, a more politically correct title. In that optimistic post-war period, the UN hoped that it was in the process of taking steps toward a world of lasting peace.)

The discretionary category, besides the spending on the military, includes transportation, education, law enforcement, natural resources, housing assistance, and science, among other expenses. In 1970, the U.S. military budget was $80 billion. Over the next twenty years, that figure increased to $300 billion. For 2019, Congress approved a budget in which over 50 percent of the discretionary spending was attributed to the military, a total of $1.25 trillion. Then, the U.S. administration introduced a budget for Fiscal Year 2021 asking that the American people support devoting 55 percent of the federal government discretionary spending to the military. By 2030, that percentage was predicted to rise to 62 percent.

The proposed 2021 budget came at a time when a pandemic was sweeping across the country. Rather than redirect funding from the military toward some alleviation of the country's human suffering, whatever relief legislation was passed simply added to the national debt. Between 2013 and 2022, the U.S. is projected to spend $392 billion on nuclear weapons, $97 billion on missile defenses, and $100 billion on health and environmental costs.

In that 2021 budget, the Pentagon's share for nuclear programs increased substantially, with a 16 percent increase to $29 billion, in order to "modernize" its nuclear arsenal. The National Nuclear Security Administration, the division of the Energy Department that develops nuclear technology, asked for an additional $20 billion. Nuclear site cleanup was projected to cost $5 billion, and the troubled missile defense network wanted $20 billion more. The latter, derided as "Star Wars" when it was hailed by President Reagan in the 1980s, has managed to spend more than $250 billion since then for a system that has failed most of its tests against intercontinental ballistic missiles. Even an efficient system, according to experts, could be fooled by decoys and other countermeasures.

For five years beyond the 2021 budget, the Pentagon wants to spend at least $170 billion on modernizing nuclear weapons and nuclear technology. This massive upgrading includes new production facilities, warheads, bombs and delivery systems. Spread over the next three decades, the cost will be perhaps $2 trillion. These plans represent an insatiable demand for overkill, adding to a lethal arsenal of nuclear weapons capable of being launched from land, sea and air with more than enough firepower to destroy most life on earth.

Among the targets for modernization is the fleet of 400 intercontinental ballistic missiles (ICBMs). There are plans to create a new generation of ICBMs by 2030 at a cost of $100 billion, and the price tag is expected to increase for this "Ground Based Strategic Deterrent" program. The total "life-cycle" cost of maintaining the missiles over their expected lifetime into the 2070s is estimated to be around $264 billion.

Beyond the ICBMs, taxpayers can expect to cover $109.8 billion for 12 new nuclear ballistic missile submarines, new nuclear-armed submarine-launched ballistic missiles at

$16-$18 billion, and 100 B-21 Raider stealth long-range bombers at $55 billion.

Budgets reflect needs and priorities. In 2019, the Pentagon spent $55.9 billion on research and development. In that same year, research on health amounted to $38.9 billion, energy $4.4 billion, and environmental research was allotted $2.8 billion. The proposed 2021 budget would slash hundreds of millions of dollars from public health agencies, with the National Institutes of Health losing $3 billion. The Centers for Disease Control funding would be reduced by 19 percent. Over the next decade, Medicare was slated to lose $500 billion, and Medicaid and the Affordable Care Act $1 trillion. Meanwhile, during the height of the Virus pandemic, nearly 90 million Americans were without any, or with inadequate, health insurance.

Beyond the issue of health, but intimately connected to it, is the fact that the military is one of the world's worst polluters. There are more than 4,000 Defense Department sites across the country. These are home to 39,000 contaminated sites, 141 of which are on the Environmental Protection Agency's list of the most polluted in the nation. Similar environmental problems are scattered across the military's 800 installations overseas in more than 70 countries. As well, the military is the world's top petroleum consumer. Between 2001 and 2017, the five branches of the armed forces poured 1.3 billion tons of carbon emissions into the air, twice the yearly output of all the nation's passenger vehicles.

The new Poor People's Campaign, inspired by the movement led by Martin Luther King Jr., in 2020 called for reducing the U.S. defense budget by $350 billion. Those dollars would be redirected to programs countering "systemic racism, poverty, ecological devastation, militarism, and [the]war economy plaguing our country today."

Also in 2020, Marshall Billingslea, the Special Presidential Envoy for Arms Control, speaking of a "three-way" arms race among the U.S., China, and Russia, said, "... we have a tried-and-true practice here. We know how to win these races. And we know how to spend the adversary into oblivion."

CHAPTER 9

Father John sat down on the wooden bench just outside the monastery side door. At 11 o'clock on this bright August day, he already could feel, in the warm sun, a hint of that familiar passage from a fading summer to the approaching fall semester. He smiled as he thought, I have measured out my life, not with coffee spoons, like Prufrock, but with semesters. I've been in school pretty much all my life, so I guess that makes sense.

The day before, he had taught his last summer school class. The last few weeks with his students had gone relatively well, he thought, ever since he had surprisingly escaped public notice by his visit to the BAE site. He had come perilously close to becoming a local TV star, but Father Jim's dramatic arrival had shifted attention away from him. Of course, that meant that poor Jim bore the brunt of the attention, sparked by the breathless TV account of his appearance as a "radical priest" at the construction site. Letters to the Editor labelled him as a "turncoat," and "deranged," or more gently, a "rebel without a clue."

At first, all this hoopla had made John begin to feel like a Saint Peter. When the reporter had turned to him and told him he looked familiar, he had to admit to himself that he had been preparing a denial. "No, you do not know who I am," he pictured himself as saying. But that guilty feeling had passed quickly. He was no Saint Peter in any category, and in the heat of the moment he had no idea of what he might have otherwise said. Besides, he had accomplished what he set out to do. He had joined the protest and added himself to the group that was arrested. There was plenty of publicity surrounding that, and it gave Eddie a chance to explain in the press why we were demonstrating.

By some minor miracle, he thought, the whole incident had escaped the attention of the abbot as well as my students. Of course, there was always the good Monsignor O'Malley, who might be able to wring the whole story out of Jim. However, the Monsignor had, according to Jim, "gone on retreat" without speaking to him.

Summer school had come to a welcome end, with the beginning of a new semester just around the bend. John's summer class had settled into a routine by the third week. There were the participators, the reluctant but willing, and the uninterested. Despite the monk's enthusiasm for poetry, and his valiant attempts to stir up at least a modicum of emotional feedback for the selections he offered his students, once again he recognized a phenomenon marking contemporary college students. They were polite listeners—most did the readings, and save for a few, attempted to answer the questions asked in class and on exams.

But, again, with a few notable exceptions, the students seemed to respond with what his colleague Professor Austin described as "benign indifference." In John's case, they did not object to the selections on his syllabus, or to his often dramatic and colorful interpretations of those poems. In the end, they appeared to be strangely neutral observers, sometimes almost quizzical as to why he was getting so riled up about rhymes.

Well, he mused, as he sat in the relaxing warmth of the sun, they are young, and perhaps they will look back on these times with another perspective. All we can do is soldier on ... Darn it, there I go again. After Labor Day, it's back to class with a fresh bunch. And maybe things will quiet down in the protest scene. If not, what to do next? Have I gone too far already? Well, I'm still here, the sun is shining, and this is the feast day of Saint Rose of Lima. My mother has always liked her. She used to ...

John's meditations were interrupted by the sight of Brother Isaac walking towards him, newspaper in hand.

"Hi, John, just the devout monk I've been looking for. Are you back into Sun worship again? Remember, moderation in all things."

"Isaac, I don't think I've ever seen you reading the Union Leader, and here you are walking around with it. What's up?"

"You're right, Father, I don't read it as a rule, but I do find it quite useful for shading some of my more delicate seedlings in the spring, or for wrapping up small bits of trash I want to toss. But this one's for you. Check out the headline."

He handed the paper to John. The front page featured a large stock photo of a submarine—one of those pictures where there are a few sailors perched on top, looking as though the next ocean swell might pitch them into the sea. The headline read, "Nuclear Sub Headed to Portsmouth." The story went on to explain how the huge vessel, one of the Navy's SSBNs—the ones carrying nuclear-tipped missiles—was cruising off the New England coast when one of the seamen aboard tested positive for the Virus. The sub, although it stretched almost two football fields in length, had to accommodate 150 crewmembers and five officers, making the notion of "isolation" an impossibility. The commander, in conjunction with the Portsmouth Naval Shipyard, planned on docking at the Yard and turning over the one sailor to the local medical staff, then releasing the others on board for two weeks of quarantine, leaving only a skeleton crew to maintain the submarine. The newspaper article explained that the plans included importing a few sailors "trained in maintaining the missiles and firing the nuclear weapons in case they might be needed."

"So, what do you think of that, mister peacenik? All that firepower parked over on our coast. I hope you don't get any ideas. In the first place, the security there is as tight as a drum, and it's federal property. You know what happened to those poor Kings Bay protestors. Some of them are in the clink. Not that I like the idea of that thing being so close, but it's only for a couple of weeks and then they'll be off to who knows where? Not to get all political on you, but I've read where those subs have nukes that are incredibly powerful, and they can travel thousands of miles, so those subs are the best protection we have against war. Anyway, the paper belongs to the library, so you can return it when you decide to haul yourself up off that nice bench before you get too comfortable. I've got to go and put on my hair shirt. See you later."

"Thanks, Isaac," John replied, laughing, "I hope you don't get a rash. If you do, just offer it up."

He went back to the news article. It turned out that, by some fortuitous chance, the sub happened to be the USS *New Hampshire*. It was one of the fleet of 14 SSBN submarines, six of whom were assigned to cruise somewhere in the Atlantic and the rest in the Pacific, at least when they were not undergoing refueling and maintenance. The submarine christened after the Granite State, according to the newspaper article was, ironically, too large to be serviced at Portsmouth. John bristled, as he always did, at seeing the term "christened" in conjunction with the naming of a weapon of war designed to kill.

Well, he said to himself with a sigh, at least we won't have to undergo the spectacle that his Uncle Alex had described to him when John was a kid. His Uncle had told him about a demonstration he had joined over in Portsmouth when a controversial sub was there for maintenance. By that time, the Navy had changed the name of the ship from the USS *Corpus Christi* to the USS *City of Corpus Christi*. It turned out that the original name was particularly irksome not just to liberal Catholics in general, but also to House Speaker Thomas P. O'Neill. He asked his friend President Ronald Reagan to see to it that the Navy make the name change. Reagan did it, according to Uncle Alex, over the objections of the Secretary of the Navy. His uncle was proud of the fact that he had joined with a large group of demonstrators standing on the bridge near the shipyard, protesting as an honor ceremony was underway, in which a priest solemnly prayed over the submarine, blessing it as an "instrument of peace." He showed the young John the sign he had carried that day, still hanging in his garage. It read, "It May be a Sub, but it's no Hero." Alex, his mother's late brother, was probably the reason she was not upset when she saw John's recent Union Leader picture. Instead, she sent him a box of cookies.

So, almost forty years later, another controversial submarine would be over in Portsmouth, John mused. This time, its name would be a source of pride to many, but the deadly Trident nuclear missiles it carried would certainly spark loud protests from a vocal minority. And I'll bet I will be hearing from some of that minority before long. So much for that peaceful semester I have been looking forward to. Darn, I hate ending a sentence with a preposition.

John did not have to wait long before hearing from his newfound co-conspirators. That evening, he found a voice message on his room phone. It was from Eddie, describing the Granite State Peace Action plans for a public response to the unexpected visit:

> Father, I was over in Portsmouth today, and already the locals are draping flags all over the place. They've even put up a big banner in Market Square that says, 'USS New Hampshire: Welcome Home!' Looks like we'll never get near the thing, but we're going to have to get the usual suspects together to demo over in Prescott Park and on the bridge. It was a good thing we got the word out about BAE, but this sub is the real deal. Those nuclear missiles on board pack enough power to kill millions, and folks are cheering them on like it's the Navy football team. Looks like it will be around for a few

weeks, so we're getting the word out—I'm already hearing from people from here to New York who want to join us. It will probably go down a week from Sunday. Of course, what you decide is up to you. I just wanted to let you know. Just give me a call or text when you can.

John put the phone down and sat on the edge of his bed. Well, it looks like Eddie is trying to recruit a fearless monk to man the ramparts, he thought, barely noticing the unwelcome military metaphor. I'm sure the abbot will encourage me to go over to Portsmouth and yell at a submarine in public. Lots to think and pray about here.

His thoughts were interrupted by the ringing phone. Probably Sister Eileen, he guessed. Eileen it was, as cheerful as ever. Didn't this woman ever worry about anything? He remembered her repeating on the drive down to Waltham, to his surprise, his mother's expression, "Worry is a useless emotion." Maybe that helped her sleep better than he did.

"Hi, John, hear about the boomer coming to town?"

"Hello, Eileen. Well, I do know about the submarine Portsmouth is welcoming with open arms. Hey, that almost sounded like a joke. You know, arms?"

"Not bad, John. Google tells me that these subs are called boomers because the missiles they carry can go 'boom' in a big way. Isn't that cute? Another factoid—their missiles can hit targets over seven thousand miles away. Ironic how they always say, 'targets' instead of 'people.' So, in case you haven't heard, the GSPA is getting together as many bodies as they can to go over there and be a loud voice against this monstrous war weapon."

"Eileen, I appreciate the call. I just listened to a voice mail from Eddie. He wanted me to know about the plans. I'm still kind of lying low after the BAE scene. I'm pretty sure I can keep it quiet around here but going to Portsmouth might just be the last straw."

"John, I have a pretty good idea what you're going through. It's above my pay grade to comment on your relationship with your abbot. Looks like you'll have to work that one out. Maybe I had better stop handing you these temptations to get in trouble. I mean, you guys blame Eve for the apple thing, but that's another story. Listen, you do what you decide is the right thing, and just get in touch and let us know where you're at."

"Thanks, Eileen. I'll do that. And say hello to Mary for me."

"Ok, will do. And listen, you may have some problems, but just think of those poor Trappists down in Gethsemane—making rum-soaked fruit cakes every day. Now there's a temptation!"

Two days later, when he checked up on his email on a library computer, any hopes of a tranquil fall semester disappeared. The abbot, in a brief email message, informed him that he would not be teaching classes in the coming academic year. Instead, Father John was to assume a newly created position, that of the college archivist. The abbot reassured him that his classes would be taken over by several part-time professors, adjuncts who were "fortunately newly available after their contracts were finished at a nearby liberal arts institution."

The college had "long needed" according to the abbot, "a diligent scholar to efficiently collate and store the college's permanent records and historically valuable documents." His message offered John "the opportunity to research and possibly publish facets of the college's long, proud history here in New Hampshire that might otherwise go unnoticed."

John was unused to such a peremptory command from his abbot, the prelate to whom he had vowed obedience. The abbot was far from an ordinary "boss." He was called Abbot from the Greek *abbas*, meaning "father." According to Saint Benedict's Rule, the abbot's commands should "permeate the minds of his disciples."

This was the first time that John was literally angered by an instruction from his abbot. John always had assumed that Abbot Flynn respected his teaching abilities. After all, hadn't he encouraged and supported John in his years of graduate studies, and assigned him to teach in the English department every semester? What about the pressing need to have the monks maintain a prominent presence on campus? At this point there were only six monks numbered among the one hundred or so faculty. And now, in his wisdom, the abbot had decided that John could best serve the college by shuffling old papers over in the library basement.

As he walked slowly back towards the monastery, he turned and entered the college chapel. He sat in his familiar seat in the rear row. He could see a lone novice, Cecil, methodically vacuuming the carpet in the sanctuary, with the slow, careful movements of someone scrupulously "doing small things with great love" as Saint Thérèse advised. Was there any real difference between vacuuming a rug and becoming an archivist, leaving behind his beloved teaching?

It had taken John only a moment of reflection to realize what the abbot was thinking. The good man was concerned that his rebellious monk may have become so radical that his liberal ideas about the defense of our nation, ideas that had gone beyond theory and propelled him out into the streets with a sign-waving bunch of demonstrators, would now be passed on to Saint Oliver students in the classroom. Only the day before, John had been told by Father Anthony, a confrere who worked in the Alumni Office, and a monk who seldom talked to him, that he had seen five letters from alumni, all veterans, threatening to stop contributing to the college because of, as Anthony put it, John's "antics."

Any thought that the storm had passed was in vain, apparently. Thank goodness he had escaped notice at the BAE site, he thought, as he watched the novice move from vacuuming to polishing the already gleaming gold candle holders on the altar. Forget worrying about changing jobs, centuries ago I'd be dressed in sackcloth and ashes in the public square. You know, I never really knew what sackcloth really is—maybe burlap?

The monk's irrepressible sense of humor made him grin. He was grateful that the novice was not watching him. Maybe he'd report that John was going around the bend. Well, John considered ruefully, maybe I am, in a way. What's around the bend for me now? Of course, I want to remain obedient to my vows. But I feel the tug of a higher duty, one that I began to answer in the streets of Waltham and Manchester. Am I needed to join my voice as a priest

to the voices, Catholic or otherwise, who literally are answering the call of the pope and many bishops, to speak
out against the very possession of nuclear weapons and any
intention to use them? But who do I think I am, anyway,
some hero who is needed at this moment in history? Maybe
I should "stick to my last" as my dear father Brian used to
say. Be a good monk, be obedient, and pray for the world
in this comfortable church. Even the carpets are clean.

John got up and walked outside, into a light sprinkling
of rain. "A Hard Rains a-Gonna Fall" he sang to himself, re-
membering only the first few lines of the old Dylan classic.
Was there a sign of what was coming, now moving silently
under the chill Atlantic waters, making for Portsmouth?
He felt sorry for those sailors and their officers, now unsure of the dangers to their health. Of course, they were
shepherding a bunch of gigantic nuclear missiles, each of
which made the Hiroshima bomb seem small. Now, there
was a threat to the health of many millions …

He remembered, as a kid, picnicking with his family
at Prescott Park, and looking across the Piscataqua River
at what the locals called the Portsmouth Navy Yard. The
tidal currents at the mouth of that river, where it emptied out into the sea, was a notoriously treacherous pas-
sageway for vessels. And this vessel, as technologically
advanced as any on or under the seas, was treacherous
almost beyond description.

Before John could speak with the abbot about his new
assignment, news broke about the USS *New Hampshire*
in the form of a front page spread in the Union Leader.
He had formed a new habit of going over to the library

periodical room to check up on whatever might be going on over in Portsmouth. He enjoyed the "old school" feeling of picking up one of the daily newspapers hanging there on wooden rods. Of course, they were full of yesterday's events, unlike the "breaking" internet news.

That day's Union Leader featured the plans of the New Hampshire bishop, the Most Reverend Jonathan Farrell, aimed at "honoring the presence of this great example of our blessed nation's defenders." The bishop was so impressed that the submarine, named after the Granite State, would be moored for a few weeks in that very state, although the shipyard actually was located in Kittery, Maine—a mere technicality. The bishop had written a letter to be read at every parish in New Hampshire, announcing that he and "a gathering of clergy from across the state" would meet with "local Navy and government officials and selected representatives of New Hampshire citizenry" to "conduct a ceremony on Saturday, August 22 at 11 a.m. at Portsmouth Naval Shipyard, at which time I will confer a special blessing on the vessel, honoring its vital role in protecting our way of life, and keeping all of us, of whatever religious persuasion, from harm's way."

After that news, he needed some fresh air. He walked over to the quad and paced back and forth, all the while kidding himself that he could not possibly take the chance of joining what would surely be a major demonstration against not just the sub itself, but all that it represented. It looked like even his chance to influence students might be over, at least for now. How could he remain silent?

He heard the slow ringing of the bell calling him to the noontime Mass. And at that same moment, he thought about Jerome.

He and Jerome Eisner had been close friends when they were both novices at Saint Oliver. That is, as close as one could be in the novitiate, where there was limited discussion with one another. About one month before they were to take their simple vows, Jerome was gone without a word. Eventually, he got back in touch with John, explaining that he was drawn more to the diocesan priesthood than to the monastic way of life. He had entered Saint Oliver monastery already having earned a Ph.D. in Theology, and now, years later, he was working in the chancery office in Manchester as a special assistant to the bishop. He and John got together about once a year, around Christmas time, and shared a meal at the local Pizza Hut.

That evening, John went to the library and wrote a long email to Jerome. He thought he knew his friend pretty well, at least well enough to know that Jerome was somewhere on the left side of the political spectrum. But when he read what John was asking for, would he suspect his motivation? That was quite likely. How would Jerome react? He hesitated for a moment, then hit "send," and went back to his room.

CHAPTER 10

The day arrived for the blessing ceremony. The sky was bright and clear, presaging a hot day. The ceremony was slated to begin at 11, but by eight o'clock a crowd had gathered, filling Prescott Park and extending all the way back up to Market Square. Vendors offered a wide array of flags, balloons, and other tchotchkes, all bearing some likeness of the honoree. For the children, there were soft, stuffed submarines, each complete with a tower topped by a small LED light, and with two rows of twelve red circles, representing the tops of the nuclear missile tubes.

It was obvious that there would be tight security surrounding the event. Ranks of State Police and local officers lined the streets within a mile of the shipyard. Here and there, clusters of armed men walked through the crowd. They wore what looked like some kind of camouflaged military outfit. Each of the jackets bore a large American flag, and a patch that read, "NH Militia." There did not seem to be an obvious reason for them to be carrying automatic rifles.

At 10:15, a phalanx of large, black SUVs appeared, moving slowly down State Street, heading for the bridge. Cheers erupted as the flag-waving crowd spotted the purple-clad bishop in the lead car. This was followed by 10 other vehicles, each appearing to be carrying clergy and a few laypersons. The procession moved over the bridge and turned toward the shipyard entrance. There were no onlookers allowed within a half-mile of the entrance, ensuring strict security. According to reports earlier that week in the Union Leader and also in Foster's Daily Democrat, the local publication, the authorities had been put on notice that "peace activists" and "anti-war groups" threatened to protest the ceremony, but there would be "ample security to protect the celebrants."

As each SUV approached the entrance, Navy guards carefully inspected the occupants' credentials. The invited participants each had been given a red, white and blue card which they were instructed to wear around the neck on a lanyard. This process slowed down the proceedings a bit, but within a few minutes all the vehicles had entered, and the gate closed behind them.

As the vehicles emptied and the guests streamed toward the dock, the assembled reporters could see various dignitaries, including the governor and several mayors, in addition to several dozen priests and a few nuns. A wooden platform had been constructed next to the dock, and the group climbed the few steps and sat down. They found themselves facing a unique and impressive site.

The USS *New Hampshire* stretched out in front of them, an imposing, dark presence, bobbing ever so slightly in a gentle swell, looking for all the world like some giant humpback whale. The ailing sailor and his shipmates had left the ship, and a new, temporary, small crew had been airlifted from the Naval Submarine Base Kings Bay in Georgia. Those sailors were now standing topside, at ease in a single row. The visible hull was a fraction of the massive vessel hidden beneath the dark water.

The sub's commander spoke over the loudspeaker from his quarantine, welcoming the bishop and the other assembled dignitaries and guests. The crowds gathered on the bridge and across the river could hear the ceremony clearly. When the commander completed his remarks, the bishop and the others gathered on the platform seemed startled for a moment as cries of protest drifted down from the bridge and from Prescott Park. It was unclear at that distance exactly what they were saying, but the message was unmistakable. The news accounts later reported that "less than one hundred protestors in the Park, and a dozen or so on the bridge expressed their disapproval as the bishop prepared to bless the USS *New Hampshire.* However, the bishop remained undeterred as he continued with the impressive ceremony, that is, until ..."

The accounts went on to describe what happened next. His Excellency the bishop, clad in a flowing purple cape—described more accurately as "magenta" by the Union Leader, approached the submarine, accompanied by three priests in black cassocks and white lace surplices. The bishop raised his right arm, and in a firm, loud voice prayed, "We are set in the midst of great dangers, and we cannot be faithful to the trust placed in us to keep our beloved country safe and secure without the help of Almighty God. Let us pray for His blessings upon this ship. May God the Father bless her. May Jesus Christ bless her. And may the Holy Spirit bless her. All please respond, 'Bless this ship.'"

As all those who wished to respond to the bishop's request did so, three figures stood up from their seats on the platform, filed down the steps, and walked quickly toward the edge of the dock. This appeared to be part of the ceremony, because the trio consisted of a priest and two nuns. The priest was described later as "a somewhat dumpy, short man, wearing what appeared to be old, scuffed black shoes." The nuns were dressed in classic habits, each complete with a long, black tunic secured with a belt from which hung a large, wooden rosary, and a white headpiece with a black veil draped at the back.

They paused momentarily at the water's edge. Suddenly, the priest reached inside his coat, while the nuns reached inside their habits. They pulled out what turned out to be small glass bottles, each filled with a reddish liquid. In unison, they threw the bottles against the side of the submarine hull. The glass containers broke almost simultaneously, and their red contents flowed slowly down along the side of the hull, before mingling with the incoming tide.

The three knelt and began to pray in unison. Witnesses later reported hearing the words "peace" and "forgive," but no one could give an accurate account of the brief prayer, which was speedily terminated as the nearby security force approached from both sides of the plat-form, guns drawn. The priest and the two nuns were seized from behind and pushed down. Their wrists were bound with plastic cuffs, after which they were pulled to a standing position. The officials quickly searched them. No weapons were found. During the commotion, the sailors standing topside remained motionless. The remnants of the red material, which the three admitted later was their own blood, remained as a bright crimson stain on the dark hull of the submarine.

Meanwhile, the bishop and the assembled guests were hustled off the platform and led back to the waiting SUVs, which soon departed out the shipyard gate. According to the shipyard Naval Security office, this was done on the chance that the perpetrators may have had accomplices nearby, or perhaps had left an explosive device in the area.

The three were hustled off to an office some distance away from the dock. Thirty minutes later, a gray van entered the gate. Two FBI officers emerged. They collected the trio quickly, placed them in the back of the vehicle, and sped off. As they drove over the bridge back towards Portsmouth, Father John, Sister Eileen and Sister Mary could not see out through the van's tinted windows, but they could hear the muffled applause of the hundreds of protestors still lining the roadway.

CHAPTER 11

Manchester Union Leader
Sunday News

Trio arrested after
USS New Hampshire vandalism

By John Daly
August 23, 2020

Portsmouth police and U.S. Naval security officers arrested three people yesterday morning after the trio threw glass bottles containing blood at the nuclear submarine USS *New Hampshire,* docked at the Portsmouth Naval Shipyard.

The three arrested are the Reverend John Fain, OSB, Sister Eileen Healy, RSM, and Sister Mary Lyons, RSM. Father Fain is a Benedictine monk from the Saint Oliver Monastery, associated with Saint Oliver College in Manchester, New Hampshire. The two nuns are Sisters of Mercy serving in Nashua.

During a ceremony in which the Most Reverend Jonathan Farrell, Bishop of the Diocese of New Hampshire was blessing the nuclear submarine, the three perpetrators left the stand erected for the occasion, walked to the edge of the dock, and proceeded to throw the bottles at the ship, where they shattered. The three then knelt down and appeared to be praying when they were seized by authorities.

Authorities say the trio had been admitted to the Naval facility along with several dozen others yesterday, along with the bishop, who was there to bless the submarine, named after the Granite State. According to a diocesan spokesperson, invitations to accompany the bishop had been screened through their office.

After their arrest, they were turned over to FBI agents, who transported them to their Portsmouth office. They were later brought to the Strafford County House of Corrections, where they remain in custody, pending arraignment.

Mark Brooks, public affairs officer at the Naval shipyard, said, "At no time was there any threat to the USS *New Hampshire* or its complement of nuclear missiles."

The Navy's fleet of Trident submarines are armed with about half of the U.S. active strategic nuclear warheads, according to military analysts. Witnesses said those arrested cooperated with authorities and did not offer any resistance.

The Portsmouth Naval Shipyard (PNS), often called the Portsmouth Navy Yard, is a United States Navy shipyard located in Kittery on the southern boundary of Maine near the city of Portsmouth, New Hampshire. PNS is tasked with the overhaul, repair, and modernization of U.S. Navy submarines. The shipyard is home to approximately 1,000 naval officers/enlisted personnel and their family members. PNS employs around 8,000 civilians.

The USS *New Hampshire* is ordinarily serviced at Kings Bay Naval Submarine Base in Georgia. It is currently docked at PNS during an emergency evacuation of its crew due to an outbreak of the Virus. It will remain in Portsmouth until the completion of the mandatory quarantine period.

Manchester Union Leader

Trio arraigned
after Navy Shipyard incident

By John Daly
August 24, 2020

Three Catholic peace activists were denied bail during a court appearance on August 24 in the United States District Court for the District of New Hampshire in Concord, two days after they were arrested at the Portsmouth Naval Shipyard. They face charges of criminal trespass, conspiracy, and willful depredation of Government property. The first is a misdemeanor, while the latter two are both felonies.

The Honorable Rebecca Trainor ordered the accused to be held without bond, citing their recent arrests in Manchester, New Hampshire. The trio are currently released on bail pending a hearing on charges stemming from a demonstration against the construction of the new BAE Systems facility in Manchester. She also stated that the accused could not be trusted in the community because they were a threat to continue their public protest activities.

The Reverend John Fain, OSB, a monk at the Saint Oliver monastery, associated with Saint Oliver College, Manchester, New Hampshire, and Sister Eileen Healy RSM and Sister Mary Lyons, RSM, both of Nashua, were represented in court by Thomas Emmonds, attorney for Saint Oliver College, as well as attorney Walter Kelly from Kelly, McIntire and Burns, Manchester, New Hampshire. That law firm has joined the defense team on a pro bono basis.

A motions hearing was set for October 12.

Manchester Union Leader

Indictments against
USS New Hampshire protestors

By John Daly
September 1, 2020

A federal grand jury has indicted three New Hampshire residents in connection with their actions during a ceremony honoring the USS *New Hampshire* at the Portsmouth Naval Shipyard on August 22, 2020. They each are charged with conspiracy, destruction of property on a Naval station, willful depredation of Government property with damages exceeding one hundred dollars and trespassing on a Naval installation for a purpose prohibited by law. The first three charges are felonies, while the fourth is a misdemeanor. The charges carry a penalty of up to 20 years.

The Reverend John Fain, OSB of Manchester, NH, and Sister Eileen Healy, RSM and Sister Mary Lyons, RSM, both of Nashua, NH were arrested on August 22, 2020 at the Portsmouth Naval Shipyard after throwing bottles containing blood at the nuclear submarine. The incident took place during a public ceremony at which the Bishop of the Diocese of New Hampshire, the Most Reverend Jonathan Farrell, was blessing the nuclear submarine, waiting at the shipyard during the quarantining of its officers and crew.

They remain in custody pending a motions hearing on October 12.

Manchester Union Leader

Motions hearing delayed
for Portsmouth protestors

By John Daly
September 15, 2020

Assistant U.S. Attorney Matthew Lewin has advised that a motions hearing set for October 12 has been postponed until November 15 at the request of the defendants' attorneys, citing the need for time to prepare.

Attorney Walter Kelly disclosed that his three clients, the Reverend John Fain, OSB, Sister Eileen Healy, RSM and Sister Mary Lyons, RSM will seek to defend their actions on several bases, including their religious freedom rights and their contention that they "acted in accordance with the 1996 declaration of the International Court of Justice that any threat or use of nuclear weapons is illegal." He also informed the court that the defense intended not only to file motions related to potential defenses but also a motion to dismiss the charges entirely.

The defendants are charged with multiple counts stemming from their actions on August 22, 2020 at the Portsmouth Naval Shipyard. They threw containers of blood, which they later admitted was their own, at the nuclear submarine USS *New Hampshire*, currently docked at the Portsmouth facility.

They are being held while awaiting trial.

The Boston Globe

Motions to Dismiss
filed in NH Shipyard case

Barbara Glenn and James Buck
October 22, 2020

Yesterday, attorneys for three NH residents filed Motions to Dismiss all criminal charges against their clients in federal court in Concord, NH.

The three Catholic members of religious orders are charged with three federal felonies and one misdemeanor for their actions in entering the Portsmouth Naval Shipyard under false pretenses and, according to the indictment, damaged government property on a Naval installation. They are the Reverend John Fain, OSB of Manchester, NH, and Sister Eileen Healy, RSM and Sister Mary Lyons, RSM, both of Nashua, NH. The Motion to Dismiss all charges stresses several arguments. First, international law, a part of U.S. law, holds that any use or threat of use of nuclear weapons is illegal. Second, the defendants' actions were a result of their sincerely held religious beliefs that nuclear weapons are both illegal and immoral. Thus, the government, in prosecuting them, is violating the Religious Freedom Restoration Act. In addition, the Motion argues that the defendants' actions were necessary, considering the threat that these weapons pose to the health and safety of humanity. Assistant U.S. Attorney Matthew Lewin, in an interview with Globe reporters, stated that this Motion would be discussed at the pretrial hearing to be held on November 15 at the U.S. District Court in Concord, NH. He explained that, after the hearing, the Magistrate would rule on the admissibility of the defendants' arguments at the trial, whose date is yet to be determined. According to Lewin, there is an "increasing interest in the legal proceedings" in this case. He cited "many requests" for admission to the upcoming hearing from a number of news outlets.

⚛

The Boston Globe

Pretrial hearing
defends Portsmouth protest

Barbara Glenn and James Buck
November 16, 2020

Attorneys for three New Hampshire residents provided arguments in U.S. District Court in Concord yesterday that the charges against their clients be dismissed. The Reverend John Fain, OSB of Manchester, NH, and Sister Eileen Healy, RSM and Sister Mary Lyons, RSM, both of Nashua, NH have been indicted on three federal felony counts and one misdemeanor. They were arrested on August 22, 2020 at the Portsmouth Naval Shipyard. Authorities say they entered the facility under false pretenses and threw glass bottles containing their blood onto the side of the USS *New Hampshire*, which is docked at the facility while its officers and crew remain under quarantine after a Virus outbreak on the vessel.

In a packed courtroom, Attorney Walter Kelly maintained that under the Religious Freedom Restoration Act (RFA) of 1993, the government cannot infringe on a person's exercise of their religious faith, unless there is a compelling governmental interest in doing so, and that infringement must be done in such a way as to place the least possible burden on religious freedom.

In this case, he argued, the government dismissed all alternatives, such as ban and bar letters, or civil

244

suits, or charging with only a misdemeanor. He described as "totally inappropriate" the possibility of the imposition of a sentence of up to 20 years. He pointed out that the RFA has protected religious motivated actions under other circumstances—for example, exempting employers from the contraceptive mandate of the Affordable Care Act.

Attorney Thomas Emmonds detailed how his clients will use the "necessity" defense, based on the principle that they had no other choice but to act in order to prevent a much greater harm. He cited an example of seeing someone drowning in a pool at a private residence, arguing that one would be justified in trespassing in order to save the individual. He cited the example of the Kings Bay Plowshares 7, decrying the fact that they had been denied the use of this defense in their trial for breaking into a naval submarine base in Kings Bay, Georgia in 2018 and vandalizing the military complex to protest the fact that it housed nuclear weapons. They are the same Trident missiles that the three New Hampshire defendants "symbolically disarmed" in Portsmouth.

The "necessity" of their actions in Portsmouth, he explained, was based on the fact that the existence of thousands of nuclear weapons, and the open threat by the U.S. government to use them under a variety of scenarios, poses an existential threat to humanity. He pointed out that the use of 50 to 100 nuclear weapons could kill as many as two billion people, and cause global cooling leading to widespread famine. This real threat required a dramatic, public, non-violent symbolic action to draw attention to this danger. He pointed out that the USS *New Hampshire* carries those same Trident missiles that were the objects of the Kings Bay Plowshares 7 nonviolent action, one that he termed "heroic."

Attorney Emmonds explained why a third line of defense would be used at trial, citing statements by legal scholars that international law, a part of U.S. law, holds that any use or threat of use of nuclear weapons is illegal. The accused will argue that the spirit of the law expressed in international treaties is aimed at preventing what amounts to mass murder on a global scale. He cited the compelling evidence for this offered by Francis Boyle, a highly respected professor of international law.

Professor Boyle's contention, that all humans possess the basic right under international law "to engage in non-violent civil resistance activities for the purpose of preventing, impeding, or terminating the ongoing commission of these international crimes" was not allowed as a defense argument in the Kings Bay Plowshares 7 trial.

Attorney Walter Kelly, on the question of illegality, pointed out that the U.S. has been bound since 1970 by the Non-Proliferation Treaty, which is aimed at the "cessation of the nuclear arms race and to take effective measures in the direction of nuclear disarmament."

The three defendants were allowed to give statements summarizing their positions on the justification for their actions. Sister Eileen Healy SJM cited their "sincere and heartfelt religious beliefs," and explained how the practice of their religion has been unduly burdened by the government's response to their actions. She pointed out that the statement of Pope Francis in 2017 condemning nuclear weapons: "The threat of their use, as well as their very possession, is to be firmly condemned," spoke to the primacy of conscience, so that their actions were fully consistent with Catholic religious teaching.

Sister Eileen Healy quoted Clare Grady, one of the Kings Bay Plowshare 7, who maintained at a Court hearing, "We cannot build, possess, maintain and threaten the use of nuclear weapons and love God ... I see in our/my action, as inspired by Jesus and the Gospels, a loving response to this systemic harm of the 'least,' that is being done in my name." She also cited testimony of Elizabeth McAlister, another Kings Bay activist, who maintains that "The government has set up a religion of nuclearism. It is terrifying and dead, dead wrong. It is a form of idolatry in our culture, spoken about with a sense of awe. It's a total contradiction to our faith."

Sister Mary Lyons maintained that their actions in Portsmouth were in keeping with a long tradition of nonviolent symbolic actions, especially those of Plowshares activists over the last 40 years. She explained that the name of that organization refers to the lines in Isaiah in the Old Testament in which swords are turned into plowshares. There have been over 100 actions in that same spirit against nuclear weapons since 1980. She stressed that the three activists, in their "simple demonstration" in Portsmouth, were acting in response to a higher authority than the government—God's voice speaking to their consciences, committing them to respond, especially to the needs of the poor and oppressed, and all who daily live under the threat of nuclear annihilation. She quoted Dr. Martin Luther King, Jr.: "The greatest logic of racism is genocide," adding, "The Plowshares movement says the ultimate logic of Trident is omnicide."

Father John Fain spoke briefly. He has been under treatment for pneumonia during his imprisonment. The Benedictine monk said that "regretfully" Christians have had a long history of cooperating with military authorities, blessing acts of violence. He pointed out that Jesus never taught or suggested to his followers that it is possible to express love for one's neighbors by killing them. He explained the trio's symbolic actions at the Naval Shipyard as those of "Christian pacifists." He also quoted the Plowshare's activist Clare Grady: "Nuclear weapons eviscerate and violate the possibilities of loving God and neighbor."

Father John concluded with the words of Henry David Thoreau, speaking of the U.S. Government in *Civil Disobedience*: "Why is it not more apt to anticipate and provide for reform? ... Why does it cry and resist before it is hurt? Why does it not encourage its citizens to be on the alert to point out its faults, and do better than it would have them?" Father John added, "And may I say for the three of us, in the spirit of the great Father Daniel Berrigan, our apologies to the good bishop and the other observers of our simple, heartfelt gesture against that great behemoth, now floating only a few miles from this courtroom. In its presence, 'We could not, so help us God, do otherwise.'"

At the conclusion of the hearing, the presiding magistrate, the Honorable Rebecca Trainor, informed the defendants that she would consider their testimony carefully, and inform them of her decision on the Motion to Dismiss, as well as determine a trial date. She ruled that the three defendants would remain in custody.

The Boston Globe

Motions to Dismiss
denied in Portsmouth submarine hearing

Barbara Glenn and James Buck
December 1, 2020

The Honorable Rebecca Trainor, Magistrate of the U.S. District Court, District of New Hampshire, denied all Motions to Dismiss yesterday in the case of the activists who, on August 22, 2020, were witnessed splashing blood onto the USS *New Hampshire,* a submarine carrying Trident nuclear missiles, as the vessel was docked at the Portsmouth Naval Shipyard. The action occurred during a ceremony in which the Bishop of the

Diocese of New Hampshire, the Most Reverend Jonathan Farrell, was blessing the submarine.

Attorneys for the Reverend John Fain, OSB, a Benedictine monk from the Saint Oliver Monastery, associated with Saint Oliver College in Manchester NH, and Sister Eileen Healy, RSM and Sister Mary Lyons, RSM, both of Nashua, NH had filed Motions to Dismiss the charges which included three felonies and one misdemeanor, on the bases of religious motivation, necessity, and the illegality of nuclear weapons as stated by U.S. and international law.

Magistrate Trainor concluded that while the three were sincere in their religious beliefs, and the government had burdened that belief by prosecuting them, the government had a "compelling interest" in the security of the nuclear weapons aboard the USS *New Hampshire*, as well in keeping unauthorized people out of the Naval facility. She held that to be the least restrictive means of protecting the safety of the base and the submarine.

She further denied any use of arguments based on notions of illegality or necessity. She indicated that no reference could be made to the use of international law as a defense. She forbad the defense from invoking any law beyond U.S. law, and not "other laws that someone else might want to believe in."

Pending any appeal, a trial date was set for March 7, 2021.

U.S. policy on nuclear weapon use is spelled out in the Defense Department's 2018 "Nuclear Posture Review." In substance and tone, the 2018 document leans more heavily toward nuclear weapon use than the previous 2010 version. Below are passages taken directly from the 2018 Preface and the Executive Summary.

"We must look reality in the eye and see the world as it is, not as we wish it to be."

"This review calls for a flexible, tailored, nuclear deterrent strategy ... the diverse set of nuclear capabilities that provides an American president flexibility to tailor the approach to deterring one or more potential adversaries in different circumstances."

"To remain effective, however, we must recapitalize our Cold War legacy forces."

"This review affirms the modernization programs initiated during the previous administration to replace our nuclear ballistic missile submarines, strategic bombers, nuclear air-launched cruise missiles, ICBMs, and associated nuclear command and control. Modernizing our dual-capable fighter bombers with next-generation F-35 fighter aircraft will maintain the strength of NATO's deterrence posture, and maintain our ability to forward deploy nuclear weapons, should the security situation demand it."

"Ensuring our nuclear deterrent remains strong will provide the best opportunity for convincing other nuclear powers to engage in meaningful arms control initiatives."

"At the end of the day, deterrence comes down to the men and women in uniform—in silos, in the air, and beneath the sea."

"The requirement that the United States have modern, flexible, and resilient nuclear capabilities that are safe and secure until such a time as nuclear weapons can prudently be eliminated from the world."

"The United States remains committed to its efforts in support of the ultimate global elimination of nuclear, biological, and chemical weapons."

"The highest U.S. nuclear policy and strategy priority is to deter potential adversaries from nuclear attack of any scale. However, deterring nuclear attack is not the sole purpose of nuclear weapons ... U.S. nuclear forces play the following critical roles in U.S. national security strategy. They contribute to the:

- Deterrence of nuclear and non-nuclear attack;
- Assurance of allies and partners;
- Achievement of U.S. objectives if deterrence fails; and
- Capacity to hedge against an uncertain future.

Potential adversaries must recognize that across the emerging range of threats and contexts: 1) the United States is able to identify them and hold them accountable for acts of aggression, 2) we will defeat non-nuclear strategic attacks, and 3) any nuclear escalation will fail to achieve their objectives and will instead result in unacceptable consequences for them."

"Nuclear and non-nuclear aggression against the United States, allies, and partners will fail to achieve its objectives and carry with it the credible risk of intolerable consequences for potential adversaries now and in the future."

"The United States has formal extended deterrence commitments that assure European, Asian, and Pacific allies."

"The United States would only consider the employment of nuclear weapons in extreme circumstances to defend the vital interests of the United States, its allies, and partners. Nevertheless, if deterrence fails, the United States will strive to end any conflict at the lowest level of damage possible and on the best achievable terms for the United States, allies and partners."

"Today's strategic nuclear triad ... consists of submarines (SSBMs) armed with submarine-launched ballistic missiles (SLBMs); land-based intercontinental ballistic missiles (ICBMs); and strategic bombers carrying gravity bombs and air-launched cruise missiles (ALCMs). The triad and non-strategic nuclear forces ... provide diversity and flexibility as needed to tailor U.S. strategies for deterrence, assurance, achieving objectives should deterrence fail."

"The triad's synergy and overlapping attributes help ensure the enduring survivability of our deterrence capabilities against attack and our capacity to hold at risk a range of adversary targets throughout a crisis or conflict. DOD and National Nuclear Security Administration (NNSA) will develop for deployment a low yield SLBM warhead to ensure a prompt response option that is able to penetrate adversary defenses."

"The United States must have an NC3 system [Nuclear Command, Control and Communication] that provides control of U.S. nuclear forces at all times, even under the enormous stress of a nuclear attack. NC3 capabilities must assure the integrity of transmitted information and possess the resiliency and survivability necessary to reliably overcome the effects of nuclear attack."

"Today's NC3 system is a legacy of the Cold War, last comprehensively updated almost three decades ago. It includes interconnected elements composed of warning satellites and radars, communications satellites, aircraft, and ground stations; fixed and mobile command posts; and the control centers for nuclear systems. While once state-of-the-art, the NC3 system is now subject to challenges from both aging system components and now, growing 21st century threats."

"The United States will ... provide the enduring capability and capacity to produce plutonium pits at a rate of no fewer than 80 pits per year by 2030 ... Fully fund the Uranium Processing Facility and ensure availability of sufficient low enriched uranium to meet military requirements."

"Although the role of U.S. nuclear weapons in countering nuclear terrorism is limited, our adversaries must understand that a terrorist nuclear attack against the United States or its allies and partners would qualify as an 'extreme circumstance' under which the United States could consider the ultimate form of retaliation."

"The United States remains willing to engage in a prudent arms control agenda."

In mid-June 2019, the U.S. Joint Chiefs of Staff published the Pentagon's official doctrine on the use of nuclear weapons. The next week they removed the document—Joint Publication 3-72, "Nuclear Operations"—from the public website. It is now available on a restricted access site. A copy remains publicly available on the Federation of American Scientists (FAS) website.

Below are passages taken directly from Joint Publication 3-72, "Nuclear Operations," June 11, 2019.

"This publication ... provides military guidance for use by the Armed Forces in preparing and executing their plans and orders."

"Developing nuclear contingency plans sends an important signal to adversaries and enemies that the U.S. has the capability and willingness to employ nuclear weapons to defend itself and its allies and partners."

"The employment or threat of employment of nuclear weapons could have a significant influence on ground operations."

"In crisis or conflict, there may be a requirement to strike additional (follow on and/or emerging) targets in support of war-termination or other strategic objectives."

"Survivability operations take on increased importance in a nuclear environment ... The commander must employ appropriate protective measures to ensure mission-critical operations can continue after exposure to nuclear effects."

"The President authorizes the use of nuclear weapons."

"U.S. nuclear forces provide the means to apply force to a broad range of targets in a time and manner chosen by the President."

"Effectiveness is achieved by commanders training the joint warfighter to survive, fight, and win in a nuclear environment."

"Possibly the greatest and least understood challenge confronting the joint force in a nuclear conflict is how to operate in a post-nuclear detonation radiological environment. Knowledge of the special physical and physiological hazards, along with guidance and training to counter these hazards and effects, greatly improves the ground forces' ability to operate successfully."

"Unlike SLBMs [submarine-launched ballistic missiles] and ICBMs [intercontinental ballistic missiles], bombers are recallable."

"A weapon may be set to detonate at or near the Earth's surface. Some weapons may be employed at higher altitudes. Selection of HOB [height of burst] enables planners to take advantage of the incident blast wave, with resulting dynamic air pressures to vary the effect on the target."

"US policy on the use of nuclear weapons complies with all law of war requirements."

The U.S. government continues the policy as stated in the "Congressional Commission on the Strategic Posture of the United States, 2009": "[The U.S.] should not abandon calculated ambiguity by adopting a policy of no first use."

According to the 2020 Ploughshares Fund Study Report No. 5 by Akshai Vikram: "Retaining these policies is an unacceptably dangerous choice. [They] increase the chance of a miscalculation, which could precipitate an accidental nuclear war."

In John Bolton's 2020 book, *The Room Where it Happened*, the topic of the UK nuclear arsenal came up at a 2108 meeting of the president with Prime Minister Theresa May. The president asked her, "Oh, are you a nuclear power?" Mr. Bolton said he could tell it "was not intended as a joke."

The U.S. president possesses sole, veto-proof authority to launch nuclear weapons. The president can exercise that power at any time at his discretion.

CHAPTER 12

Early September. A new semester had begun on the Saint Oliver campus, with the usual anticipation and enthusiasm, and a sense of optimism that would last for at least a few weeks until the daily grind set in and the question arose—when is the next break? Even the weather matched the transition. True, the bright sunshine felt warm, but somehow, even so soon after Labor Day, there was an edge to the air, a certain crispness to the early morning that signaled the sad loss of summer.

This was a familiar and welcome rite of passage for the faculty and students at Saint Oliver. But this year was unique. In the happy reunions and excited conversations there was only one topic. One of their own—a monk, priest and professor had committed acts a few weeks earlier described by both students and faculty, as well as the staff and employees, as actions that ranged all the way from treason to heroism, depending on who was passing judgement.

That person, Father John Fain, was now sitting in a jail awaiting trial in a federal court, along with two nuns from Nashua, who had aided and abetted this terrible crime—or admirable act of nonviolent civil disobedience. All over campus, arguments developed that mirrored the controversy. Fights broke out, spasms of violence aimed at settling arguments about pacifism. Names were tossed about—Gandhi, Martin Luther King, Jr., Thoreau, Merton. The president of the Debate Club waxed eloquently about "the rule of law" and "No man is above the law," while his female listeners demanded the term "persons" rather than "man."

There were numerous defenders of Father John, particularly among his former students. It was clear that he had given them at least the basics for understanding the actions of the three over in Portsmouth, even though they might not have agreed with what was done. But it appeared that the majority of the students were not willing to put Father John in the fellowship of principled activists. There was a growing consensus that he had committed a public act that was embarrassing, altogether puzzling, pointless, and offensive to the proud traditions of the United States military. The three had sullied the reputation of their fine Catholic college and deserved whatever punishment would inevitably be handed out to them. By the second day of classes, Father John, Sister Eileen and Sister Mary had become "the Bloods," "the terrible trio," the "sub slayers," or "the religious rioters," among a variety of other colorful epithets.

Meanwhile, in the Faculty Lounge, the mood was far more restrained. Their universally respected colleague, Father John, had surprised them all. They certainly knew the flavor and sincerity of his pacifism, but even after his actions at the Raytheon and BAE Systems facilities, they never suspected that he would put his freedom on the line with such a bold act. And those nuns? Well, certainly it was no surprise to see them in the front row of civil disobedience actions. That had become almost expected of them.

At a gathering of faculty in the lounge during the first day of the semester, Mary Shea, the diminutive theologian, opened the conversation with a plea. "OK, everybody, we all know what the topic *de jour* will be. Given the nature of the stories plastered all over the Union Leader and the Globe, not to mention the fact that this has even leaked over into the Gray Lady, can we promise that this discussion will not be too divisive? We all know John and love the guy, but as far as I am concerned, I think it would be better to talk about Adam rather than atoms. What I mean is, what went on in Portsmouth comes down to what amounts to an immoral act. He and his nun friends, during a ceremony in which the bishop was blessing a nuclear submarine named in honor of the Granite State as well as the fine men and women serving on board, a vessel whose sole purpose is to keep our country safe, defiled that very submarine in what seems to me to be a pointless act. It appears that after their display, they knelt and began to pray the Rosary. Was our Lady supposed to be pleased? John is an intelligent man. What did he think their shenanigans would accomplish?"

"Well, Mary, I can offer my answer to your 'non-divisive' question, if I may." Professor Austin rose slowly, and stood, supported by his cane.

"This dramatic incident draws me back to my younger days. Father John and his associates in civil disobedience remind me very much of myself and my fellows with regard to actions we took many years ago not far from Portsmouth. If you will allow me to draw back the curtains of history for just a moment. In nineteen seventy-two, when I was considerably younger than I am at the moment, and filled with youthful ardor of various sorts, I lived in beautiful Hampton, New Hampshire, hard by the Atlantic Ocean. At that time, the Public Service Company, producers and purveyors of our electricity, announced their ambitious plans to build, not one, but two nuclear reactors smack in the middle of that serene salt marsh in the Hampton-Seabrook estuary.

There was an immediate outcry of opposition, at that time based mainly on the potential desecration of that fragile ecosystem, particularly because the plan involved discharging great quantities of heated water directly into the adjacent Hampton River. In addition, it became obvious that that there could never be an adequate evacuation plan for the area in case of disaster. Mind you, all this was before Chernobyl and Three Mile Island, but the potential for disaster was very much in our minds. After all, a meltdown at the plant when thousands were crowded onto the beaches, and a couple of small roads to handle the escape? Not likely.

At any rate, I joined the band of activists known as the 'Clamshell Alliance.' In the Spring of seventy-seven, I believe, several thousand of us massed at the construction site to nonviolently reclaim the land and declare the marsh 'nuclear free.' This burst of idealism resulted in scores of arrests, including my own. There were so many of us that we were hustled into several armories, where we waited for days before we could be put on trial. The upshot? Many, including myself, eventually had their cases dropped, the Seabrook Station Nuclear Power Plant finally went online years later, and the brouhaha had cost the Public Service Company so much that they went bankrupt. So there sits the single nuclear power unit out there in the marsh, at least until it is forced to shut down in twenty-fifty, at which time there will be an enormously costly and complicated dismantling of its radioactive skeleton—and of course there will have to be a decision as to what to do with the radioactive waste stored indefinitely on site."

"With all due respect, Professor Austin, we can appreciate how you might have been upset about the salt marsh being despoiled, but objecting to an unsightly power plant does not seem to be analogous to attacking a beautiful nuclear sub designed to protect us all."

"Mary, if I may, let me speak to that," answered Bill Johnson. "This gets us to a subject that I take up in my intro physics class. I went through some of this when we talked with John last summer. What you've got happening in a nuclear power plant is fission. You start with a particular form of uranium that you get by first digging it out of the earth, a messy, polluting business—just ask the Navajos in New Mexico—and using a process called 'enrichment' to get it into a concentrated form. You pack it into fuel rods, and you have the fission from that uranium create heat. You use the heat to make steam that turns a turbine, and that generates electricity. In the process, there is another element that is created by the fission, and that's plutonium. Sound familiar? Uranium was used for the Hiroshima bomb, and plutonium for the Nagasaki bomb. This just adds to the mess we have on our hands with the piles of radioactive waste we have generated. Why do you think so many are concerned about selling nuclear power plant technology abroad?

The same technology that makes 'peaceful, clean atomic energy' can make nuclear weapons. Every power plant annually creates enough plutonium that could be used to make dozens of bombs. In fact, the UK's first nuclear power plants were built mainly to make material for nuclear weapons during the Cold War. So, yeah, the nuclear power plant world and the nuclear weapon world are intertwined.

Oh, and by the way, and this is a pretty important aside, there are more than a quarter million tons of highly radioactive waste sitting in storage at nuclear power plants and weapons production facilities all around the world, with over ninety thousand tons in the U.S. It is enclosed in various ways, none of them permanent, and this stuff poses serious risks to health and the environment. It will have to be safely stored somewhere indefinitely, but nobody knows where yet. Where is Seabrook's nuclear garbage? Right there onsite."

Ruth Conerly spoke up. "Bill, I see your point about the connection, but still, on the one hand you've got Professor Austin here joining the mob yelling at a nuclear plant construction site, and John crashing a bishop's blessing to throw blood at a nuclear submarine. I mean, the difference seems pretty clear to me. At Seabrook you get dismissed charges, and in Portsmouth the government is threatening John and the nuns with twenty years."

Professor Austin, still standing, answered her. "Ruth, I submit that the difference is not one of kind, but of degree. I can assure you that, in my case and that of my fellow protestors, we had the same enthusiasm as John and his fellow activists to stop the madness, as we perceived it, before the plague of radioactive waste and possible meltdown became widespread. We were proven prescient with Chernobyl, Three Mile Island, and more recently, Fukushima. Incidentally, as we speak, the Japanese government is planning to release over one million tons of radioactive wastewater from that disaster into the Pacific. The action at Portsmouth, by its decidedly more dramatic nature, was the very point. They wanted to turn the eyes of the world on the threat that nuclear weapons pose to humanity.

I hesitate to say this, but I fear that the same forces that disregarded the near and long-term dangers of nuclear power are even more powerful today, as our government presses on with the 'modernization' of our vast array of nuclear armaments. I applaud the Portsmouth trio, but I suspect that their idealism will culminate in their lengthy incarceration. We shall no longer enjoy the friendly presence of Father John here in the lounge, and the poor of Nashua will miss the saintly ministrations of the good Sisters." He sat down, slowly.

The first semester moved on, with the faculty, staff and students finally freed of any serious concern about the Virus. Occasionally there was word of an occurrence here and there, but seldom in New Hampshire. The trial for the Portsmouth protestors would not occur until March 7, 2021, and attention drifted away from its original intensity. There were a few modest attempts by the campus Pax Christi chapter to organize a rally to inspire support for the jailed activists, but there appeared to be little enthusiasm among the students, beyond the half-dozen chapter members, to make a public commitment to their cause. On the other hand, the ROTC hired a bus to take students over to Portsmouth in early October for a tour of the Navy Shipyard. It turned out to be a rather limited experience for the 45 students who signed up, given the many restricted areas surrounding an attack submarine then undergoing maintenance. They were especially disappointed that the USS *New Hampshire* was no longer docked there. It had slipped away without fanfare, headed for a cruise whose location was carefully guarded. However, they were allowed on the dock, and were soon laughingly recreating the incident that had led to their professor's imprisonment.

Back in Manchester, at Saint James parish, Monsignor O'Malley was feeling quite satisfied with himself. Father Jim had, as the Monsignor put it, "moved on," and the good bishop had sent him a priest fresh out of the seminary—a young fellow who had graduated from Madeline College, only a short drive away from Manchester. Father Auger had spent a good deal of time there reading the "Great Books" and had deeply immersed himself in the seminal works of Saint Augustine and Saint Thomas Aquinas. Augustine had argued, in the fifth century, that God had given the sword to government for good reason. Aquinas, in the 13th century, laid out the principles for a just war.

Armed with those insights, and three years of seminary instruction, Father Thomas Auger was eager to pass on his accumulated wisdom to his parishioners. Monsignor was delighted with his curate, secure in the knowledge that he would be a shining example of fidelity to the magisterium and certainly would not be frolicking about with nuns on some sort of fancied "peace" protests. The youthful priest's homilies were indeed models of restraint and avoided any mention of contemporary issues. By October, the Monsignor felt like his old self again. He had been forced to spend three weeks recovering at his sister's house at Hampton Beach after the "incident" at Portsmouth.

Another victim of Father John's adventures was Abbot Flynn. The repeated shocks of Father John's "indiscretions," as the abbot described the monk's public protests, had left him confused and deeply dismayed. He had been besieged with requests for interviews from a variety of media outlets. His only recourse had been to leave all that business to Paul Downes, Saint Oliver Public Relations Director. He instructed Paul to report only that Father John had been put on "administrative leave," pending the conclusion of his upcoming trial. Within the monastery, as well as the college community, the abbot let it be known that the monk was persona non grata.

Father John's return to Saint Oliver College, and the welcoming embrace of his monastic community after his years in graduate school at Notre Dame, had been followed, a few years later, with the first year of the presidency of Ronald Strump. The man who had been known primarily for his flamboyant social presence among the glitterati in New York, and for his purported fabulous wealth, garnered from a variety of sources including his ownership of thousands of substandard housing units, had suddenly emerged as the leader of the free world.

John admitted to only a passing interest in the political scene, but in the friendly rhetorical jousting in the Faculty Lounge, a recreation he soon came to love, there was no escaping the puzzlement over the ascendancy of Strump. College and university professors for the most part tend to be either Democrats, or at the least, Independents. However, the new president inspired a fierce loyalty among the majority of Republicans, leading to a polarity between left and right. The give and take in the lounge took on a sharper edge, while the student body drifted from their typical indifference to politics to open clashes between the Young Republican Society and the Democrats Club.

It had not taken the American people long to get caught up in the pressure to take sides in what evolved into a bizarre loyalty test. One either pledged allegiance to a president who gained his office and presided over it by repeating an endless series of lies and distortions, or engaged in an exhausting, daily refutation of this unprecedented dishonesty.

Given his background and behavior, neither friend nor foe of the president understood how Strump had managed to corral sufficient supporters and votes to win the presidency—that is, until a lengthy Congressional investigation revealed a complex, widespread collusion among himself, his political associates, and Russia. And why would Russia, a country who even the most ardent Republican recognized as a potent adversary of the United States, see any advantage in championing the cause of Ronald Strump, American playboy and slumlord?

While the probing of the Congressional committees revealed an unmistakable pattern of contact and chicanery between Strump and his people and various Russian officials, the president had managed to gain sufficient loyal adherents that even the disclosures of his traitorous behavior were ignored. Instead, in the court of public opinion, his accusers became the objects of derision and suspicion. Rumors of a conspiracy against the president deep within the Democratic party, and extending even to the F.B.I., caught hold in the American public, and led to frequent verbal and sometimes physical battles.

It was clear to any objective observer of the scene that was playing out in the final days of the Strump administration, now contemporaneous with the arrest and imprisonment of Father John, Sister Eileen and Sister Mary, that there had been something terribly wrong in the relationship between the president and the Russian leaders throughout his tenure. He had never, not in any instance, been critical of any aspect of Russia's behavior. His collusion with Russia had been consistent, but its exact details had never been unearthed by even the most determined investigators and journalists.

The man derided by many as an ignoramus, who possessed surprising political skills, and parlayed his business expertise into a successful election campaign, became the target of an intelligence system which, in its sophistication, was able to create a puppet who surpassed even its most optimistic aims. Over the course of a decade before he took on the title of president, he had been carefully and gradually courted by each of the three Russian intelligence services. A combination of constant praise, financial assistance, and promises of enticing business opportunities earned Strump's unswerving loyalty towards Russia. For a man whose sole interest was himself and his advancement, that country's attention, despite its history, was irresistible.

None of the Russian spies would have wasted any time with Ronald Strump, save for the fact that he had periodically, and with great fanfare, announced that he was planning on running for the office of President of the United States. His combination of buffoonery, naiveté, and attention-getting abilities landed him on the target list as someone who, at the very least, would be fair game for the accumulation of a detailed *kompromat* dossier.

When Strump began to seek out influencers in Moscow who might be useful in his grandiose ambitions to build a luxury hotel there, Russia was presented with an opportunity to draw him into its net. And when his loud, right-wing braying began to draw increasing political support, all three intelligence agencies began an unusual cooperative effort to assist him with all their various techniques towards his future election.

One of their methods resided mainly in the work of the Russian Federal Security Service, the FSB. There, men and women highly skilled in the complex world of information technology—"cyber" experts—spooled out a web of information gathering and misinformation peddling, aided by their knowledge of the tools of "hacking." The latter proved to be successful in penetrating the Democratic National Committee files in 2015. Further inroads into a wide variety of sites swayed the electorate sufficiently to garner him a slight but decisive majority of electoral college votes. Ronald Strump became the President of the United States.

Scarcely one month after the heady days of the election celebrations, his inauguration, and his gathering together of Cabinet officials, purported "advisers," and Department heads chosen for their fealty to his ambitions, President Strump met with one of his long-time FSB contacts, Alexei Petrov, in the Oval Office. Alexei was introduced as Yusif Varga—his cover as an international businessman and trade envoy.

The president was accustomed to his friend's relaxed, casual attitude, always marked by a complete deference to Strump's opinions and preferences of the moment. Alexei had been a frequent golf partner, just good enough to almost keep up with Strump on the fairways, but not quite good enough with the putter to best him on the greens.

Today, however, was different. There was none of the usual banter, or the off-color jokes that were part of the Russian's repertoire. Alexei entered, sat down without a word, and handed the president a blue folder. He said, "Open it, Ronald." Surprised, but suspecting either a gift or some sort of joke, he opened the folder. The Russians, knowing that Strump's attention span was remarkably short, did not offer him even one page of text. Instead, there were images—the kind that he might otherwise have savored—except for the fact that all of the pictures, page after page, included himself in the scenes.

He recognized the women and the hotel rooms. All of this had occurred during his visits to Moscow, where he had been flattered over the years to discover that even an aging, overweight businessman was attractive to such exotic females. At times, he had been married, or sometimes in between marriages, but whatever the case, his other relationships had lacked the excitement and intrigue provided by these encounters. And they had asked nothing in return. They were delighted to be in the presence of this rich, powerful American.

He looked up at Alexei, his affable golf buddy.

"I don't understand. How did you get these, and why are you showing these to me now?"

The president stood up behind his desk. His expression had quickly gone from quizzical to enraged, and his voice grew louder. "What the hell is this, some kind of sick joke? You know, if you're trying to blackmail me, I could have you arrested right now, Mr. Varga."

The Russian remained calm.

"Please, Ronald, sit down and relax. Of course, I would never try to blackmail my old friend. Don't forget, I was with you at some of these parties, and I was the one who introduced you to Natasha. By the way, she looks forward to seeing you again. No, no, I show you these pictures—and by the way, I did not want to bother you at the moment with the audio recordings or financial records. We have all those, of course, but I am simply here to let you know that all we want from you is a bit of harmless information now and then. That's all. And I do mean harmless. After all, Ronald, Russia and the United States are the two preeminent military powers in the world—and I know that you are a very intelligent politician and incredibly rich and successful business-man—so you understand that the continued prominence and success of both of our countries is vital to our people's safety and well-being. We need to work together to stymie the growing ambition of China. That country is our common enemy. But of course, I am not telling you anything you don't know. I have always been impressed by your uncanny insight into international relations."

The president was sitting again. His expression had mutated dramatically from rage to curiosity.

"Of course, I do have that talent. But what about these pictures? I mean, they do bring back some pleasant memories, but ..."

"Mr. President, I must confess to you that even though I am connected to levels of government in my beloved country far beyond the ordinary, I and my colleagues who work on behalf of Mother Russia are still beholden to the very highest authorities. I am sure you can understand. After all, you are in the process of selecting departmental officials who will cooperate with you to forward your agenda, and if they do not, then, as you say in this country, 'heads will roll.' I can assure you, my friend, that I will keep these images and other information close to me. Only the most egregious acts towards Russia would ever force me to pass them on to other hands."

Ronald Strump looked somewhat puzzled, but also relieved.

"You mean, Yusif, that all you want is a few harmless secrets from me here and there, information that will really benefit both of us, and you will keep this stuff," he said, pointing to the folder, "completely secret?"

"Of course. I would never ask you to betray any vital secrets. You are a loyal patriot, just as I am. And of course, don't forget, after your remarkable presidency is over, there are any number of rich business opportunities awaiting you in Russia. But more on that later. We will be in touch periodically. By the way, we no longer need to concern ourselves with these folder matters."

"Well, Yusif, you've always been a loyal friend. But I have to warn you, I will never tell you anything that might hurt my followers. Millions of Americans have put their trust in me, and I won't let them down. Now, listen, I'm going to be setting up a schedule that will free me up to play golf as often as possible. I'll keep in touch so we can hook up. You've been trying to beat me for years. Let's see if you can do it with these Secret Service guys watching ..."

After the initial Oval Office meeting, President Ronald Strump, now the Commander-in-Chief of the U.S. military forces, met with Yusif, businessman and golfing buddy, almost monthly. The subject of those revealing images was never raised again. The requests for information coming from the Russian were few and far between and seemed to the president to be quite harmless. For example, during a particularly close match on the president's Scotland links, Alexei explained to him that the information he was particularly interested in on that occasion was not simply details that the Russian government wanted to know about our military capabilities, but those few facts also would be quite useful to them to bolster that country's capabilities for defense against China. Not only that, there were also European countries that remained a distinct threat to Russia's "territorial integrity." He followed that last remark by missing a putt, giving the President the match. Strump was not sure what that phrase meant, but he was reassured that the help he was giving his friend would certainly benefit America in the long run. After all, China was their common enemy, and those European countries? They certainly had not treated him with the respect he deserved as the leader of the world's most powerful country.

Now and then, the president passed along a few details about government contracts with major defense companies, and a phone number or two. Only once did he supply a password, but that bothered him enough so that he let Alexei know that asking for passwords would be out of the question in the future. The Russian agreed.

The president's most enjoyable moments during his ceremonial duties were the occasions when he donned his tailored leather flight jacket emblazoned with the presidential seal and reviewed the troops—"his" troops, as he liked to tell his friends. Strump's Russian friend was fond of regaling him with his harrowing experiences during his days in the Russian military. Strump, being unable to match Alexei's exploits with his own modest adventures in military school, was happy to offer him details here and there of the movements of his forces or boast of new developments of how this complex mix of land, sea and air might was learning how to more seamlessly communicate with each other. "My soldiers tell me everything," he told his friend on the first tee, one sunny day in Florida, "They can tell I understand. I know the lingo."

On an unusually chilly mid-September evening, at precisely three bells, the enormous bulk of the USS *New Hampshire* effortlessly and silently got underway. It was slack tide at that time—the brief interval when vessels could safely enter and exit Portsmouth harbor, where the Piscataqua, the third-fastest tidal river in North America, spills out into the Atlantic.

The submarine, almost the length of two football fields, remained just beneath the surface of the dark, choppy seas as she moved slowly to the south of the Isles of Shoals. The sub's commanding officer could not help but think of how they would be passing close to the grave of another submarine—the USS *Thresher*, built at the Portsmouth Naval Shipyard. She had embarked from that very same port on the way to the first test of the sub's deep diving capabilities. The *Thresher* unexpectedly sank to the sea floor on April 10, 1963, killing all on board. Its nuclear reactor remained there, 300 miles off the New England coast, presumably still intact. He thought as well about other submarines with a connection to Portsmouth. Back in 1945, four captured U-boats were towed to the Navy Yard. The German prisoners were housed briefly at the giant naval prison that remains, abandoned, on Seavey Island in the harbor.

He had read of those incidents but had never expected to be docking at that historic site. The shipyard, begun in 1800, was the site where over 70 submarines had been built during World War II. Now, the work at the busy shipyard involved the overhaul, refueling, and modernization of the nuclear-powered submarine fleet. However, the submarine under his command was simply too large to be serviced at Portsmouth. Instead, its home base was Kings Bay Naval Submarine Base in Georgia, the east coast home to the Ohio-class submarines.

Only a few months earlier, the USS *New Hampshire* had completed its scheduled maintenance period at Kings Bay—the same site where the "Kings Bay Plowshares 7" had expressed their protest against the presence of the nuclear warhead-tipped Trident D5 missiles. The commander had been on site when what he called the "rabble" had defaced government property and railed against what he was convinced were vital weapons for the nation's defense. To his relief, the base remained secure, and the offenders were on their way to jail, or already there.

The work done on the submarine, which took a frustrating 14 months to complete, involved not only a nuclear refueling, but extensive upgrading of its communications and launch capabilities. This was not the first time the ship needed modernization, particularly in her electronics—she had been built in 1983 in Groton, Connecticut—the same year that Motorola introduced the first cell phone. Every system on board, from the oxygen generators, filtered air circulators, ballast tanks, and even toilets, to the missile launchers and communications systems, had digital components ranging from simple to remarkably complex.

Now, as his submarine descended deeper to 500 feet below the surface, and veered gently off to the south, heading down along the coast, he took comfort in the fact that it was carrying a state-of-the-art set of nuclear weapons—20 Trident II D5LE missiles, each armed with four individual warheads. The DLEs were an upgraded, life-extended version of the Trident II D5. The extended stop at Kings Bay had allowed a full complement of these newest missiles to be loaded. They were equipped with the improved Mk6 guidance system. Each warhead could be programmed to head off to separate targets. Some packed an explosive power equivalent to 90,000 tons of TNT. The bomb that devastated Hiroshima had erupted with a force of a "mere" 15,000 tons. The commander was pleased that four of his missiles carried the W88 warheads, each equal to an almost unimaginable 455,000 tons. Once launched, these missiles would streak towards their destinations at speeds of over 1,300 miles per hour and could travel at least 7,000 miles.

On this deterrent patrol, the *New Hampshire* would be on "high alert," ready to launch her missiles at a moment's notice. Patrols were typically planned to last about 77 days, but this time there had been those few weeks delay at Portsmouth, so the length of this voyage would be extended. All of the officers on board were well aware that, on this trip, there was more than the usual complement of new crewmembers aboard, half-jokingly referred to as NUBs, or Non-Useful-Bodies. They would be put through their paces until they were familiar with every aspect of the workings of the submarine and its unique subculture. Even the Weapons Officer was a last-minute addition. Two others familiar with the USS *New Hampshire* had fallen victim to the Virus back in Kings Bay. The commander was confident that everyone on board would be faithful to the mission and return home safely. As for the "incident" back at Portsmouth, as far as he was concerned, those characters would get what they deserved.

On a bright fall day, almost exactly three years earlier, a young man smiled broadly as he signed the papers admitting him as a Computer Systems Engineer at the Kings Bay Naval Submarine Base in Georgia. His new employers were delighted that he had applied for the position, considering the fact that their expert worker with similar skills had come down with a mysterious illness, and the Base was under pressure to finish its busy schedule of submarine upgrades.

Jan Crowden, according to his credentials, had graduated from Stanford with honors. His former professors had nothing but praise for his work ethic and expertise. His friends at Stanford jokingly called him "Stanley" because of his slight accent that he claimed was the result of his mother having been raised in Poland. His timely request for employment at Kings Bay was a relief to the harried technicians working on what they hoped were the final stages of installing new electronics on the SSBN USS *South Dakota*. It didn't take Jan long to fit in to the system, and by the time that job was finished two months later he was already established as a valuable and talented member of the team.

When the USS *New Hampshire* docked at Kings Bay two years later, Jan was the leading figure in his team, the self-styled "Transformers." They had been preparing for this job for months. The Transformers took over, and the cramped quarters of the submarine became a maze of electronics, whose installation was presided over by the seemingly ubiquitous Jan. Months of upgrading was followed by six weeks of intensive training with the new systems for the sub's officers. Now, the *New Hampshire* was as ready as she could be for whatever challenges lay ahead. As Jan and his fellow geeks joked over beers, the night after the submarine got underway, "She's ship-shape and squared away from stem to stern, me hearties." Not long afterward, Jan left for what he told his disappointed friends was a "lucrative" position. It seemed strange that the email address he left behind turned out to be invalid.

As the fall advanced towards the dark winter months, the political season turned to another presidential election. The upcoming challenge had evolved into an especially difficult one for President Strump. While he boasted about his "accomplishments," for the most part imaginary, he was particularly proud of his reputation for toughness, especially with other nuclear powers. He refused to admit to himself that those countries showed him public deference, but in private regarded him as a dangerous fool. However, in the case of North Korea, the facts were indisputable. Without question, its despotic leader, Kim Jong-un, a man who had promised his loyalty to the president and had pledged to destroy North Korea's nuclear weapons, was now flaunting new, more powerful intercontinental ballistic missiles. But what could be done?

The polls, even though he considered them simply an extension of the lying press, pointed to an overwhelming defeat for Strump and many of his fellow Republicans. That was correct. He was defeated resoundingly. His future after leaving office looked to be grim, punctuated by a backlog of legal actions destined to land him in prison.

Ordinarily, Strump would get at least four or five hours of sleep, but at this point he managed only two or three. He could not wipe away the image of himself, defeated, and no longer regarded as the world's "most powerful person."

At two a.m. on the morning of December 7, 2020, the President woke from an uneasy sleep with a start. A solution to not only his dilemma, but as he saw it now, that of the entire free world, was at hand. He hauled himself out of bed, put on his slippers, and called out to his body man. There was work to be done.

"Billy" he shouted, as his aide entered the room, sleepy-eyed and disheveled. "Where's the damn biscuit?"

"In your drawer next to the bed. I'll get it."

"OK, I need the football."

"Alright, Jim's just down the hall. I'll get him. Are you sure ...?"

"Goddamn it, of course, I'm sure. Get him in here."

By the time the uniformed young man carrying the football, a black leather satchel, entered his room, Strump was reading the laminated card retrieved from the bedside table.

"Open the damn thing and get me the phone."

"But shouldn't you ...?"

"Give it to me. Now what button do you push to get the Pentagon?"

"Uh, it's this one here."

The president grabbed the phone, hit number three, and within a few seconds the senior officer in the Pentagon War Room answered.

"This is your president speaking. I want a heavy strike immediately on North Korea."

The officer hesitated briefly, then answered.

"Your challenge code is Charlie-Echo."

"OK, OK, um ... right, the answer here is Delta-Zulu."

"Hello, Mr. President. North Korea?"

"Right. Look, I just had a briefing on this, and you've got a sub out there with some of these really big nukes—you know, I think they are eighty-eights or something like that?"

"Sir, the *New Hampshire* has been fitted out with those. Right now, she is in the Gulf. We have a Pacific fleet of ..."

"Never mind, the *New Hampshire* is perfect. I won the primary there. They like me. That's it then. I want everything that sub has got headed to North Korea now. Don't let anybody else fire—that sub should do the trick. Is that clear?"

Within three minutes, a 148-character encrypted message was on its way to the USS *New Hampshire*, gliding gently just off the coast of Mexico, near Vera Cruz. The launch order was complete with the necessary authentication codes and codes to unlock the missiles. The ship's officers and crew followed the protocol in stunned silence, save for the necessary commands. The moment was here, but there was an air of unreality to it. They were in the process of killing unseen millions of human beings. But there was no hesitation. The orders were clear.

The commander, executive officer, and two other officers had authenticated the orders. They now had the combination to the on-board safe holding the "fire-control" key needed to deploy the missiles. All hands acted with precision, and within ten minutes, the first missile was ready to launch.

The sub had been deliberately moving upwards through the warm, turquoise waters of the Gulf, and was now balanced just beneath the surface. On command, an explosive charge flash-vaporized a tank of water instantaneously to steam. The resulting pressure ejected a 44-foot-long, seven-foot wide, 130,000-pound missile from its tube, up through the water, and out into the balmy air. As the missile began to feel the tug of gravity, motion sensors monitored its precarious balance, and the first of its rocket stages ignited. It roared into the night sky, followed, one after the other, by the remaining 19 Tridents. The Pentagon, at the order of the president, had transmitted the unlock codes for all 20 of the *New Hampshire's* nuclear weapons.

As the salvo continued, the commander could only repeat, "God help those people, God help those people."

CHAPTER 13

After the launch, there was a stunned silence aboard the *New Hampshire*. All had performed as trained. The commander ordered a descent to 600 feet. Would there be retaliation from North Korea? Would they detect the incoming missiles about to destroy them in time to send at least some of their own towards the United States? There was nothing left to do but wait.

Meanwhile, in the White House, the president acted decisively. After giving orders to the Pentagon, he had dressed quickly in his favorite dark blue suit, white shirt, and red tie. There was no time to tend to his hair. He donned a red baseball hat and glanced approvingly at his image in the full-length mirror. His body man was waiting anxiously in the corridor. Strump ordered him to gather the president's family and whatever staff happened to be on duty and meet him at the bunker entrance.

Five minutes later, seven people descended an elevator. They emerged deep underground, still half asleep, some in pajamas. They hurried along a wide, concrete lined corridor and met the president standing at the massive steel doors leading to the bunker. It had been built 10 years earlier, when it became obvious that, in case of a nuclear attack on Washington, it would be unsafe or impossible to leave the White House. The shelter, complete with its independent air supply and enough food to last for months, was intended to serve as a safe command center and living quarters for the president, family and staff. It was sealed off from the possibility of radiation contamination.

From inside, a waiting military aide opened the door, and they entered the brightly lit interior. The aide said, "The vice president is coming over now." At that moment, they heard the elevator door open, and the vice president came running down the corridor.

"I'm sorry, Mr. President, I was staying next door at the EEOB and I got the call, so I came right over. You've made a brave decision, Mr. President, and I support you one hundred percent. I'm pleased to be able to join you here. I'm sure the stay will be a brief one."

It took only a few seconds after each missile was ejected from the submarine for the microchips recently embedded by Jan in its control system to activate. The timing had to be precise. The guidance system that Jan installed during the Kings Bay upgrade featured a new electronics assembly and an inertial measurement unit (IMU) containing the system's sensors. The assembly was designed to interface with the submarine's fire-control system and the missile's flight-control electronics. The IMU's task was to track the missile's motion, transmit signals to the flight-control computer, and convert them into steering commands to keep the missile heading towards its target.

The twenty enormous missiles, one by one in rapid succession, began to turn in an eastward direction.

They were already over the Pacific, straining towards the planned apex of their flight to North Korea. Instead, each turned in a graceful arc and streaked towards the west coast of North America. Their trajectories were far lower than usual. By now they were moving at four miles per second, only a few miles above the Earth's surface. As the flock of missiles spread out, separating from each other, a few released their warheads, while the others waited for their turn. The warheads were listening for the electronic signals directing them to specific targets. The new microchips sent out predetermined commands quite different from those programmed much earlier under the direction of the United States Navy.

In the Pentagon, officials at the National Military Command Center were beginning to gather. They were stunned as satellites began reporting airborne objects streaking eastward from the Pacific. They had not expected North Korea to be capable of launching retaliatory intercontinental missiles—but even if they had been, these things were on a trajectory far lower than any Korean missile would take. Certainly, there was nothing approaching from Russia. The only thing that could possibly travel at this speed were ballistic missiles—but the only missiles in the air at the moment should be arriving in North Korea at any moment.

Suddenly, the computer screens were alive with reports of a massive attack on California. It appeared that Los Angeles and San Francisco had been … the screens faded into gray. And then the lights went out.

The Trident missiles each carried four nuclear warheads. Each of the 80 demonically powerful weapons was destined for a specific site. The planners in Moscow had patiently mapped out a target pattern that included all of the U.S. principal population centers. Fifty cities were on that list, headed by New York City. Those with the largest geographical areas were assigned at least two warheads. The W88 warheads were sent to sites including Washington, D.C., San Francisco, and to Boston, where there were so many liberals who had been outspoken in their opposition to Russia.

As the thunderous blasts rolled across the landscape of America, from the coastal bluffs of California, eastward across the Rockies and out onto the Plains, across the fertile fields of the Midwest, and into the teeming Northeast megalopolis, most of the victims were torn asunder before they were even aware of the sound. Millions were killed by the ferocious blasts of heat or were consumed in the fires which incinerated everything even remotely combustible. The whole country, within a few minutes, was a raging inferno. Many who survived the blast and immediate fire suffocated, as the flames consumed the oxygen from the air.

Any hope of rescue was gone for those who survived. The hospitals and clinics and medical personnel had vanished. In the ensuing months, here and there across the country, roving bands of starving humans who had escaped the lethal effects of radiation sickness would fight each other over whatever food could be found.

☢

The small group clustered in the spacious meeting room in the White House bunker was not sure of what to do next. Most of them were pretending that they had not heard the noise that filtered through the tons of earth enclosing the fortified concrete walls of the bunker, or felt the room shudder as though it had been struck by a mighty blow. The first time this happened, they managed to remain silent. The second time was even more forceful. The President's wife began to sob.

"Ronald, what's happening? Are we being attacked? And why?"

"Please, control yourself. I'm sure there is a good explanation. Just calm down. Ike, let's go take a look."

The vice president hesitated.

"Mr. President, we have a military aide here. Perhaps we should have him see what's going on. Besides …"

"Damn it Ike, don't be a wimp. We'll head up the stairs to the nearest emergency exit and just peek out. If it's all clear, we can all get the hell out of this prison."

Both men left the room and headed down a narrow hallway towards a bright yellow door marked EXIT. The vice president opened the heavy door and held it for the president to enter. They stood at the foot of a set of metal steps leading up to what appeared to be some sort of round steel plate, several stories above.

"There's the escape hatch, Ike. I saw it on the tour I took down here last year. Now, haul your ass up the stairs and look outside. They said you just have to push a big handle and the thing will pop up like the hatch on one of those missile launchers."

"Of course, sir."

The vice president climbed slowly up the stairs, each step clanging loudly as he labored upward. Reaching the top, he grabbed the black handle and pushed. Nothing happened. He tried again. Again, nothing. Climbing down, he faced an enraged president. He pushed the vice president aside and made his way up the stairs.

He returned 10 minutes later, breathing heavily.

"Must be stuck. I'll get my body man to yank the damn thing open. Let's get him in here. Ike, go get me a diet soda. I'm dying of thirst."

Far above their heads, angry yellow flames had erupted where the White House had been. Now, the beautiful grounds were deep in the shattered, smoldering remains of the nation's capital. In a bizarre juxtaposition of demolished landmarks, a severed section of the Washington Monument lay stretched out across the former White House lawn. The monolith's tons of white marble covered both exits from the presidential bunker.

Deep under the surface of the Gulf of Mexico, now littered with debris and ash, the crew and officers of the USS *New Hampshire* could not understand why they could not communicate with anyone or receive messages from Command. All shipboard systems were operating without a hitch, but they were isolated from the outside world. Earlier, they feared that they had struck something because the sub had suddenly begun to shake—or perhaps the cause was an earthquake to their north in California? At any rate, the tremors were brief, and now all was quiet again. The commander broadcast a simple message to the crew. "Attention—due to some difficulty with our communications systems, we will head for home. We should arrive in Kings Bay without delay. Congratulations for your service to our country. God Bless America, and God Bless President Strump."

When the warhead struck not far from Portsmouth, Father John, Sister Mary and Sister Eileen were in the prison meal room. Officials had given the monk permission to offer Mass there that morning. Thirty prisoners had gathered for the welcome celebration. Father John began a short homily.

"Oh God, grant us peace for the world. Help those in power to heed your words and lay down those weapons meant only to destroy, and learn to love ..."

At those words, a light shone in through the bars of the prison windows—a light brighter than the Sun, blinding those who reflexively looked toward it. A sound followed the light, a sound far louder than they might have imagined the sound of God's voice to be ... and then they were gone.

APPENDIX

Organizations whose goals include nuclear disarmament:

ananuclear.org	Alliance for Nuclear Accountability
agapecommunity.org	Agape Community
afsc.org	American Friends Service Committee
theatomproject.org	The Atom Project
armscontrol.org	Arms Control Association
preventnuclearwar.org	Back from the Brink
baselpeaceoffice.org	Basel Peace Office
thebulletin.org	Bulletin of the Atomic Scientists
beyondnuclear.org	Beyond Nuclear
armscontrolcenter.org	Center for Arms Control and Non-Proliferation
christiancnd.org.uk	Christian CND
carnegieendowment.org	Carnegie Endowment for International Peace
ctbto.org	Comprehensive Nuclear Test Ban Treaty Organization
liveableworld.org	Council for a Livable World
paceebene.org	Campaign Nonviolence

ratical.com	The Committee for Nuclear Responsibility
dontbankonthebomb.com	Don't Bank on the Bomb
daisyalliance.org	Daisy Alliance
eastwest.ngo	EastWest Institute
fas.org	Federation of American Scientists
globalzero.org	Global Zero
gsinstitute.org	Global Security Institute
gzcenter.org	Ground Zero Center for Nonviolent Action
globalphiladelphia.org	Global Philadelphia
ialana.info	The International Association of Lawyers Against Nuclear Weapons
icanw.org	International Campaign to Abolish Nuclear Weapons
inesglobal.net	International Network of Engineers and Scientists for Global Responsibility
ippnw.org	International Physicians for the Prevention of Nuclear War
lasg.org	Los Alamos Study Group
www.mayorsforpeace.org	Mayors for Peace
peacecouncil.net	Nuclear Free World Committee
nti.org	Nuclear Threat Initiative
wagingpeace.org	Nuclear Age Peace Foundation
nevadadesertexperience.org	Nevada Desert Experience
nukefree.org	NUKEFREE.ORG
nuclearfreeschools.com	Nuclear Free Schools
nukewatch.org	Nuclear Watch New Mexico
nukeresister.org	The Nuclear Resister

nuclearban.us	NuclearBan US
nukewatchinfo.org	Nukewatch
nhpeaceaction.org	New Hampshire Peace Action
ploughshares.org	Ploughshares Fund
paxchristiusa.org	Pax Christi
paxforpeace.nl	Pax
psr.org	Physicians for Social Responsibility
peaceaction.org	Peace Action
peacefarm.us	The Peace Farm
peaceworkskc.org	Peaceworks Kansas City
pugwash.org	Pugwash Conferences
reachingcriticalwill.org	Reaching Critical Will
sipri.org	Stockholm International Peace Research Institute
thesimonsfoundation.ca	The Simons Foundation
spaceforpeace.org	Global Network Against Weapons and Nuclear Power in Space
tridentploughshares.org	Trident Ploughshares
trivalleycares.org	Tri-Valley CAREs
ucsusa.org	Union of Concerned Scientists
vandenbergwitness.org	Vandenberg Witness
wilpf.org	Women's International League for Peace & Freedom
wslfweb.org	Western States Legal Foundation
wildfire-v.org	Wildfire-The Geneva Nuclear Disarmament Initiative
worldfuturecouncil.org	World Future Council

Thomas F. Lee, Ph.D. retired in 2002 after thirty-five years as a biology professor at Saint Anselm College, Manchester, NH. His special areas of interest include microbiology, molecular biology, and genetic engineering.

Several of his seven nonfiction books have received noteworthy attention, and he has been a frequent contributor to *Encyclopedia Americana*. His book, *Conquering Rheumatoid Arthritis: The Latest Breakthroughs and Treatments* (2001), was featured in the *New York Times* Health Section. The Spanish translation of *The Human Genome Project: Cracking the Genetic Code of Life* (1991) was selected for listing in the *Limites de la Ciencia* collection, which also included a book by famed physicist Richard Feynman, who contributed to the Manhattan Project. The noted historian Howard Zinn praised Lee's 2005 *Battlebabble: Selling War in America*.

Professor Lee lives in Goffstown, New Hampshire with his wife Eileen. They have six grown children and six grandchildren. This is his second novel.

Made in the USA
Middletown, DE
01 August 2021